WILEY O'WARY

Wiley O'Wary

A Novel

LIAM SEAN

LEGALESE

ALSO BY LIAM SEAN

<u>Novels</u>
Donald's Inferno
A Tragedy Wrapped In A Comedy Inside A Fiction
<u>Screenplays</u>
Ameriking
with Paul Lamb
<u>Stageplays</u>
Deathbed: A Comedy
with Dean Wilson

DEDICATION

For Mom Anne and Mom Karen

And Mary Corofin
For Yip, Bean and Rabbit
and mostly Marilyn,
Life and Love
Like Earth and Trees
Without any one of you,
I would not be

In memory of
Seamus Duffy

With Gratitude
To Bill Cashman for editing this novel

1

It's amazing where life takes you and even stranger how it gets you there. These thoughts occurred to me as I wandered down Market Street toward the downtown. The West Michigan sky was racing in several directions at once, not unlike the West Michiganders, and the sun was having a difficult time keeping up, not unlike me. I had just stepped off a Greyhound bus from Chicago and the proverbial dart striking the map had brought me to Grand Rapids.

Now, the map had been in a tavern in Boston, plastered to the dartboard with the splintered pieces of an Irish pound coin. On the board beside it were my divorce papers, held in place by just about every dart in Boston. In my hand was the dart in question, and as I closed my eyes, the image of the map seared upon my retinas, I let fly the dart. With the satisfying, soft thump of dart penetrating cork, I opened my eyes and beheld my destination.

How odd. The subtleties that could have sent me to, say, Poughkeepsie, or Peoria or even Chicago. Was it fate? Blind luck? Doesn't really matter now, I am here, walking down Market street and have been directed to the corner of Monroe and Pearl to a tavern that serves Guinness by the pint. Simple we men are, or so we seem.

I have never been further west in my life until now. Before this the end of the Green Line on the outskirts of Boston would have been as far from Ireland as I had ever been. The disinterested looks of Chicago have given way to the quizzical and sometimes condescending looks of this town. I feel the part, a stranger in a strange land, but shake it off to the many miles of travel.

The sky looks Irish: low clouds dark with rain, wind pushing them faster than they care to go. March is March is March; spring trying to yield to the old man, several warm days brought to an abrupt end by snow and a bitter north wind. But today is fair and it makes each step that much easier.

The pub is nearly vacant, and as it is the middle of the afternoon on a Monday, this seems fairly reasonable. There are some lads in suits in the corner by the big window, and judging by their volume they have forgone the afternoon's work and are continuing the weekend. An empty bar greets me, the barmaid wiping its surface in slow, lazy circles with an ancient bar towel. I call for a pint, my Donegal accent as thick and incomprehensible to her as calculus was to me. In the spirit of Geneva, *Glasnost,* and the European Union, we resolve the language barrier and she brings me a pint of the black stuff.

The bar is decorated for the coming holiday that celebrates the patron saint of Ireland. In spite of the silliness of the leprechauns, the harps and shamrocks, the overall feeling makes me feel a bit wistful. I fish out my wallet and open it to a picture of my mother. Her dark hair is spilling over her face in curls and she holds up a hand as if to say, 'Jaysus would ya put that thing away.' I stare out the window and order another pint.

Hours will go by. Some people will talk to me, ask me about Ireland, and then return to their mates or to the telly. As dusk settles into night, I leave the pub and walk down Pearl to the river. Wandering down to the water's edge, there is a boardwalk that seems to run on in either direction. I crouch down onto one knee and peer into the river known as the Grand. Lights from a bridge cast enough light for me to see my face, and I can't help but wipe away a tear.

Behind me, in a few days, the streets will fill with people. The buildings will echo with the screech of bagpipes and the cadence of drums. Green shamrocks will be painted on faces, gold harps hung in bars, and one hundred thousand glasses will be lifted. At that moment many people will never feel closer to the land of their heritage. But for me, three thousand miles from Donegal, by the banks of this river, I just cannot feel further away.

Still, the sound of the water is soothing, with the lights twinkling across its surface, the arch of the bridge is reflected as a smile. I return the favor, pull myself up, turn, and walk away from the river in search of a mission or a YMCA. Strange this life is, strange and wonderful.

2

The view out the seventh-floor window from my perch, top bunk, corner room, YMCA, is quite expansive. I can look out over Veteran's Park, high atop the empty maples and sycamores, across Fulton Street, and on and on until the sea of rooftops blurs into the horizon. Wisps of smoke and vapor stream from chimneys in the cold March air, and it doesn't take much to place oneself in the background of a story by Dickens.

Below, on the brick-paved streets, participants in the city's St. Patrick's Day parade are marshalling before they step-off. There are fire trucks, police cars, and lorries for shipping beer; there are convertibles with dignitaries beside flatbed trucks lined with musicians; throngs of people are making their way to a place in the parade or a spot along the route. A vista of green, shamrocks and Tricolors, highland pipes, drums, wee step dancers, and babes in prams pushed by smiling mothers, it is a wonderful array of people.

It seems strange to be staring out the window at the festivities and not making an attempt to join in them. I mean, having come all this way from Boston, and with a thirst to match the journey, it would only seem proper to be down there pressing the flesh, rubbing elbows, following the tumult, and then getting right bloody pissed. However, as the wind blows a sheet of snow across the marchers, with men holding hats to their heads and women keeping their skirts from looking too much like Marilyn Monroe's, I remember that the last look I had at my finances was more than a little depressing.

I take a peek at the stack of library books at the end of the bed. My first bold move as a new Grand Rapidian was to cross the street from the Y and obtain a library card. Easy stuff! Having remained virtually sober, other than the wee bottle of Jameson smuggled in the other night, I have managed to saw through a number of books already.

Today, on St. Patrick's Day, I was going to celebrate the holiday by reading more of Joyce's *Finnegan's Wake*. Now, however, the sudden need to smoke and walk around takes hold of me. Trundled up and out the door, I walk the still streets of downtown Grand Rapids, thoughts of St. Patrick's Days past coursing through my head.

Going back in time, St. Pat's after St. Pat's, I eventually arrive in Donegal as a child. The holiday is more somber in Ireland, particularly back then, with pubs shut down and Mass the highlight of the day. There would be gatherings at neighbors' houses; a few casual toasts made, and a family dinner as if it were a Sunday. As I trod the snow-drifted streets of this American city, I wince, having gone too far back, remembered one St. Pat's too many.

There was the screaming, my brother hollering in response to my father, who was yelling as well. My sister running to find somewhere to hide, my mother crying from a bathroom, trying to fix make-up that will continually run all afternoon long. And then there was me, the youngest, trying to sort the whole thing out. When the noise got this bad, I would always go to the window at the top of the stairs and look out past the town to the pier. Staring at the endless rows of waves marching into Ireland, while I sat on the ledge wishing and dreaming on how to ride them out.

These memories, the deep ones, the ones that cause my hands to shake, my throat to become parched, the images that bring a sweat to my temples, will take a hold of me now. Drown them. That's the only way. Drown them in deep green water, drown them in endless pints, walk them out of the head and show them the door.

In my mind I can still look down from that window and see it all in great clarity: the Atlantic wind blowing trash and debris up the hill, a cat crossing the street while a dog runs out from an alley to greet it, the men and women in blue and black grimly walking to the church. Several men exit the back door of The Midway Bar, cigarettes puffed hurriedly to cover the smell of whiskey and porter. Low, dark clouds sealing us off from the heavens, the continuous sound of the surf just under the wind, under the conversation. It seems to me now like a painting, or one of those glass balls with a diorama glued into place.

I can still hear the shouting. Still hear the names being yelled at one another, the very thing they bade me never to do. Actions and words, cliché after cliché, what is a small boy to do but dream about the ocean and what may lay on the other side.

As I turn the corner from an alley that backs the Y, the sudden screech of pipes snaps me from this daydream. The parade is stepping off, marshals moving the groups, bands and vehicles into their proper queue. I check my pocket for cigarettes, pull out a meager clump of dollars, and look up at the host of Tricolors.

"Ach," I say to no one in particular, crossing the street to follow the parade, "better to be poor and happy." And set out to inscribe another St. Pat's into my memory. *Finnegan's Wake* tossed aside to let the green water break over the bow, a smile washing over my face.

And the wind? The snow? Memories? They soon will fade, tucked safely away beneath the weight of each pint.

3

A strong, warm wind wraps around me like a glove, pushing me up the street with a confidence I haven't had in months. What a couple of weeks can do this time of year. The St. Pat's parade was so bitterly cold I thought the good saint had fallen out of grace with Christ himself. Yet now, the sky contemplating a deep blue, the sun just starting to remember this hemisphere, life seems to have a new lease. The buds on the trees are matched by the spring in people's step, their voices confidently talking of the promise of summer. So this is Grand Rapids as April dawns.

I am experiencing my own bit of renaissance. From the wistfulness of first arriving here, unsure, alien, I now strike out from my home at the Y in any direction of the compass and know my way around. One of my favorite things to do in Boston was to walk. I walked everywhere. Boston is still a city of neighborhoods, places where distinct ethnic backgrounds, classes and all of the tapestry that goes along with those are plain to be seen. This is true here as well, that separation of enclaves. And that's why the place I really enjoy walking through is known as Heritage Hill. It is a *Crayola* box of people, a dozen types of music on every block.

The fresh vernal energy has pushed me in the direction of employment. I have gained a position in a local eatery not too far from my humble abode. Dishes and food prep. I tried to convince the Chef that there were indeed great cooking schools in County Cork and that I had attended one of the best, the Ballymaloe Culinary School in Shanagarry; but my accent had already sealed my fate. It's no worries though, with the lack of responsibility comes greater time to think, and if you're an Irishman you can spend entire days inside your head.

I have adopted the pub on the corner of Monroe and Pearl as my local, and upon entering am greeted by familiar looks. My Donegal brogue met with kindness and curiosity instead of consternation and puzzlement. I met a bloke from Australia in here one evening and between the two of us we had the staff in fits. It seems that the people of Grand Rapids have a bit of trouble with foreign accents. Once your man from Ballarat inquired as to why it wasn't very busy and the barmaid thought he was asking directions to Chicago.

There has been a lot of confusion over my accent. People at work have pegged me as being from New Zealand, an Aussie, English, that didn't go over very well, even South African. My new friend the Sous Chef realized I was Irish, but when I clarified my Donegal brogue, he couldn't believe there were different accents within Ireland. To which, in mockery I alone understood, I gave him a brief tour of Ireland via the brogues. Still, he was the only one on the right tack.

At first, the Chef had asked which part of Scotland I was from and I'm in too good of a mood to discuss my first reaction.

I walk up to the bar, take my usual seat at the end nearest the big window, and order a pint of Guinness. I am basking in the glow of my new direction and in having begun the transition from successful, married Bostonian to starting all over, divorced Grand Rapidian. I open my wallet to the picture of my mother, thank her for the wonderful gift, and then close my eyes, thinking of spring in Donegal.

The tiny flowers on the heather are starting to open. The sky is a schizophrenic mix of rain and sunshine alternating every fifteen minutes or so. The clouds are close to the ground and mimic the sheep running up and down the hills at the equally schizophrenic will of a border collie. There are whitecaps on the North Atlantic and a bit of beach sand in the wind. Along the roads the rhododendrons are starting to bud, as are the hazels growing out of the ancient, wet stonewalls that divide the farmers' fields.

I open my eyes to the pint of Guinness in front of me many miles from those rolling hills. The entire pub is lit up with West Michigan sunshine as the sun has crawled out from behind a bank of clouds. I thank the barmaid for the pint, am about to raise it to my lips when the fella beside me can't help but notice my accent, loved the film

Braveheart and promptly asks me what part of Scotland I am from.

I shake my head to myself, take a long cool draw of the black stuff, and tell him Glasgow. Wiping the foam from my upper-lip, my wistful face reflected in the mirror behind the back-bar, I catch my eye and wink at myself with a sideways nod. The sun is wonderfully warming through the immense, glass window, as are the easy smiles of patrons, blue cigarette smoke drifting to the tin ceiling in fat, lazy circles. I settle back into my bar stool, empty my mind, and float along.

4

The evening sun streaming in through the window by the prep table was all the excuse I needed. The window faced west and the light was a constant irritant, although the reason for the tears welling up in my eyes had nothing to do with the last rays of sunshine or even the onions I had just finished slicing. It had everything to do with the miraculous events that took place back home in Ireland this past week.

I had wanted to finish work early, buzz down to the local and celebrate Easter weekend. In Ireland, St. Pat's has nothing on Easter weekend for a good time. The reason is that the four-day weekend celebrates the Christian holiday, the beginning of the Irish revolution and the start of summer. And this year there is even more to celebrate with the new peace accord signed in Belfast.

I set my chef's knife down, rub my eyes with my apron, and return to my task. I have been given the honor of preparing the night's special, and it is just that which has nixed my hope of cutting work early. Oh well, a chance to flex my culinary muscles, despite the fact my mind is far away.

I remember the eyes the most, cold and hard. Distant. Those men at the far end of the bar, or at a table in the corner by themselves, drinking slowly in dark pubs in towns like Letterkenny or Monaghan. Upon making contact, those eyes would either dart away, or look right through you. They'd been over the border, and you couldn't pay me to see what those eyes had seen.

In Derry you could pick out the Special Branch men right away. And the Brits, they stood out like the carrots I'm slicing right now. But the men from East Belfast, or the Shankill, the ones with the same eyes as the IRA men, they were the ones you could never quite spot. And if you did, it was probably too late.

Brushing away the carrot slices I slide over stalks of celery and begin working on them. I slice them lengthways as I had the carrots, and then crossways to make everything the same size, all the time being careful that the knife doesn't slide down onto my fingers.

We had the sunshine here in Grand Rapids. I phoned my mother back in Donegal and from her tone you would have thought it was still February. My sister assured me it was merely overcast with a light mist and quite fair altogether. She said Mom was suffering from having lived too close to the North Atlantic for too long, thus producing a good dose of Irish melancholy.

My sister told me the mood in the North was skeptical, but upbeat. She had just come from London by way of Belfast at the moment the accord was being signed on Friday morning. She met some friends in the Ardoyne to have tea and chat. She said they were very happy, but also quite cautious. I guess you don't wipe away thirty years of war in a few weeks.

Still, I can't help but feel optimistic, can't escape the conclusion that this time it will work. It seems all the pieces are in place, and that not only will peace be given a chance, but a peace on an even playing field.

I finish jotting down the recipe for the sauté cook who will prepare the dish tonight: how much butter, sherry and garlic, when to add the scallops, the ratio of pasta to main ingredients. All the stuff most people take for granted, but makes them roll their eyes in delight.

With the clock punched, the day firmly behind me, I race out the back door and into the last bit of sunshine. Trying not to appear too eager, already tasting the Guinness on my lips, I trot across the busy street and up into Veteran's Park. I always slow up here. There is a solemnity about this place that I respect. The names on the monument seem to echo of lives lost, duties served, honors bestowed; men and women who paid the ultimate sacrifice to protect the freedom of not just America, but of the world.

Several minutes later I'm nestled in my favorite barstool, a copy of the *Chicago Tribune* in front of me. The events of the past few days ready to be slowly gleaned over, my mouth as dry as the sherry to flavor the scallops, I hold up a hand to order a pint.

The front page has a snap of Gerry Adams, David Trimble, Tony Blair, and Bertie Ahern, the key players who carved out the agreement at the behest of Bill Clinton and the peoples of Ireland and England. I am holding the paper up to my eyes

in disbelief at the sight of Trimble and Adams so close together when a young lady asks if she can use the barstool to
my right.

'Absolutely", I say, as my pint arrives, a smile and a hello
from the bartender.

I take a long, cool sip and shake off the equally long day.
Glancing over to the young man who has joined the girl now
sitting on my right, I can see the spark in their eyes. It makes
me smile. And at that very second she looks down upon the
ring on her left hand. Her face lights up; he brushes her
cheek, leans forward, and kisses her lightly on the forehead.

At that point I am stunned with revelation. The past few
days in Ireland, the accord, three decades of war, they pale.
It is moments just like this that will cement peace in Ireland
faster and more secure than mere words.

Once upon a time I was helping my mother prepare dinner. I had just turned fifteen a few days past, and at this moment she decided to share some wisdom with a young man
who knew everything.

She set her knife down, turned to me as I blithered on in
the way young men do, and told me that love does conquer
all. Having been recently divorced, I've spent a lot of time
trying to figure out what she meant by 'conquers,' but sitting
here in my favorite pub surrounded by love on Easter weekend, I think that wise woman by the North Atlantic knew
what she was talking about. In no small way, no matter how
many miles have separated us, she has always been a touch-
stone of tranquility, a place of refuge, of calm. The sudden
image of her as the ferryman in *Siddhartha*, sitting by the

river in Buddha-like repose, brings an abrupt laugh which returns me to my pint, quizzical glances at the Irish lunatic, stout meeting thirst as the Irish stream of consciousness continues to the sea.

5

There are times when you just have to stop and shake your head. As if we are truly actors in some cosmic play, the curtain trembling to fall whilst the act's point is made all too clear. The point being made through irony, or biting satire and the audience left in shock by the sheer truth of it. This is what happened to me just the other day.

It was one of those days where the world seems to be rushing around way too fast for its own good. I've always believed that haste makes waste; and having been raised in the West of Ireland, I still try to hang onto the principal of not doing today what could easily be done tomorrow. Particularly if it is a really nice day and your favorite trout stream is just up the road and 'round the bend.

However, I no longer live in the West of Ireland, haven't for some time, and my duties this enlightening day had me hunting down product that had not been delivered earlier in the morning. All of this made absolutely imperative by the fact that a dinner party of thirty was on the books, and the missing product not discovered until three hours before the group's arrival.

In the greater Grand Rapidian scheme of things, large food markets are not placed in the city center, simply because most people do not live downtown. Even if they were, the likelihood that they would have thirty half-ducks is a bit remote. I had thus been charged, in a city I don't know, to track down said ducks and to do so in a couple of hours.

I had driven in my boss' truck, east to an area called Cascade where some ducks were found. Then dashed along this drag known as 28th Street in search of more ducks. The traffic here was atrocious but belief in my mission, and love of my pay packet, guided me forward.

On the complete opposite end of that street, more ducks were procured, bringing the total number of fowl to nineteen, still eleven short of the quest. I then raced up US 96 to US 131 to Alpine Street to continue the chase. This was not an easy task given the crab-like note of directions my boss had handed me, writing in one hand while pulling out hair over handing a foreigner his truck keys with the other.

Two stops on Alpine had yielded nine ducks. As I paid for several of the fowl at this one store, a woman who happened to be from Dublin noticed my accent and had to say hello. It turned out that when she was a child, her family holidayed in Donegal just outside Dunfanaghy, not far from where I grew up.

Now if you were in the middle of Donegal, surrounded by Irish, and suddenly a bloke from Grand Rapids tugs on your sleeve, you would probably do exactly what I did: forget completely about the bloody ducks and have a great conversation.

It seemed just a few minutes to me. The woman was charming, having grown up a generation or two ahead of me, and her recollections about my county watered my eyes. In looking away, I noticed a large clock on the wall and realized I had twenty-five minutes and was still two ducks short. I made my good-byes, ran out the door, leapt into the truck and was off to Plainfield Street.

Rush hour loomed in front of me and traffic slowed down to below the speed limit. It seemed the slowest drivers were always just in front of me, or pulling into my lane.

I found the remaining two ducks, that being the easier part, and then realized I had lost the paper with the directions. Having already driven the roads away from the city center, I thought I could figure my way back. I needn't have worried, traffic was moving so slow I had plenty of time to retrace my footsteps.

What I didn't have was plenty of time. While one half of my brain analyzed the path to take, the other agonized over the digital clock, which was constantly reminding me of futility and unemployment.

I exited the freeway, slowly made my way to Fulton, naturally catching every traffic signal, and was only five minutes late when Eastbound Fulton on the bridge ground to a halt. I had just turned my head, something odd having caught my eye, when the backside of the car in front of me was nearly right on top of me.

Both feet went to the brake pedal instinctively. The truck's front end nosed downward, tires squealing, the back end sliding to the left as I turned the wheel to avoid the accident.

I closed my eyes, inhaled deeply, and slowly exhaled muttering both a curse in Irish and a small prayer as well. The ducks, loosely wrapped in haste in their protective white butcher's wrap, were all on the floor, my duffel bag and its contents littered atop them.

As I looked up, I saw what had held my eye. Hanging from a power wire by a fisherman's line, hung a wild duck suspended above the river and perfectly silhouetted against the deep blue sky.

I could not believe it. All of the hassle, the time, and blood pressure in search of ducks seemed reduced to nothing in the face of this poor creature's demise. Whether snagged, tangled, or having eaten the hook by accident, the line had wrapped itself around the wire sealing the fate of the animal. How long, I wondered, had it struggled, feebly and impossibly, to free itself.

Well if this isn't a metaphor for my life," I said to myself, waiting for the light to change and the snarl of traffic to uncoil.

I looked about me, trying not to look up at the hanging duck, put the truck into drive as the car in front pulled away, and drove back to work.

The rest of the night wore on as slow as the traffic had previously, my mind's eye continually reminding me of what I had seen. I craved a pint of Guinness to wash it all away and perhaps a wee one of Jameson to help make some sense of it. Instead, I took some old baguettes, crumbled them into a paper bag, walked to the river, and fed the ducks. The stout could wait that night. It may have been a feeble gesture, and in the face of everything, probably meant nothing at all. But to me, and as I am who I wake up with each and every morning, it did.

6

I am waiting for a perfect pint of Guinness at a pub called Bantry Bay, deep in Chicago. A traditional music session is about to happen; and there are three lads from County Roscommon on the barstools next to me. The barmaid herself is from Howth, and I just couldn't be any happier.

Work makes its own rewards. I have just finished a brutal week of four doubles in a row and nine days without a break. The restaurant had had some staff roll over and the rest of us picked up the slack. For all of this toil, the light at the end of the tunnel would be three days off and a bit of the extra bob to spend on me own self.

My first thought was to race back to Boston and see some of my old mates. Unfortunately, time, distance, and the fact that the ticket was a bit too dear, led me to Chicago. I needed to hear an Irish accent, to have some connection with home. There is a comfort that comes with being with one's own kind. The ability to converse about everything and then nothing at all, so that in mentioning a particular county, or football team or politics, or even simply the weather, there is innate understanding.

The barmaid has just set a beautiful pint of the black stuff in front of me when all heads turn to the far side of the bar. There is a great host of people making toast after toast in celebration. Most of them are policemen and policewomen still in uniform, clothes slightly disheveled, cheeks flushed, they seem carried away by the moment.

And so am I. The pub could have been cut right out from Irish soil and dropped here in Chicago. It is brilliant: wood floor with the traditional low tables and stools, a cushioned bench running the walls, stained glass depicting the flags of each province. The bar is pitted and stained by a million pint glasses. They even sell packages of crisps and Bacon Fries, as well as Majors, Silkcuts and Sweet Aftons.

I have waited the appropriate length of time before addressing my pint, one need not rush headlong into anything, and as I'm reaching for it, another peal of cheers erupts from the far end of the bar. I turn to my new mate, Conor, and ask if he knows what's going on.

"Jaysus, but I don't have a clue. What part of Donegal are you from again?"

"Dungloe," I answer.

"You probably had as few cops up there as we did."

"Bloody good way to grow up", pipes in another of the lads, "after all, there's no need to guard the bog." We howl with laughter.

The truth behind this rings a loud bell with me. The simple fact that places like Donegal and Roscommon are so desolate is why so many Irish men and women made their way to America. Sitting here in Chicago, a city with a vast Irish population, I am struck by all of this in a profound sort of way, feeling some undercurrent but unable to put my finger on it.

Chicago's finest explode in another toast, pints ringing together, Guinness and lager spilling to the floor. Seeing so many police officers in uniform, and most of them being so young, leads me to believe that they have just graduated academy and are out celebrating the event. However, I could not have been more wrong.

As another pint is set in front of me, the band stops for a moment and one of the young officers holds up his hand to quiet everyone down. The barmaid sets down her towel and stops working. The musicians lay their instruments to rest and the din of pub noise falls away like mist in sunlight. A young policeman raises his glass.

"To Jimmy McIntyre, and the fuckers that killed him."

"They've just come from the funeral," Conor says, leaning in close to the rest of us.

We all drink to Jimmy. The officers having just laid the lad to rest, stopping by what was most likely his local pub before going to the wake. Their cheeks wet with tears, their top lips covered in foam mustaches from the Guinness, the echoes of the toast like a bell reverberating, I close my eyes and fall silent.

This young man who has died, be he third generation or right off the boat, he had followed in the footsteps of an entire legion of Irishmen. From the bogs and poverty of Ireland, or in this century, to simply look for more opportunity, they had left their homeland and come to America. Now he was gone, his life cut short, dreams discarded, his memory lying just behind the eyes of his mates in this pub.

It reminded me of some lines from a Pogues' song:

Did you work upon the railroads,
or did you rid the streets of crime,
Were your dollars from the White House
or were they from the five and dime.
Did the old songs try to cheer you,
or did they just make you cry.
Did you count the months and years,
or did your teardrops quickly dry.

So, hoisting the pint in front of me, my own history as fresh and similar as all the people around me,

"To Jimmy."

An answer of three dozen 'ayes', pints are finished and set toward the back of the bar, the barmaid begins drawing more, and the musicians, tapping the collective Irish heartbeat, return to the reel as thoughts of home, of my brother, neatly fall into the wheel of music.

The officers shortly filed out, hugs, handshakes and goodbyes silhouetted in front of the open door, the early afternoon sunshine making a blinding rectangle. The pub was reduced to a few small groups and then, as the lads about me trailed-off to different parts of their lives, I found myself alone again in a pub, quiet contemplation revolving around home and loss, the stout giving way to whiskey and the laughter to tears.

7

I'm at the end of the bar in my local and I must have looked like a loon. Thoughts racing through my head like wildfire, I would throw my head back in laughter or simply shake it from side to side. They say things happen in threes and by God if that's not the way it seems. The three odd events that happened to me, completely unrelated, resulted in remembering a boy I went to school with and an incident long forgotten that had left a lasting impression upon me.

The day began bright and cheerful, a fine May morning filled with promise, the day budding-out just like the trees. Hours before work, as I went flat hunting up in Heritage Hill, I had walked by a hole in the sidewalk where someone had taken the time to plant several petunias. The hole and the flowers were on someone's walk from the sidewalk up to their front porch, safely away from treading feet, yet in plain view. A nice touch, thought I.

As I walked back by the same area an hour later, I noticed that the flowers were gone and all that remained were three little petunia stumps. That's a pisser, I thought, someone having gone to the little extra work to plant them, water them, and then to have some gobshank nick the end result.

This buggered me for quite awhile, not that pinched petunias will have me running to Greenpeace, but it just wasn't all that decent of a thing to do. As I worked at my station, hands turning romaine into Caesar, leaf lettuce into house, and endive into special, I let the old Irish thought process play with the event and before I knew it, the night had ended.

As I sat down at the bar in the restaurant where I work, my service pint of porter washing away the evening's stress, a young man sitting next to me started to pull my ear. He'd been sitting there for some time, frustration building in him to talk, so he turned to me and let go.

He explained that he was recently married, wonderfully so, but that something odd had come to light which had transpired at his wedding. Apparently two young women had gone up to the bride's father and wanted to reveal something about this chap that the father needed to know. The father, being a gentleman, brushed the two busybodies aside telling them to take it up with the groom or the bride or both.

The young man shook his head in disbelief, grabbed his cocktail, and consumed the rest of the clear liquor in several large swallows. He looked over at me, eyes imploring for an answer, and asked how some people could find the nerve to do such a thing at his own reception. I couldn't help but agree that just when you suspect that people can't move any closer to proving Darwin correct, they do so with great verve and gusto. I related the petunia story to which he was unable to find the parallel, gave me an odd look questioning my sexuality and slid his barstool a couple inches away while turning his back just so. I took that as my cue to buzz down to my local for a pint of Guinness.

The place was nearly empty for a Saturday night. My barstool was occupied, so I stood next to it trying not to look bothered. I ordered my pint, accent hanging around my head like a name tag, when the fella in my barstool spins around and in perfect mid-western twang, "Jesus, your Irish, so am I. My name's Donahue, how 'bout yours. Hey what about that referendum"

To this the mishaps of the day drifted away, the overwhelming 'yes' vote in support of the peace process back home had watered my eyes when I had heard it on the telly. I was ready to engage in heartfelt conversation, naysayers of the world be damned.

Not to be. He went on for what seemed like hours about how the peace process could never work. He offered various theories on sectarian conflicts, all of which were lengthy and monopolized the conversation. His diatribe sounded more like Ian Paisley and less like an Irish-American with a name from County Cork. The end result being that all of this negativity brought me down lower than the stems of the violated petunias.

At some point however, his litany increasingly becoming white noise, I tuned him out by simply staring into the foam of my pint in what could best be described as the meditation of contemplation. Suddenly, as always happens to me in meditation, I was astonished by remembering a face I had not thought about in a very long time, one of those random thoughts that float down the river, waving its arms about hoping to be noticed.

It was of a tinker's son with whom I had gone to grade school. Of dark complexion, tall and wiry, he always seemed older than the rest of us, as if he were a step faster and a foot above. If it rained, he would be in school. On fair days he could never be seen, the hills, streams and ocean calling his name in a chorus that tugged at all the boys in class. But he, without our punitively learned restraint, would answer.

His family was very poor. All of their possessions were crammed into their wee caravan, or hanging from its roof by string. The gossips in the town would make them the butt of a lot of ill-humor, the rumors nearly as loud as the clattering their pots and pans made as their old horse pulled the caravan from one side of town to the other. But to me he was a hero, having saved me innumerable times from the older lads who seemed to have nothing better to do than bloody my nose.

One day, he came to school wearing a beautiful pocket watch tucked into his torn and dirty vest. It was gold, with a white face and black, Roman numerals slightly raised from the watch's face. And it ticked.

A group of us had gathered, taking turns holding the watch to our ears, himself never letting go of the chain, carefully monitoring how long each of us held the watch. His eyes filled with pride knowing for once he had something that others would envy.

All at once the headmaster came up, saw the watch, grabbed the tinker boy by the scruff of his neck, and hauled him down to his office.

The gossip followed, children sounding all too much like their parents. The consensus was that he had stolen the watch. There was no way a tinker lad could possibly afford such a nice watch and his family didn't really work properly at all anyway. Accusations and names filled the air, myself ostracized for defending him, the unthinkable happened when the principal adults in town supported the headmaster's decision to have him expelled.

The shame of it forced his family to pack up their caravan and move to another village. The busybodies stood beside their doors, or stared out their windows, watching the family leave town, feeling vindicated by the course of events.

Until one day, at the end of term, when the truth came out. Our village's postman had been talking to another postman in Letterkenny when the story of the watch was mentioned. As it turned out, the watch had been a gift to the lad from a woman whose husband was in hospital. They lived in a village just up the road, and the boy had helped with the farm chores for the time the husband was laid up. Every weekend he would go down to the farm and help out as best he could. In his quiet, shy way, he had told no one what he was doing. The watch had been his reward.

So, sitting here in my local, many miles from Dungloe, many years from those events, I nurse a pint of Guinness and chuckle like a loon. My thoughts of petunias, gossip-mongers, and watches neatly wove into a Celtic pattern, I come to this resolution: It seems to me, that the people whose glass is half empty persist in trying to convince those of us whose glass is half full, that, sorry, it really is half empty. To this I toss back my pint, which was just slightly one quarter full, and order an entirely new one, determined to play hooky the first fine day that comes my way.

8

They said she was a runner. They said that when she drank, she became someone else; she would grow sullen, distant, and before you knew it, she would be gone. She would just take off. Running from the memories in her head. Running from the pain in her heart. A dead sprint turning into long strides, into a jog and finally just walking. This was how she dealt with things. In the never-ending whirlpool of idle chatter that is the background buzz of any restaurant, these things were said to me about her. I'll be honest. It intrigued me.

It was the busiest night since the restaurant had opened. Between a prom, a wedding reception, an anniversary and the fact that it was Saturday night, we were up to our arses in food and plates from three p.m. until nearly one in the morning. It was one of those nights in the restaurant business where you wished you had chosen any other possible field of employment.

At about half one, the staff sat down at the bar, which was closed, and made a bold attempt at taking the evening's stress out on their livers. I knocked back two pints of porter as if I was headed to prison in the 'morrow. No one said a word. For ten minutes there was silence, save deep breaths, sighs, and the clinking of ice.

She was a waitress at the restaurant. Tired and whipped like the rest of us, she was drinking vodka and not saying much. In her eyes, all night long, you could see she was someplace else. I could only hope it was someplace nice.

At two a.m. the bartender produced a set of cards and suggested a round of euchre. By this time, most of the staff had left, heeding the warnings of ill weather that the cable weather station had been prophesying all evening. This left us with six people, four to play and two to watch. The waitress decided to watch, as well as the closing manager, who was going over the evening's tapes anyhow.

In Donegal, when you come from a family that fishes and grow-up along the Atlantic in a small village, cards take on a special place in the household. You must understand, even in the best of weather, there simply is not all that much to do. When it's winter, and the winds are coming off the Atlantic in excess of thirty knots an hour for a week at a time, there are only so many things you can do besides drink and make babies.

I dove into the game with a load of gusto, fixing a cup of tea and cracking knuckles. We were playing a dollar a trick. The Sous Chef and myself were representing the back of the house, while the hostess and the bartender stood for the front. The tension was just beneath the surface, not unlike the wind which was growing as steadily as the warnings from the telly. The restlessness of the waitress going unnoticed, a bottle of Absolut now beside her glass.

I had just laid down my cards to go alone, yielding a quick kick under the table from my wide-eyed partner, when we noticed she was gone. It was that quick. A ghost could not have disappeared with more ease. Her best friend the hostess stood up and looked about the room in a panic.

"Where the hell'd she go," she said, her head swiveling.

"I don't have a clue," said the bartender, the manager turning his head to see what was going on.

"Probably just a bit of fresh air, now about these jacks," I said, attempting to bring levity.

"You don't understand. She could be anywhere. Anything could have happened We've got to find her."

In the silence that followed that request, the wind howled and the voice on the telly told us of the twisters in Wisconsin. We set our cups and glasses down, donned our jumpers and jackets, and looked at each other wondering what to do. For the first time all evening we noticed the windows lighting up with the bluishness of lightning; a sudden gust of wind barreled into the front of the building, shaking the windows and stretching the canvas on the entryway into an ugly, uneven shape.

"Where would she run to, I mean, where would she go? Does she have someplace special?" the manager said, walking over and tidying up the table.

"She likes parks. She's from the country, and she likes to be among trees."

"Let's go, how far could she have gone, I mean its only been ten or fifteen minutes."

"Right, then, which direction?"

"Veteran's first, then up Fulton to the cemetery."

And away we went, the four of us card players piling into the bartender's car and the manager staying put in case she came back to the restaurant. The rain falling in large drops, lightning high up bouncing from cloud to cloud, and the thunder in the distance was the backdrop for this sudden drama.

But it was something unseen and unheard that made the hairs on my neck stand up. There was that strange stillness. A feeling of emptiness, like all the air was being sucked away. I paused, a memory flitting across my mind, and then jumped into the car.

We were at and through Veteran's Park in minutes, it not being far from the restaurant. All of us slightly winded from scouring the park and the nearby streets. Heads shaking and hands being held up as if to say, 'No, she's not here.'

It was about half two, almost quarter of three, when we leapt back into the car and dashed up Fulton to the cemetery. This search would take much longer, as it covered many times the area with loads of places to hunker down and not be seen.

We spread out, four abreast, about twenty feet apart, and did a slow trot from the west end to the east. There was just enough light to see the tombstones, and despite the pressing concern, the eeriness of our surroundings was not lost on any of us. The tall oaks were waving back and forth as the wind picked up, casting dim shadows from the streetlights on gravestones and grass. It was an old cemetery, and though well kept, it still had a roughness to it. Our heads were constantly turning to see where she could be, and despite looking down, there would every few minutes come the yelp from one of us having banged a shin into some poor soul's final resting marker.

When we reached the far end of the graveyard, the hostess yelled for us excitedly. We ran over, hoping she had found her.

"What is it?"

"I know where she is."

"Where?"

"Riverside Park. It's her favorite place. There's an old bridge there, I'm not sure where. It's all rusty. She climbs a fence to get to it. I know she's there. She's probably sitting on it, right now, watching the storm come in."

And that was that. We ran back to the car, hearts pounding, lungs burning, and were off back down Fulton Street. The sky in front of us was black, the rain more steady, and I noticed that the power lines were starting to rock back and forth with the trees.

By the time we got to Riverside Park, the storm was mounting. The wind had to be over fifty knots an hour. Twigs and small branches were coming down with the rain. We didn't quite know where to go, as none of us had really been to the park before, so we pulled into the south entrance and started running up the walkway.

As we ran, the storm intensified. The trees were no longer rocking, they were being lashed straight east by the gales. The thunder was audibly closer, the rain stinging when it hit.

At the next park entrance we slowed up as a giant limb split from a poplar tree and landed not twenty yards in front of us. We exchanged worried glances.

"Whaddya think?" asked the bartender.

"I've been on the Atlantic in gales," I panted between breaths, "and I'm telling you, this one is just getting started. We've got to hurry. Follow me, lads."

Over a bridge, on up the walkway, in a dead run we went. The trees thinned out, which made us a bit more comfortable, but the wind, easily over sixty knots, almost knocked us off our feet. In the flashes of lightning, a building could be seen up ahead, and beyond that, the dim silhouette of a bridge.

We ran past the building and up the path to the bridge. In the strobes of lightning, it loomed in front of us for an instant and then would sink back into the wind, rain and darkness.

It was surrounded by fencing, eight feet high, a relic serving no purpose other than being too big to move and too old to be useful. It was maybe twenty feet or more tall, and had several rusty rails running perpendicular to its span about two-thirds up. About five feet below these there were matching rails on its topside. It was in one of these corners that she sat. Her legs wrapped around the perpendicular rail, she was facing another rail, which went vertically from bottom to top, and her arms were wrapped around this. Her long hair was matted into dreadlocks that stood straight back from her head. She saw us running up to the bridge as we called to her, our voices lost in the gale.

The Sous Chef and myself scaled the fence, leapt over and started to climb the bridge to get to her. She was good enough to meet us half way, apologies falling from her mouth like tears. We helped her back to earth and over the fence.

As we stood there, the two girls locked in an embrace only best mates can ever understand, we heard what sounded like a snap from the other side of the bridge. My curiosity piqued, I rounded the fence. There, as if placed, lay an entire tree, roots and all, stretching some sixty feet from where it had been in the ground. From the other side of the pond I heard another two "snaps."

"We had better get feckin' movin'."

The five of us took off in a run. The wind was ferocious. It had to be approaching nearly eighty knots with peak gusts well beyond. In the open spaces it might be topping a hundred. The thunder was nearly on top of us, the rain hard and sideways. Branches blew into our faces, along with sand and dirt.

We crossed the bridge and had only several hundred yards to make the car. Behind us I heard the "snap", a tree hitting the ground muffled by the roar of the wind. I winced as a branch hit me in the face. It felt like I had been punched.

The lights of buildings at the park's south entrance were becoming brighter. There were less than one hundred yards to cover when a deafening "snap" happened just in front of us. The tree landed half way between the car and us, its mass blocking out the lights.

Without any hesitation, we jogged over to the left and skirted the fallen willow. In a few more moments we were at the car, scrambling to get in. The bartender started the engine and we were off, away from the park, from the trees, heading south towards downtown and away from the storm.

The wind shrieked around us, the car being buffeted violently. Our breath was coming in gasps, a towel being passed around to wipe wet faces. Fingers rubbed bruises or checked cuts and scrapes. I closed my eyes and remembered the memory that the stillness before the storm had stirred up in me.

It was a long time ago. I was twelve, standing on the pier at Dungloe. The sky to the west was black, and the same eerie stillness rippled across the water. The gale that would pound Dungloe that day came out of the southwest. It had winds in excess of one hundred knots and it would save most of its fury for the open sea. Out on the sea that day was a trawler called *Leannan Si,* and my uncle Colm. Neither one of them would come home that day. When my mother told me Colm had drowned, I became very angry, and ran up into the blackthorn in the hills overlooking the sea. My brother would later come find me, offer me my first cigarette, and do his best to explain what had happened. He wouldn't stay long, just checking to be sure I was okay, but the time that he had spent slowed my heart, stopped the tears, and gave me room to sort things out.

In the car, driving back to the restaurant, we were all too tired to say anything to the waitress for doing what she had done. But in my heart, I could never be mad at her, for I knew why she ran.

9

How many times in the sporting world, no matter what sport it might be, have you heard that oft-spoken cliché about being ready to step in when a man goes down. I hadn't; and I wasn't.

It was one of those nights when the number of times the jam-side of the toast will land jam-side down is a perfect ten out of ten. Old Mr. Murphy and his confounding law were working overtime tonight.

I was working at my back prep table, safely away from the din and chaos of the line on a busy Friday night. The way of it was like this: I would process whatever foods or sauces the teams working the hot line and the cold line needed. They would call out a food item, and I, knowing what they meant by the one-word or two-word bellow, would quickly produce the end result and run it to them. It works out well. On the theory side, if one of them has to leave their station, say from injury or more likely, the threat of acquiring over-time, I would step in. The only wrinkle being that the pace of the line is far quicker than that of prep, and when one hasn't been on the line in some time, the rust shows right through the paint.

While I whisked together a bowl of pesto, the garlic hovering above the table while the Romano cut straight through, I heard someone react in pain and then a commotion from the line. "Wiley!"

I had only a few more turns to finish the pesto.

"Wiley! Godammit!" It was the Chef himself.

I ran around the corner. "Do you need that pesto?"

"I need you on sauté. Finish the pesto and get over here now!"

"Aye. One minute."

"Well hurry the fuck up"

"Aye, aye."

Pesto whisked. Oil added. Pesto whisked. Touch more cheese. Pesto whisked.

"Wiley! Are you back in Scotland or what? Get your ass out here!"

Now, my relationship with the Chef is strained to say the least. He is one of those people who is always yelling, always in your face, always throwing something, be they words or pans. I rounded the corner with the pesto as the Chef rounded it the other way, an explosion of viscous green liquid enveloping us.

"Godammit, Wiley!"

"Jaysus! You scared the livin' shite out of me."

"Sous! You've got broiler and expediting while I change my goddamn shirt. Move it, Scotty! Sauté, now!"

I bit my tongue, unclenched my fist, the sneaky left one, and went to the stove.

On the mat at my feet was a kitchen towel covered in blood. This was not nearly as horrible as the six pans bubbling away on the stove in front of me.

"You must be fecking kidding me."

"A big hello, Wiley," my mate the Sous Chef said, a goofy grin on his face and sweat filling a do-rag on his brow. "We are getting our ass kicked tonight, bro."

"Which of these do you need and when," I said, pointing at the pans burning on the stove.

"All of them now, of course. Adam sliced his thumb, had to leave the line. Head honcho freaked and couldn't swing it."

"So he called in the Irish, very wise." And off I went.

The menu has six sauces that must be prepared from scratch when the dishes are ordered. Here they all were: Creole, lemon-caper, a fiesta with cilantro and lime, béarnaise, an apple far-east with chutney, and the Chef's own specialty, an eight-step sauce that he called Ambrosia.

"Would you happen to know at what stage any of these sauces are?"

"Not a clue, man. You're going to have to use your finger, and I do solemnly swear not to tell a living soul."

As I plunked my left forefinger into the pan closest to me, the printer on the hot line began to chatter out several orders. The Sous Chef started calling them out while all of us at our stations grimaced.

"Ambrosia. Fiesta. Porky chops with the apple-India. Two more ambrosias. Hey, how about another ambrosia and a lemon-caper. Have fun, Wiley. See ya in an hour."

The hour turned into four. There was never an end in sight. For every pan that I prepared to perfection, it seemed one went into the garbage. All six burners were on the entire night; it seemed every patron ordered a dish involving my station. In the middle of this horror, dressed now to leave but before vacating the kitchen, the Chef decided to stand next to me and critique my work. In language only a sailor could appreciate and at a level only a drill instructor could re-create, he spent some twenty minutes yelling at me in front of the staff while I tried to cook. I thought to myself at one point, maybe slicing a finger wasn't such a bad way out.

It was so busy that time actually stood still. I could complete several tasks, turn all the pans on the stove, walk the dirty ones over to the disher, who by this point was swearing at me in Spanish, look up at the clock, and realize that only a few minutes had passed.

When it finally ended, four ambrosias being poured over angel hair pasta by the Sous Chef, I took a step back from the stove and leaned against the line. The area I had been working in resembled the GPO in 1916, replete with blood, gunpowder, and prisoners. There was a good two inches of blackened cream, oil, and butter covering the entire stove. I knew it would take an hour to clean up; I knew I didn't have the energy to do it.

"Wiley," said the Sous Chef, leaning against the line beside me, arm about my shoulder, "call it a night, man. You've been here longer than us and well, it sucked to be sauté tonight."

I had no words with which to reply. I almost felt like crying. It was one of the kindest gestures I had experienced since moving to Grand Rapids. Before he could finish the sentence, 'you don't need to thank me,' I was out the back door, cigarette already lit.

I crossed the side street in a jog, crossed Fulton in a sprint, and was halfway through Veteran's Park when the obelisk with the names of those who had fallen stopped me yet again in my tracks. I lit another cigarette, exhaling and sighing as I leaned against the monument.

"I am going to drink this town dry!" I said to the sky.

"And I am with you, my man," said a street person whom I hadn't seen lying on a bench not fifteen feet away.

"Sorry, lad, didn't mean to wake ya."

"No, no, not sleeping, just going over some figures in my head."

"Anyone's I know?"

He laughed. "Well now that you mention it, I was earlier thinking of this pretty little waitress I used to know in Flint."

"Waitress! Shit! I was supposed to meet the Waitress at the local. Cheers, lad, thanks for reminding me."

The Waitress had rung the restaurant earlier asking the Sous Chef and I to meet her for drinks. We hadn't seen much of her since the storm, she was working mostly days, and she had wanted to say thanks for braving the winds by standing us a round or two. I dashed across the park, down the block, and made my way to the local in hopes of still being able to catch her.

I was walking in the door as she was leaving, being all but pulled out the pub by a rather large gentleman in a biker's jacket and a goatee.

"Wiley," she said, "what took you so long. Were you guys busy?"

"Like you wouldn't believe."

"I left some money with the bartender so you and the Sous could drink."

"Ya won't come in and have one as well?"

"No, we've got other plans. Maybe we'll stop back though."

I could see the big fella roll his eyes at this.

"I'm Wiley," I said, sticking out my hand.

"Butch, pleased," he replied, in a voice that seemed anything but and a handshake that should have been served with chips.

"Well, maybe next time, like. I'm on me way in, I've got the thirst tonight."

"That bad, huh?" the Waitress said, hoping for Butch to relinquish.

"It was unbelievable. Truly. Come on in and I'll tell ya all about it."

She looked back to him.

"Let's go. We're late."

"Sorry, Wiley."

"Alright, lads. All the best, thanks for the rounds."

"Thanks again for the rescue." She laid a hand on my shoulder and was abruptly pulled down the street and around the corner.

"Treat her nice, ya bruiser," I said to myself, pulling out a cigarette and walking into a hail of drunken welcomes.

"Wiley, I've got two pints of Guinness and two shots of Jameson right here waiting for ya," the barman announced, one hand laying cocktail napkins down and the other setting up my first round.

"Jaysus, Jimmy would like to marry me," as the laughter and stout quickly extinguished the night's fire.

The Sous Chef strolled in as round number four was placed in front of me.

"Christ, Wiley, there must've been a gallon of butter, oil, and cream on that stove."

"One drop for every drop that went out the door and into the waste."

"Hey, Jimmy, Bud and a Crown. Was the Waitress here?"

"She was indeed. And she left a pile of money for us to drink on."

"Really. That was nice of her. What'd she have to say?"

"Not a thing. She was dragged out the door by some big geezer as I walked in."

"She did leave this, besides the money," said Jimmy, handing over a card.

"Let Wiley read it, I'm too fucking tired."

"A card! Lovely. I haven't received a card from a woman since my wife divorced me."

"Your wife sent you a card on your divorce?"

"Yes, she couldn't thank me enough." More laughter. More stout. More whiskey.

"Hurry up, Wiley, I'm falling asleep."

"Do ya spell sous, s-o-u-s, or is it s-u-e."

"Read the card."

I pulled the card out from the envelope. On the front was an impressionist rendering of a tree. I opened it up, and on the left side it simply said, 'Thank-you both so very much for coming to my rescue. I'm very sorry for having been so foolish. I guess sometimes I just can't help myself. Friends always.' On the right side was a pen and ink drawing she had done herself of the five of us running through the wind-blown trees. There was the bartender and the hostess on the left, a great willow tree bending toward them, the Sous Chef on the right, another tall tree leaning beside him, and there, in the middle, were her and I, holding hands and running.

"Wiley, if it's not in Irish, please read the card."

I didn't say anything, my mind now wandering down an avenue it had not been down in quite some time.

"Wiley," the Sous said, taking the card from me. "Thank-you both for, yadda, yadda, sorry for being foolish, blah, blah, blah, and what do we have here. Hey! How come she's holding your hand? Wiley, what gives with this drawing. Wiley. Hey, is that a blush."

"I think that's a blush," replied Jimmy.

"Wiley, you're blushing," the Sous said turning to look at me.

"I am not. I'm flushed."

"Flushed! You're blushing."

"You're on crack. It's just this cheap whiskey."

"So, you're calling my whiskey cheap," Jimmy stood to his full six-four.

"I produce phlegm with a higher alcohol content."

"It's a blush," several voices rang out in unison.

They continued to have a go at me, telling me how red my face had been, making fun of my sauces, and describing in great detail how impossible it was to understand me as I became more intoxicated. As the night slid into morning, I would turn my head to the big window, the lights of downtown Grand Rapids making haloes from a mist that had settled, and did my best to retrieve my mind from walking too far down that avenue, from thinking too much about her. The effort was in vain, for as surely as one pint followed the other well past closing and into the short hours of the morning, I took up the card and tucked it into my jacket pocket, one hesitant footfall following another.

10

Let me begin by saying that I share an Irishman's love for all things wild. Someone once told me that the difference between England and Ireland is that in England things are groomed to a fair-thee-well, whereas in Ireland those things are allowed to run free. As an Irishman, I have always taken this to heart with great pride. However, this love of wildness would be sharply tested by a two-pound kitten and the mother of all mulberry trees.

I would like to say it was a dark and stormy night, and, well, it was. The fine June day had clouded over late in the evening threatening much-needed rain. My good mate the Sous Chef and I had finished up work earlier than expected, purchased a bottle of Jameson's, and were prepared to wile away the evening at his flat playing cribbage.

He had just flipped over the most perfect card I could possibly imagine, my impish grin hiding behind my glass of whiskey, when we heard a mewing coming from just outside the kitchen window. We looked at each other, shrugged, and went back to the game.

In my head I was already rounding the street, my crib adding up to what had to be the most unbelievable point total ever, when once again the mewing caused us to pause. There seemed to be a desperate kind of plea at the bottom of each whine. We set our hands down and crossed the kitchen to the window above the sink in order to get a better listen.

"Whaddya think? Have a look?"

I shot a forlorn look over to my point-bulging hand.

"Och, sure. Bloody cat. I was just set to skunk ya."

We went out the kitchen door and into the night grabbing a flashlight on the way. As we walked across the lawn, I asked him what it was we were stepping on. He pointed to the largest mulberry tree I had ever seen. The grass was so thick with mulberries that it not only made walking difficult, but you could feel the juice seeping in through your shoes.

We had crossed the lawn and just as we stepped up to the bushes, the mewing stopped. We got down on our hands and knees to get a closer look when the shrubbery parted in a burst of leaves and fur as the cat split us down the middle, dashing off to another thicket. We decided to give chase and crossed the yard a second time.

Kneeling down in front of the thicket, the Sous Chef shone the flashlight on the feline and we could see that it wasn't a cat at all, but a calico kitten no more than ten weeks old. It had perfect markings and was just dirty and wet enough to elicit a warm, squishy feeling from even the most hardened of IRA operatives. I looked over at the Sous Chef who met my eyes with the most pathetic, I-have-to-have -this-kitten face I had ever seen.

"I've got to have this kitten. Look at the poor thing. If we can just get her out of the bushes."

"You get to the one side of the bushes and I'll stay here, start walking towards me to flush him out, and I'll nab him."

This seemed like a sound plan. As the Sous Chef noisily careened through the bushes to force the kitten toward me, it darted to my right, my left, and then straight at me. All of this caused me to shift my body weight in several directions at once, resulting in a sick, flopping sort of dive as the kitten ran past me and back to the first set of bushes.

I picked myself up, wiping away mulberries and grass, only to see in the streetlights that I was covered in purple stains. I rolled my eyes to heaven and jogged back over to my colleague who was already trying to force the kitten out of those bushes.

Just as I got to the first thicket, the bushes opened suddenly with the Sous Chef carrying the kitten hissing and spinning around in his arms.

"Give me a hand!"

"Whaddya want me to do!"

"Jesus, this thing's got some claws."

And with that, the kitten ran up his chest and down his back as if he were a tree. It spun around in a circle and ran toward me, veering off at the last second just as I dove at it. I landed with the wet thud of mulberries, face down and hands holding only the palms God had given me.

"Maybe we're going about this the wrong way," the Sous Chef said in consolation.

"Is it illegal to use firearms in the city?"

"That's not nice."

We walked over to the second thicket of bushes and shone the light on the kitten. It let out a long, lonely mew.

"It's laughing at us."

"No, Wiley. It's hungry. Hungry and scared."

"Do you know of anyone who has some cat food?"

"Yeah, the woman in the apartment above me has a cat. Give me half a minute."

"Bring a blanket, too."

Now we had a plan. We would place a small bowl of food in front of it, and while it was distracted, throw the blanket over the kitten and that would be that. What, could possibly be more simple?

When the Sous Chef returned with the gear, we crouched down in front of the bushes just a scant few feet in front of our quarry. Slowly he placed the food in front of the kitten and watched with delight as it eagerly ate from the bowl. The Sous Chef lifted the blanket up to toss it, when the sudden movement startled the kitten and it darted. It dashed between us, each human making a vain attempt at catching it; gravity taking the place of grace, we both slammed once more to earth. I picked up the food dish, pulled the blanket from his hands, and tossed it on the back steps.

"You were close enough the last time to grab it. Just take your time, be steady. The poor thing is half-starved, it should just sit above the food."

We walked over to the first set of bushes. I crouched down, gently set the food bowl by the kitten. I slowly inched back to my right, turned the flashlight on, and shone it in the kitten's eyes.

The Sous Chef just as slowly moved into the bushes on my left. We sat for some time and let the kitten eat. It nervously looked up, searching for the two bumbling people who had been trying to catch it.

The wind began to rise, causing the mulberries to start raining down on top of us. By this time, we were so covered with purple stains that we paid no notice to it. The sound of them hitting the parked cars, however, was loud enough to spook the kitten.

"This is it, lad. One chance. Take a careful aim and try to trap it to the ground so you can get your other hand over."

The Sous Chef slowly reached over, the kitten still eating, and opened his hand. He was about a foot away, inching closer through a tangle of branches. At the last second, he looked over to me with eyes seeking reassurance.

"Just grab the shaggin' thing."

He set his face in determination, causing me to laugh at the absurdity of this. He shot me a stern look, his gaze returning to the kitten, and his hand then lunged downward.

In a burst, the kitten leaped skyward. Where once there had been feline, now there was only space and an empty clutching hand. The Sous Chef let out a dull howl as he hit the ground on a twist of roots.

We looked around the base of the bushes, the kitten mewing frantically, but could find nothing. Crouching down, I shone the light up into the bush. The kitten was there, three feet off the ground, tangled in a mass of branches. Legs bicycling, eyes wide, it was snared in the very bush it had used for protection. I simply stood up, took two steps, bent over, and gently pulled the kitten free.

As we walked back to the flat, the wind rising even more, mulberries falling like large, purple raindrops, I handed the kitten over to its new friend. He held her tight, but with care, his free hand stroking her between the ears. You could actually see her body go slack with exhaustion, an audible sigh slipping from her tiny mouth.

We sat back down at the kitchen table, covered head to toe with purple stains and sweat, each of us looking like poster children for some weird tropical disease. I topped off our watery glasses of Jameson's, rubbed my eyes with purple hands, and looked down at the kitten. She had drunk what seemed like a gallon of water, finished the dish of food, and was now curled-up on the table, beside the cribbage board, sleeping.

The Sous Chef, eyes full of love, looked up from the kitten to me.

"What do you think I should name her?"

"Bushes, berries or bugger, play your bloody hand."

And with that, I began counting: "fifteen-two, fifteen-four, fifteen-six..."

11

In 1776, the First Continental Congress signed The Declaration of Independence declaring the separate and sovereign rights of the new America. This act would fuel a rebellion into a full-blown war, and would create two documents that would forever change the course of human history.

Two hundred and twenty-odd years later, I find myself, an Irishman having lived in this country for five years, wiping down the year's collective gunk off of various kitchen appliances. Far removed from the nuances of sovereign rights, my independence hinged to my pay packet and my constitution in desperate need of a pint of Guinness, I try to keep a focus on what I'm doing despite the heat.

The restaurant is closed for lunch today, opening this evening in hopes of attracting people coming downtown for the fireworks. We took advantage of the break to let those of us not working this evening catch up on some well needed cleaning. The Sous Chef and myself had already taken apart and cleaned everything on the line, and were now wiping down the prep area.

While I took apart the meat-slicer, I thought about all this day stood for. I had hoped there would be lectures or film festivals or other events centering this most important day in the nation's history. However, beneath the glow of long weekends, of summer trips planned around the Fourth, there didn't seem to be a buzz of excitement for the day itself. There just didn't seem to be a clear recognition that this was the birth of their nation.

I remembered when I was a child, seeing the fireworks in New York City on the telly in the pub. Though the set was bloody awful and only black and white, you could imagine the colors as the shells exploded behind the Statue of Liberty. Our next door neighbor, Mrs. Dolan, would exclaim time after time how her son Danny lived in New York and just had to be down there in the crowd. Her face would beam with pride when she would say that he had taken his oath of citizenship to become an American.

Standing behind me in the pub that day was my cousin Padraig. My Uncle Colm's oldest boy, he would announce his intentions of crossing the water not two weeks later. His reason for this was his being in Derry during one of the Orange parades. He and my brother had been chased through the city center by some Loyalist thugs who caught up to them on the edge of the Bogside, the Catholic ghetto, and beat them. After that, despite living in the Republic, he decided to leave for America.

My Uncle Colm was very close to his oldest son, and with the announcement of his impending departure, Colm carried a heavy heart. Because of his great love for Padraig, he threw him an old fashioned American wake, a going away party that mixes happiness and sadness, because very few of those who leave ever come home again.

At that party, hanging next to the Irish Tricolour, was the American flag. It was the first time I had ever seen it. I loved the way the white stars jumped out at you from their deep, dark blue background, my cousin telling me that each of those stars represented a State, and each of those States was the size of Ireland. But secretly what I loved best about the flag was that it represented a country that had whupped the English. Not once, but twice.

I called the Sous Chef over to help me move the food chopper to a different table. We lifted carefully, as the rubber feet have a way of sticking to the stainless steel and then suddenly giving way. With a reassuring 'pop' the machine broke free and we swung it over. We wiped down the remaining surfaces, swept, mopped, and walked out into the brilliant sunshine of summer.

"Smoke and soak?" he asked.

"Aye, that'd be grand. Vet's?"

"Yeah. Man, what a day."

We walked over to the empty park, each finding a vacant bench, sat down and pulled out cigarettes.

"Hey, Wiley, you got a light? I left mine on my desk." His 'desk' was actually the back windowsill, the unofficial office of the Sous Chef.

"Aye," I said, lighting my cigarette and tossing him the lighter.

There was a comfortable silence. Two men sprawled on park benches taking in the sunshine, contemplating the night off. No real worries, no plans, no one ambitious enough to make them.

"Say, Wiley?"

"Yeah."

"Where you at? I mean you've hardly said a word all day."

"Just thinking about home."

"It's the Fourth. You should be thinking about your new home."

"Well I am. I mean, I was."

"Do you find yourself as confusing as we find you?"

"I was thinking about the Fourth back in Ireland when I was a boy."

"And so?"

"Just family stuff, my brother, my uncle. His son came over here about thirty years or so ago."

"Did ya ever look him up, while you've been here," he craned his head toward me.

"No."

"Your own cousin, and you didn't look him up."

"Sorry Father, but I was busy."

Silence resumed. New cigarettes lit off of old ones. Old ones flicked into the meditating pool.

"What's your brother like," he asked.

"Well, I don't really know him anymore. He left the house when I was still pretty young. But from my memories of then, like on that Fourth of July all those years back, he was my hero,"

"Not your Pop?"

I shivered, a cool breeze on hot shoulders. "Oh no. No, my brother was exactly who I wanted to be like when I got big."

"Tough guy?"

"The toughest."

"Really?"

"Oh yeah. Him and Colm, my cousin, the one who lives here now, well New York the last I knew, they would go to Derry. All the time, like. No matter if it was marching season or not. They had no fear. Got the snot kicked out 'em time and again," I explained.

"Why? What's marching season?"

"Marching season is when all the zoos open their cages and let all the animals run around Northern Ireland without any supervision. In fact, they starve them for three weeks before they release them, and taunt them with bloody big pieces of meat with pictures of the Pope painted on the sides."

I burst into a fit of laughter. The Sous Chef sat up and looked over at me.

"You are one looney fucker."

"I'm serious; it's just like that."

"Can I get the non-Wiley version," he asked.

"Marching season is when the Loyalists, Protestants that is, have loads of parades to rub in the fact that they kicked the shite out of us at the Battle of the Boyne and at the Siege of Derry. That's it in a nutshell. And so they go on the piss for three months, dressed up in layers of polyester clothing, and march around in the hot sun beating drums, beating their chests, and beating up the odd Catholic."

"And your bro and cousin would walk right into the middle of this mess."

"With glee."

"That's nuts."

"I'm sure at that age you did silly things as well."

He thought about it for a second, "Yeah, I did. How about you."

"Aye, but no. I guess I saved all my silly stuff for later in life."

"That explains a lot. Hey, let's find some air conditioning. We cooks weren't meant to be outside this long."

"Brilliant idea. Fireworks tonight?"

"Yeah. They should be good. I bet Boston had good fireworks."

"Never saw them. Always working."

"That's why they invented beer, Wiley. For dopes like us."

We left the park and walked toward the river, bypassing the local as it seemed to us that on a holiday we should drink somewhere different. While we walked, each of us lost in our own thoughts, I remembered the days after Colm left for America. My uncle had taken his boat out for over a month. The fleet had said he was nearly to Greenland. When he returned, he left the next day and sailed to Spain. He cabled from Brittany, the Orkneys, from Rathlin Island, stayed on Tory Island for a week, and then finally came home. He had done all of this without a crew.

My brother had done the same thing in his own way. He was up before light, off into the hills behind the house and not returning until after dark. Walking for hours on end, day after day. My father tolerated this until a delivery van dropped my brother off late one night. The driver had picked him up just this side of Strabane. It hadn't mattered that he wasn't in school, not to our Da; it was that he had started to get out of reach.

The Sous Chef and I spent several long hours in a restaurant beside the river. The air inside was cool; the bar was marble and there were wide glass windows with a view of the downtown, the river running towards us and by us, lazy and brown. I dodged his questions about my family as best I could, asking him about his relations, America, work.

As night settled, thousands of people began to fill the bridges and line the river. We walked out of the restaurant and onto its deck overlooking the Grand River. There was anticipation, an eagerness that was not unlike Christmas morning for children, as necks craned and faces looked skyward. I had never seen fireworks before, and I shared in this energy by shifting my weight from one foot to the other waiting for whatever would happen next.

There were three consecutive deep booms. Conversations ceased momentarily, men hurried to the bar to replenish glasses, and a rush of diners came out onto the deck. The Sous Chef gave me an elbow, myself looking at the blonde hostess opening the door for the guests, and pointed to the sky.

"Fireworks, Wiley. We're out here for fireworks. You can stare at her later."

Just then the show began. At first it took some time for me to take it in, to measure what I was seeing against what I had expected; but then, as lazy and sure as the river, a wide smile lit my face. When the grand finale had ended, the successive shells tapping us in the chest, the bright reds, blues and whites reflected in our eyes and across our cheeks, I was wiping away tears. This was much better than marching.

We finished our drinks on the deck, smiled and said thank-you to the pretty hostess, and walked through the crowds to the local. Quiet contemplation, the white noise of a thousand voices leaving he and I each alone, though we walked stride for stride. When we sat at our end of the bar, I knew exactly what he would ask.

"So, what did you think?"

"The hostess? She's very pretty."

He rolled his eyes, shook his head and sighed.

"You are hopeless, Wiley. Looney and hopeless."

"That I may be, but can I have my lighter back from this afternoon."

He looked at me from the corners of his eyes.

"You don't miss much, do you?"

"Only the big stuff."

"Wiley?" called the barman, "pint of Guinness?"

"No, not tonight, I think I'll have a Bud."

"There is hope for you yet," said the Sous Chef, sliding over my lighter, but taking a cigarette. "Yes, indeed, hope for you yet."

12

The heat has a way of working on you, the irony being that we chefs, working with all manners of heat to bake, boil, broil, fry, grill, simmer, sear, sauté, and roast, are in fact actually cooking at the same time. Kitchens are by nature very hot places, usually without ventilation or air conditioning, sometimes even without a simple fan so as to not cool the dishes we have labored to make hot. In the summertime these places become extreme, and the behavior of those who work in them tends to follow suit.

The past week had seen a ten-day long heat wave that had the entire city on edge. Civility was being openly broiled away, typically respectable people doing outlandish things, acting completely outside the usual Mid-western decorum. Even in our cozy, well-heeled bar, a fight had broken out the previous night, all sides eventually standing down, shaking hands and blaming the heat.

In the kitchen, where by the broiler it was one hundred and twenty, it was like being the caterer in Dante's *Inferno*.

Just last night, a busy Saturday as a matter of fact, this lady requests to see the individual who had prepared her salad, a main course featuring wilted endive, mandarin oranges, pan-seared tuna and a champagne vinaigrette. Would not take no for an answer, bring this person to the table this instant.

Unsure of what to expect, but hoping for the best, I set my tasks aside and was led out into the dining room, the Chef yelling at me to hurry-up.

Upon reaching the table, introductions cut in half by the woman, she shakes her head with indignation and my hopes were dashed like timbers on the rocks. I had expected glorious praise to be heaped upon me for this masterful culinary creation. Instead, and in every cook's nightmare, it seemed she was about to humiliate me in front of our teeming clientele.

Then comes the odd part. She opens her mouth, myself flinching as if from a blow, and utters, "My man, I hate to tell you this, but I can't find anything wrong with this dish."

I didn't know how to respond. I had never heard anyone put such a strange, backhanded spin on a compliment as this. Before I realized what to say, my Irish nature was already talking.

"Thank you, I think, but aren't you missing the point? I mean, you're supposed to enjoy the dish, right."

She stared back at me, dumbfounded, sweat beading her forehead despite the groaning air conditioner, her eyes seeking some sort of an answer.

"I guess what I'm trying to say is that, shouldn't you be pleased that the dish is good?"

Same look, less registering.

"I just can't find anything wrong with it."

To this I stammered a second thank you, turned, and walked back to the kitchen, my head shaking in befuddlement, wondering if she had, for whatever reason or no reason at all, just wanted to demand someone come out to the table.

As I opened the swinging door to the kitchen I was nearly pelted with a baked potato. When I realized what was going on, I had to duck again, the splat of tuber resonating from slamming into the stainless dish machine.

The Chef, working his fifth double in a row in one hundred degree heat, had finally snapped. The object of his frustration was the dishwasher who was swearing at him in Spanish and hiding behind a dish tray.

I quickly distanced myself from the dishwasher.

Panicked employees ducked for cover, openly fled the kitchen, or stood laughing and slapping knees, adding insult to injury. My friend the Sous Chef, a champion of many causes, intervened on behalf of the dishwasher. This resulted in his being struck square in the forehead by one of the potato missiles.

"That's it," he said to the ceiling, hands held above his tilted face as if beseeching God himself. The stress of his own schedule, of fate having placed him right beside the Chef for the same five brutal days, was the cause of his own impending meltdown and as plain on his face as the dripping spud.

He ripped off his apron, pulled a cigarette out of his front shirt pocket and lit-up as he walked out the back door. The Chef pretended not to notice, turned his back on the staff and began swearing at the pots and pans on the stove, imploring them for answers to questions none of us could figure out. I took the lull as opportunity, crossing the kitchen to chase down my friend, the Waitress tossing me my pack of smokes from the break room.

He was pacing back and forth beneath a streetlight, puffing furiously on his cigarette, shaking his head with anger, throwing his hands out in front of him as if he were Jack Nicholson in *The Shining*. You could feel the rage coming off of him in waves with the heat.

"I'm not going back in there. It's ridiculous. I mean ya just don't treat people like that. The bastard. Throwing things. I mean, how friggin' childish. Christ!" hands rending the cigarette in half, stopping, then punching the air and lighting another cigarette.

He looked over at me hoping for agreement, hoping I would say 'yeah, let's just leave right now.'

I said nothing.

"I'm really not going back in there."

"I never asked if you were. Just thought I might have me a smoke before ya leave."

He looked at me for a long moment.

"Yeah, right. You want me to walk back in there as if nothing happened."

"Aye. Pretty much. Come on, man, there's a pint with our names on it at the end of the shift."

"He threw a potato at me!"

"At least he had the decency to throw a cooked potato. It could've been much worse."

This resulted in a rather sharp look. It was time to dispense the wisdom of my years, himself the lucky recipient of my having worked in harsher climes than these. "Look, it's not that big a deal and no one got hurt. I mean, it could have been worse. All chefs throw things once in awhile. I once worked in a kitchen in London with a chef who threw knives. I worked in a kitchen in Boston with a chef who threw pots. I worked with a brilliant chef in Dublin who just happened to be a heroin addict and would throw-up from time to time."

"Man. But still, why do people have to act that way. Why can't they just be cool?"

I paused, the overwhelming correctness of this statement being deflated by reality as quickly as it was spoken.

"I used to live for golf." Now he was really looking at me strange. I continued, knowing, sort of, where I was going. "I mean, I lived for it. When I wasn't cooking, I was golfing. My ex's family belonged to a club. They introduced me to the game, sort of a way to drink without looking like your drinking. It became my passion. Just before my divorce, when it felt like the whole world was coming down in buckets right on top of my head, I took my set of clubs to a spit of land near Logan Airport. I teed off every ball. Flicked each and every tee. Then threw my gloves, shoes, bag, and every club into Boston Harbor." I lit another cigarette and waited for a response.

My friend looked over at me, quizzically at first. His brow furrowed, eyes looking past the brick walls for impossible solutions.

"Sometimes you just lose it," I continued, "it's just tension relief. Boom. Had enough. Sorry folks, but let me play through."

He looked away, paced off a bit, his mind racing to the logical conclusion.

"Sometimes things are just too big to hide," this the coup de grace.

He then turned back, his eyes filled with understanding.

"I know, I know. Been there myself. It was just stupid and it's so goddamned hot." He paused, then began again in a lighter tone, "Man, you must've been really pissed off." He flicked his cigarette against the side of the restaurant and a shower of sparks fluttered to the ground. "So, what's his excuse? Why's he have to be such a freak?"

"I don't know, just part of the job description, I suppose."

"Alright. Congratulations. In we go."

We walked back into the kitchen, but before we could get past the prep area, he stopped, turned and set a fist on my shoulder.

"That divorce hurt, didn't it?"

I looked at him, memories suddenly hitting harder than potatoes, pots or knives.

"Thanks for reminding me. Now there's two pints waiting with our names on them."

He gave me a nod, a smile, clapped me on the back, and we returned to our stations as if nothing had ever happened. But inside of me, in that place where we keep the things we never share, I could still feel the embers smoldering, the ache of the loss, the humiliation, the betrayal. It seems that whenever and wherever I put my full faith in whomever, whomever takes great delight in dashing that faith to pieces.

I took up my knife, not nearly as sure of myself as I had appeared to the Sous, and let the order of the kitchen pull me from these thoughts. Comfort in the time-tested, codified methods of cooking things that let themselves be cooked, preparing dishes that allow themselves to be perfect, cleaning things that actually come clean. In kitchens unlike life, even in chaos, there is, at the very least, a plan. Chop Heat. Serve.

13

The magentas, oranges and soft reds of the dusk sky hovered above the black of the forest across the lake. If you let your eyes follow a line from the blue-black of the lake, past the forest and the setting sun, higher still than the deep blue of the sky, in the emerging void straight up you could see the first stars. It just doesn't get any better than this.

I'm standing on a deck overlooking the lake. The cottage behind me is empty, my friends having taken a carload up to the local tavern. I declined, despite the Waitress imploring me with words as well as eyes. Moments like this are just too precious.

Swirling the whiskey around in my glass, ice bumping the sides making those happy little 'ting' sounds, I take the time to reflect on an extraordinary day. I feel as though I've just participated in a marathon, the runner's high slowly ebbing away with the last light of the day.

A group of us from the restaurant had taken the day off so we could enjoy the Irish festival in Greenville. I had only heard about it recently, but with the rising tide of interest in all matters Irish, it was no problem convincing four other people to accompany me up to the Fleadh.

As it turned out, one of the ladies going up with us had access to a cottage on a wee lovely lake not far from the festival. This would alleviate the long drive back to the city and make for a bit of a get-away. It would also end up providing me with this rare, Thoreau-like evening.

As we say in Ireland, the craic was mighty. Meaning it was a great, bloody time. The atmosphere was lively, din of conversations mixing with the melodies of the music. Groups were playing both ballads and traditional. There were two tents selling stouts, ales, and lagers and it was inside one of these that I spent the bulk of my time.

As I called for a glass of stout, the fella beside me turned his head sharply upon noticing my brogue.

"Jaysus," he says, "You're from the North," his Dublin accent hanging around his head like a license plate.

"Aye. Donegal."

"For fuck's sake, put it there. I'm a Dublin man myself. What brings you to this part of the world?"

"A series of misadventures. How about yourself?"

"I'm headlining this Fleadh."

"Jaysus, Finbar himself!" I said astonished, "My mother loves your music. She happened to see you in Salthill, when you were with your brothers."

"That was a long time ago. Say, come on over to the table, we've got five counties represented here."

"One more," says I, "and you can join the United Kingdom."

We walked over to the first picnic table nearest the bar. The group of faces turned to me looked like a tapestry of Ireland.

"There's Pat from Dublin, Seamus form Derry, Jimmy from Kilkenny, Liam from Belfast, and Paddy from Kerry."

I introduced myself and hands were shook all around. What would enfold is what it means to be Irish. Here, on a patch of dirt on an American fairground, beneath an old tent, picnic table creaking with the weight of us, seven lads would wile away the day telling stories and jokes. Expressing wishes, reliving memories, sharing similar feelings about Ireland and America. It was absolutely perfect.

Hearing their voices, the lilt and roll of the different accents, the vividness of the stories, the absurdity of the jokes, made me ache for home. And yet, just the few hours of it was like drinking an elixir. It rejuvenated me. It did this by showing me, that no matter how far you are from home, home has a way of showing up wherever you happen to be.

Most of the lads at the table were performing at different stages throughout the day. Our table became a bit of Ireland for them to return to after singing and playing. It felt a bit like being at the head table at a wedding. Throughout the afternoon people would come up to have tapes and compact discs autographed. Snap a photo or two. On several occasions gentlemen from a local Irish organization would stand the lot of us a round, precipitating more introductions, handshakes, and of course, stories.

I rejoined my friends from the restaurant and we took our seats up front to watch Finbar perform. He was an excellent showman, eliciting laughs and tears in that Irish way. He played effortlessly, Jimmy from Kilkenny, half his age, doing his best to keep up. Reels, stories, and ballads, all surrounded by that strange mystique that makes you feel like they have invited you here to share a piece of themselves. As if the stage was their porch, and the audience sitting on their lawn.

I put my feet up on the top rail of the deck, night having fully descended, the sun's curtain call now a memory. Finbar's last reel, only a little over an hour ago, is still spinning about in my head. Bats make insane arcs in the pale moonlight and I, in lieu of wings, refill my glass.

The grandness of the day however, is tempered by something that happened just before the last act started. As I had walked with Finbar towards the stage, I asked him to play a song that was my mother's favorite, *Four Green Fields*. He agreed with pleasure. Then asked me the last time I had seen her. I froze, flushing with shame; I couldn't remember.

"At some point my friend," he said, his hand upon my shoulder, "you're going to need to go home."

He had an odd look about him, or maybe it was just the bunting on the pole waving in front of the light in the evening's breeze, but I asked him this anyway. "Some of your people, they were travelers, were they not?"

"Aye, I have that blood."

"What do ya see?"

He took up my hand in both of his, his eyes not leaving mine, and as the showman that he is, he paused for a long time.

"You're going to need to go home soon."

"It's me ma?"

"This is strong, boy. It's someone, someone in the family. Very ill. Gravely so. But there's something even more underneath this. Something terrible, hidden."

I stared at him perplexed, an unknown wariness showing in my eyes. "Who is it," I implored.

To which he closed his eyes, shook his head, opened his eyes. Then he gave me a wink, turned, and walked towards the stage, leaving me beside the light pole, a trashcan and the sickly sweet smell of cotton candy.

At that point the next step I would take could have been off a cliff, and I would not have noticed. The implacable feeling of being alone, despite the crowds, hung for one long moment, until, suddenly, Finbar's voice from the speaker over my head, and a peal of applause, broke the spell. He had taken the stage. Jimmy from Kilkenny began to strum, and Finbar started to sing *Four Green Fields*.

Now, sitting on this deck, the night wrapped around me like a sweater, I play the mixed emotions of an immigrant, torn between this chapter in my life, and the people who helped to make me what I am. Yes, it seems that home, and everything it holds, everything it means, can show up wherever you may be. Just like the creaking of this chair on this deck could be the weight of steps on the stairs outside my room, or the rising moon reflected on this lake could as easily be mirrored off the stone of a castle. I refill my glass and bury myself in the void, neither here nor there, just now, fighting the undeniable sense that something is brewing, that the pot is about to boil over.

14

I was walking with a most unusual gait, and for the life of me I couldn't figure out why. The restaurant's produce purveyor had shorted us on onions, so the Chef had sent me down to the vegetable market on Monroe Mall. As it was the middle of the lunch rush, his sending me out of the kitchen seemed most bizarre.

Though it was well out of the way, I walked to the Mall by way of Calder Plaza. The sky was a deep blue with a hint of violet, as if evening were setting in, yet the midday heat was nearly unbearable. In my right hand I kept turning coins over and over to some invisible rhythm, a song in my head I had not heard in years.

I had just lit a cigarette when I suddenly realized there was one already lit in my hand. I noticed my friend the Sous Chef working a grill across from the produce stand. He looked up from his work, cigarette clenched between his lips, pack rolled up in his sleeve revealing a tattoo, and waved in that slow, hardly waving-at-all kind of way that only the Queen Mother can pull off.

As I walked up to say hello, my inquiries as to what he was doing ready to follow, there was a sudden rush of waitresses screaming at him and waving guest checks. He collected them with what seemed to be three hands, spindled them as if they were completed, and lit another cigarette with the butt of his previous. This sent the waitresses into a real tizzy. Exhaling, eyes never making contact with the angry throng in front of him, he wiped a ketchup-stained hand across his forehead, and returned to grilling.

I walked over to an old woman who was selling only onions. Her round face was quite ruddy, and one eye was fish-like and pale from a cataract. She wore an ancient black knit shawl over her blouse and about her head was a bar towel advertising Blackthorn Cider, a drink I had never seen in the States.

She smiled up at me, her thumbs rubbing her pointer fingers as if something were there, and told me the onions were thirty shillings. Just then, the onions somehow in my hands, their skins scratchy, a swarm of fruit flies about them, I looked up to see a man in a balaclava get into a Ford Cortina. The onion woman bellowed at me for money, myself handing it to her, and when I looked back, there was a different Ford Cortina sitting in the same spot.

It was parked, empty and running, the exhaust fumes billowing over towards the grill where my friend was working. He put down his tongs, dropped a cigarette to the ground, which seemed to fall forever, and rubbed it out with the toe of his boot. He then turned to walk over to the vehicle. The sky darkened, the clouds seeming to rush in all at once, and there was that weird yellow light you only see before really bad storms.

I turned my head back towards the Cortina, the Sous Chef now approaching the driver's side door. The car was a dark blue with significant rust. The tires were nearly worn away, one bumper cock-eyed, a large dent on the driver's side rear quarter panel. In the back seat there was a tumble of boxes. The car simply looked menacing. It sat as if awaiting judgment, as if awaiting a point in time that it or we could not avoid. And that's when it dawned on me. I shook my head in disbelief.

I ran, but couldn't, toward the Cortina. Screaming, my voice puny in the face of the wind, the din of the waitresses, the yelling of the onion lady who held onto my coattail, I swatted at her hand and turned to watch the Sous Chef reach out for the Cortina's door handle.

He lifted it, and was obliterated in the explosion. A wall of air filled with fire, metal, and pavement rushed out from the point where the car had been in a concentric circle. Windows shattered. The building closest began to collapse from the detonation. The grill, the waitresses, and the pedestrians just simply weren't there any longer.

All I could feel was heat. All I could do was scream. All I could hear was the ringing of the telephone, a thousand light years away.

I awoke with a start throwing sweaty covers aside and blinking in the darkness, the telephone ringing incessantly, at first far off, then nearer. I leaned on the nightstand for balance as I tried to find my feet. In my vertigo, I knocked a glass of water to the floor, shards and liquid spraying as it shattered. "Hello?"

"Wiley."

"Hello!"

"Wiley, it's me."

"Ma? Is that you?"

"Yes. How are you, son?" she asked.

"Jaysus, dazed and bloody confused."

"I'm sorry love, I know it's late there, but I had to call."

"Why? What is it?"

"There's been a bombing, in Omagh. Your cousins are alright. You needn't worry."

"A bombing? By who? What about the ceasefire?"

"Dissidents. Rory's boys most likely, but your cousins are fine. They'd moved out of the town's center."

She paused. I could hear her breathing. I tried to remember the sweet breath of my mother, but could only smell the bitter tang of sweat.

"Son, there's something else. Your Da, he's very sick. He's in hospital in Dublin. The cancer is in the lymph nodes. It won't be long."

I couldn't say a thing. I was shell-shocked. They hadn't spoken in years; I hadn't seen him in even longer. It was all coming at me too fast.

"Son, could you come home. Please."

"Yes. I'll ring you tomorrow, when my head's a little clearer, okay?"

"Thanks, son, I love you. All the best."

I reached out for the edge of my bed, turned and sat there in the dark. My foot began to sting from a fresh cut, my mind shaking fog away in fits like an animal caught beneath a blanket. The darkness made the room feel as if it went on forever, the ceiling and walls missing, the top of my head chilled as if by wind. I closed my eyes in spite of the blackness, shook my head without realizing it, and wished that I would awake once more.

15

We sat drenched in the late afternoon sunshine amidst a swirl of polkas, staring at our beers and wishing we could pull sentences from them. My impending trip to Ireland, coupled with my melancholy mood, had my friend thinking that I would not return.

The Sous Chef chain-smoked and sipped at his warm beer, his concern over my leaving hanging like the one dark cloud on an otherwise beautiful day. Our conversation was forced, our usual riotous laughter being reduced to half-smiles and chuckles.

My head was swimming with the idea of returning home after nearly ten years. I looked forward to seeing my mother, but didn't know what to think about seeing my father, himself the very reason why I had left Ireland in the first place. His cancer, it seemed to me, must have come right from his soul. And so, the Polish Harvest Fest here in Grand Rapids seemed very far away from where I was, and from where I needed to be.

"Alright, man, did you give your notice or what?" he said, sitting up and then taking a long drink of beer.

"For the fifth fecking time, no I did not. It's a leave of absence."

"Dude, man, you've got to come back. You're the only reason I stay at that stupid kitchen with that mean-ass chef."

"Ach, Jaysus, where you earn your living is not my fault. And even if you were to work in another kitchen we'd still be mates anyway. And besides, ya eejit, it's just a fortnight!"

"Alright, alright. But ya gotta come back. It's almost football season I'm going to take you to your first game. Come on, the Lions, Barry Sanders, twenty-four-ounce beers, we'd be famous."

"Here's eight chips for four twelve-ouncers, I'll hold the table and look famous."

He stared and said a couple of things in Polish while shaking his head.

"I'm not a shaggin' camel, off you bloody go."

He turned sheepishly, and then wended his way through the crowd to the beer tent. I leaned back with my fingers laced behind my head, and stared up at the blue sky. Maybe there were answers up there, just beyond those high white clouds.

What a mess. I had just really gotten comfortable here in Grand Rapids. The pangs of missing home were soft and could easily be put out with the handful of Irish events the community offered. If you stayed busy with work, buried yourself in some library books and went on the odd bender, you could keep the immigrant tears away. But those might just be crutches. Maybe you don't ever stop missing home. Maybe you're not supposed to.

I shook the funk from my head and drained the rest of my beer. What a day! Eighty-five with a breeze. Dusk still an hour or so away, the sun seeming to have spent a week in the sky. I could do this, couldn't I? I mean, what was it that I was so afraid of. Returning to Ireland? Seeing me ma, my old mates. Seeing how many kids my old girlfriends had, and happy not to be the da. Just what was it that I was afraid of?

My friend returned with a handful of beers. The jostling crowd had bumped him enough so that beer was dripping down his hands and forearms. It reminded me of Germany. He slammed the glasses down, sending splashes of lager in every direction and pointed his finger at me. "Hey, aren't you someone famous. No, really. You must be that one famous actor. Or maybe that sports star. Come on, man, out with it, who are ya?"

"Pee Wee fucking Herman."

"Can't be, both your hands are above the table."

We howled. We laughed for what seemed like an entire polka. The good, deep laughter that comes right from the heart and causes your sides to ache and your eyes to tear.

"Look, man, if you've got something you need to talk about, something back home you might need a second opinion on, or a little different view, I'm the guy," he said as he sat down across from me.

"Thanks," I said with a smile. Jaysus, was it that obvious?

"So that's it, huh, a little shady back history. How bad could it be? C'mon. I mean it's you. You're the peacemaker. You're the dude that always seems to do the right thing. I mean, if ya think about it, that's what pisses the Chef off about you so much. So, please, do yourself a favor, man. Talk. Get it off your chest."

"It's nothing like that at all. It's just that when ya haven't been someplace for a long time, and it happens to be where you grew up, it seems odd going back. Ya know?"

"Out with it. Quit stalling."

"I'm telling ya, there are no deep, dark secrets."

"Ho, boy! Who said anything about deep and dark, I'm talking about banging the preacher's daughter. You're the one shaking skeletons in the O'Wary closet."

"This is truly off center. I don't know why I have misgivings about going back. Probably it's just my father, we never got on, ya know. I remember him, but I guess I choose not to. So now he's dying of cancer in Dublin. I'm going to have to see him and his family and they're a bunch of jackeen bogtrotters. That's it. That's all."

He sat there, nodding his head with a small smile of success. "Don't ya feel better," he said the way a therapist would.

"Not fucking really."

"You're coming back. You're my best friend and I know you're coming back. Maybe not for awhile, but you'll be back."

His comments snapped me to sobriety, as if a bell had been rung, or I was experiencing deja vu. "What do you mean by that."

"Because," he paused, "I know stuff."

I shook my head in slight confusion.

"Because of my grandfather." He paused again, clearing his throat. "My grandfather came right from Poland. After the Nazis left, and before the Communists came in, he put everything he could on a cart. He and his family, my Grandma, an Uncle and Aunt, they walked to Gdansk and caught a ship to Liverpool and from there to New York."

I sat mesmerized, thinking about the war-ravaged European countryside, a family leaving everything but a cartful of possessions behind, and fleeing to a new world.

"For as long as I can remember, my grandfather would not talk about what happened; but he would always talk about Poland. He would talk about the lakes, or the seacoast, the mountains and forests; he would go on forever about family traditions, feasts and food, old quarrels. If he had had a bit too much to drink, the tears would well up in his eyes and he would stop talking once one rolled down his cheek. I can still see him to this day, staring straight ahead, defiantly holding back his pain."

He stopped and turned away, a tear of his own resting on the top of his cheek, the din of the festival pushed so far away as to be a murmur. The tear fell, and he turned back toward me, locking his eyes on mine.

"You're going home. And whatever it was that you ran from, you're going to that to. Then you'll come back here and honor your commitments and stew about whatever it is you faced in your odd, Irish way. And then, I think, you'll leave for good."

He stood up, fishing tokens out of his pants pocket while casting a glance over towards the food booths, picked up one of his beers, and finished it in one go.

"Say Paddy," he said, my eyes looking up from the middle distance, "just keep the front door open if I should ever make it across the puddle," and he left for the food booths.

I pushed my face into my hands and all the way through until my fingers laced behind my head. I leaned back and stretched, staring up at the darkening sky. I wished that answers would fall like rain, and then closed my eyes when they didn't.

There still seemed to be something stirring. A riddle unraveling, an answer forming to a question yet asked. I closed the box of unknown things by opening my eyes, my name being called, my nose filling with wondrous aromas.

"Wiley. In honor of my Grandfather, I have brought us a feast.'

Before me, covering one third of the picnic table, were eight large, paper plates brimming with kapusta and kielbasa, pierogis and golabki.

"Your weapon, sir," he said presenting me with a spork, draught beers being set down by the Polish Harvest Queen, who had been kind enough to lend a hand. "Damn the toilets," he bellowed, "full speed ahead!"

16

There is a sense of sleepwalking in traveling long distances on short notice. The images of the journey are abbreviated into snapshots, like memories from a family holiday long ago. The faces, places and conversations take place in the half-distance, never becoming fully formed events. Only when they are recalled shortly after having happened, do they seem to have a tie to reality. When thought upon later, even mere days later, the faces, places, and conversations sink back into a consciousness that seems more akin to *Dreamtime.*

I sit in coach, pondering these thoughts, trying to recall the images of the day. It appears I am the only soul awake, the jet having settled into it's pre-programmed flight some time ago, and the last barely noticeable bank having been performed somewhere east of Newfoundland. The remaining Scotch falls into my plastic tumbler, the liquor softening the day's driving, parking, and checking baggage. I sink back into my seat trying to figure out what had happened since I'd left Grand Rapids this morning.

The Sous Chef, in great kindness, had loaned me the use of his car for the drive from Grand Rapids to O'Hare. Chefs tend to put more emphasis on their knife kits then they do on their vehicles, and the Ford LTD, nearly as old as myself, promptly quit for the first time just outside Benton Harbor. Duct tape took care of the leaky radiator hose, the radiator itself swallowing two and half liters of Evian.

At the point where the motorway swings toward Chicago, the first tire went, a slight settling feeling on the front right side of the car coupled with what sounded like a second-hand accordion being played by a third-rate accordion player.

The second tire went in Chicago, near Madison in the heart of the Loop. More of a cannon shot then the slow, wheeze of the first tire. I drove on it anyway, there being no second spare, and made my way up the exit ramp to a garage only several blocks from the motorway. Despite the ill effects of the Polish Harvest Fest, I was more than ready to avail myself of a pint.

While the car was being tended to, and I having given myself all day to reach O"Hare, I walked up to Greektown and a pub called Dugan's.

There was a giant of a man in there, a great gregarious fella who was trying to convince me that the best food in the world was Greek. I couldn't help but agree, but after having consumed nearly a pound of kapusta a mere fourteen hours previous, the thought of food didn't settle well at all. My silence proved to be my downfall. He hoisted me by the crook of my arm and led me three blocks to a restaurant called The Parthenon.

As we walked in I could see the grimace on the staff's faces in recognizing the man. The hostess reluctantly showed us a table in the back, regular patrons turning their backs to us or openly fleeing.

He was loud, laughed loud and was always right. Even when you agreed with him he would continue to labor his point. I raised my eyes to heaven beseeching God as to why this day had to start this way, my hangover lurking just beneath the surface, waiting to breach at any moment.

I told him I had only a short time for lunch, wasn't feeling well at all, and had a plane to catch besides. This made no difference whatsoever. He wandered us through the breadth of the menu, starter by starter, until I wondered if there were any squid left in the ocean. We drank ouzo. We drank wine. We drank more ouzo. My head felt like wet cement and my stomach like the mixer. When I finally realized the time, he had fecked off to the loo while I paid the bill.

We walked back to Dugan's, himself apologizing for his lack of funds, promised me as much stout as I could drink, and asked if I had heard how England had done in the World Cup. I told him they'd been routed soundly by a girl's squad from France, Manchester United had moved to Glasgow and that the Queen Mother had declared football 'un-English'. I left him standing in Dugan's doorway as I bee-lined it back to the garage to check on the auto.

Two hundred and fifty dollars later, tire number two being "un-repairable and how the hell did you manage to drive here anyway," I was back on the motorway once more.

It was as I turned on to the Kennedy, a steady queue of jets approaching the field, the peal of turbine filling the sky, that thoughts about returning home began to fill my head. I hadn't slept well in days, a recurring dream knocking me from my sleep routinely every night since my mother's phone call. I thought heavy sedation would provide a quick end around this problem, but the stout only made the dream seem stranger, lend its images a lasting vividness.

My head jerks up, a yawn forming itself before I realize what is going on. I have an aisle seat on the right side of the plane over the wing. The seat nearest the window is occupied by a middle-aged woman who sleeps peacefully, herself impossibly tucked into a cube shape within the confines of her chair. I lean over and look out the window, there is nothing but blackness, a faint glint of light falling upon the wing as if from heaven. Another yawn, a weary glance up and down the aisle, people reposed, just slightly, the mid-flight movie forgotten. I finish my scotch and try to decipher the Irish stitched into the fabric of the seat in front of me.

It seems almost instantly that I feel myself falling, tumbling. A quiet voice in the back of my head tells me to stay crouched, stay tight in a ball. No longer cruising at altitude, I am rolling down the stairs, the old wooden stairs in the house in Dungloe.

There is only darkness, bits of light like machine gun bursts flash across my mind's eye, staccato screams, distant crying. The steps themselves are as hard as anything I have ever felt, I am in pain with each roll, the final step splits my head releasing the acrid taste of blood inside my mouth.

I pick myself up, an innate sense of survival, fight giving way to flight, my small child's hands scrambling to open the front door, wee bare feet on the outside steps, on the gravel, on the grass.

Into the trees, the blackthorn branches pulling at my bed-clothes and my face like thin, twisted hands, scratches begin to line my face, blood mixing with tears of shame, tears of rage, tears of confusion.

It is cold and unnaturally light, the landscape lit by a yellow moon, I run through and past the blackthorn, over the old stonewall and up the field toward Hooker's Hill. The ground is hard and crisp, a frost having stiffened the grass, before me the field slopes up, my breath coming in wheezy gasps.

As I crest the hill, two forces vie for control of my con-sciousness. One urges me forward to a needed conclusion, while the other deeper, more remote self tries to wake me, tries to avoid the pain that awaits this conclusion. I see the mouldering, burned-out stump of the British barracks that gives the hill its name. Its moss-covered walls are wet, black, and cold. It is a place of children's ghost stories and dares, old men's nightmares and murders. My run becomes a walk, be-comes slow and heavy with distrust. Though I knew where I was running, I hadn't prepared myself for what it would be like when it was right in front of me.

The sky darkens, distant clouds covering a more distant moon. Walls that once held the enemy seem to be the enemy now. I approach them, extend my arm, my fingers tracing lightly across long-dead stone. Light breaks free from the skies above, illuminating the single tree, which sits adjacent to the barracks. My head turns with my eyes, steps following, the walls left behind.

In the odd, canted beam of moonlight stands an apple tree, planted a century or more ago. Its thick, hoary limbs twist as if malignant, as if suffering, deep grooves from ropes weighted with bodies still clear on one limb. I walk toward it, up to it, to this particular limb, where one lone apple hangs from the leafless bough, just out of reach, just far enough off the ground.

I jump. I jump once again. Over and over, breathless and panting, the apple is unmoved by this effort. It seems to grow further and further away. Silver and round in the moonlight, in my shame, in my rage, in my confusion, I want to smash it. I want to hold it and squeeze the life out of it. I want it to decay with the barracks, with the hill, the landscape, everything. Stone after stone, rock after rock, my assault gives way to screaming, to epithets. The apple now seems as large as a pumpkin, as leering as a jack-o-lantern. I scramble about the hill until I find a stick long enough to reach it. Returning, I stand beneath it, the trump card gleaming in the light, held tight in my hands. A mocking part of me wonders if the stick itself is from the tree. I take aim and with all my might, with what feels like the strength of one thousand Cuchulains, I swing.

But before there is contact, before there is the wonderful heavy, wet thump of stick colliding with apple, I am struck from behind. The stick flies from my hands, the sky turns over in an arc, the barracks rises closer, and the ground receives me in thunderous communion.

My breath escapes in a whoosh, lungs struggling against sore tissue to breathe. My head feels as if it is stuffed with down, lopsided and heavy, my eyes droop to close. I turn to see what has hit me. A shape, black against the sky, looms over me, sniggers at my tears, at my place upon the ground.

It is then, at that point where one teeters before oblivion, the clouds part and the moonlight strains through. In the shadows from the apple tree, from barracks and from the clouds, I struggle to decipher the face. I hold this image as Percival held the Grail. The clouds part further, wind moves the branches and the face becomes...

Becomes the face of a concerned stewardess, a warm towel and a plastic tumbler of water, I wipe drool from my chin with the back of a shaking hand, a hand whose fingertips can still feel the mossy rocks of the barracks. The fear in my eyes subsides, my heart returns to my chest, and the bright blue eyes of the attendant reassure me that Donegal is still one thousand miles away.

I stumble through a thank-you, it may even have been in Irish, wipe my face with the towel, and exhale slowly. My hands rest on the tray, I stare at the water, at the verses woven into the seat in front of me, and wait for the stewardess to return to the back of the plane.

It is then, the eyes of no one on me, that I make my way to the loo. Close the folding door behind me, push the bolt to occupied, kneel before the silver commode, and throw up ropes of bitter licorice. I splash water on my face, my eyes avoiding my reflection, pull back the bolt to vacant and return to the dimmed lights of the cabin.

In the galley, on top of a scant flat surface where coffee pots, meal trays and towels rest before being stowed, lie five small bottles of vodka. I drink them in succession, the alcohol numbing my brain before the last bottle is drained. I leave two twenty dollar bills where they had been, return

to my seat, and miles above the earth I fall into sweet dreamless sleep.

17

I sit staring at the brick walls of O'Shea's Hotel Bar. A pint of Guinness, the familiar half moon of my upper lip indented in the foam, rests on an oak ledge attached to the wall. In a snug deep in the back of the bar, the cigarette smoke envelops me. It is a cloak, a shield; it is a snug within the snug rendering me invisible, anonymous.

The bar sits on the corner of Talbot and Gardiner, just barely on Dublin's North side. The Custom House, its green dome echoing the green of the flag, looms at the end of the block. Beyond it is the river Liffey, and beyond that is my country.

I've been sitting here for hours trying to erase the memories of this morning, trying to bury them in some lost corner of my brain. My father still pokes fingers in my chest. Still menaces me. No amount of time or of distance has lessened the pain, eased the confusion.

Up until this afternoon, he lay in St. Vincent's Hospital fighting a losing battle with cancer. And all the times I had wished him dead, all the times I had wanted to raise a glass to the backside of his ghost, seem to me like so many empty threats.

It is hard to believe that it has happened; that it is he who is in there, the suddenness of the event a sharp wind across the face. The tubes and machines surround him like old cronies, like allies of an old war fought well but lost. I close my eyes and I can see him in the soiled hospital sheets. The once-fierce giant reduced to a shell, to some soon-to-be written lines in the back of the *Donegal Democrat*. He seemed a long way from the tirades, the overturned tables, the drunken yelling holidays. Yet all of those hollow footfalls on the old stairs remain, like reports after gunshots.

Two hours ago the hospital called to tell me he had passed away. I sit here in a swirl of emotions trying not to feel any of them. Letting the din of the pub suck me into its white noise, hoping to find a better place in that oblivion, if only for a short while.

If only.

If only I had stood up to him once. Just once. Then wouldn't the life have gone smoother, wouldn't we all be rich and famous. The bitterest pill is that it never happened, that the need to confront him, to find those answers and then wave them in his face, remains the empty threat.

But there lies the problem. The questions themselves are unanswerable. The truth swings with the apples on Hooker's Hill. The facts are still running through the blackthorn, still tumbling down the stairs. In brave, vain attempts I search my memories, I try to crack the black wall, enter the dark clouds and see just what it was that has led us all to where we are now. But I may as well be trying to find Atlantis, trying to solve the Sphinx.

So, the man I had wished dead is dead. And the world hasn't ended. And the fire of my hatred will become like the ashes of his body, a memory.

Or so we hope.

I turn from the wall and look up at the chandelier hanging above the room. Its brass is tarnished, nearly half the lights are burned-out, and cobwebs hang between the arms. The oak beams of the ceiling, once bright and ornate with fleurs de lis and leaves, are now faded by time and smoke. These things hold memories of their own, like the cornerstone to this hotel, like the oak rail which holds my pint as surely as it held Michael Collins' in a different time. The denizens of the pub descended from earlier denizens, a dozen generations who have dwelt and thrived, perished and died on this very corner. It is, in a word, Dublin.

I leave the unfinished pint, exit the snug, exit the pub and fall into step with the rush of workers ending their day. The five o'clock crowd, heroes all for completing one more shift, push against the wind and mist, find yesterday's footprints and make their way home.

I cross the Liffey by the O'Connell Bridge and aimlessly tread the streets of downtown Dublin. Down alleys, through parks, past pubs, the light of the day tempered by the dark, low clouds, I walk. A leaf caught in a whirlwind, I have no direction. My mind is as numb as my cheeks, summer all but forgotten, the Irish Sea reminds everyone how cold autumn can be.

I stop on the Halfpenny Bridge, the black water of the river reflecting the sky, the town. The Angelus peels apart the somber mood, distant bells of a dozen churches reaching this spot in disorganized melody. I remember my mother and that I'm supposed to be meeting her at the pub I've left. I pull myself from my image floating in the water, from the serenity of reflected bridges looking like stepping stones out to sea. I turn up the Quays and back onto O'Connell, back to the front door of the hotel, the front door of the pub.

I take a fresh pint back to the snug, my old pint still sitting there, light a cigarette, and wait for my ma. In here time seems suspended. There is no real way to judge it's passing, only the barman stopping by with a fresh pint, a newspaper, or another box of fags.

From the front of the bar the wheeze of a squeezebox and the steady rhythm of a guitar begin to carry over the conversations. Through the stained glass windows in the walls of the snug I can see the two men playing, their faces distorted by the hue and thickness of the pane. The lilt of the music is that strange Celtic weave, no real beginning or end, a phrase that sounds nearly the same from any angle, yet somehow holds all the pain and joy of life. The first tear falls, and then great sheets of them.

In the midst of this, like a saint, comes a tapping on the snug wall.

"Wiley? Is that you, my boy? Jaysus, I can barely see with the lights so low."

I turn once more from the wall, and find my mother standing before me. Up, out of the barstool, and into her arms. She drops her bags and holds me. Her presence alone like a warm day, I cry into her shoulder and feel her head nod in sympathy.

"Let it go, Wiley. Do yourself a favor and let it go. Surely by now these things have passed. Never mind that old goat, that whoor of a man. He's dead now, Wiley. Pack those things in the coffin with him."

"I just wanted to once tell him."

"Tell him what, Wiley?"

"I don't know, I can't quite remember, but sure it's there."

A barman opens the door to the snug and drops off a pint and two glasses of Paddy's. I take a wad of Kleenex from my mother and blow my nose. Someone in the snug next to ours leans over and tells us to stop having so much fun. The joke lifts a burden, and I sigh, my mother smiling at me in that way only a mother can for a child long last seen.

"Slainte, Wiley, here's to a better world."

"Aye."

We rap glasses and drink the whiskey, the golden liquid completing something unfinished inside of me like the last few notes of a song. Over my mother's shoulder the musicians continue to play, the bar continues to fill, and Dublin goes right on being Dublin.

There is a hollow sense of victory, like winning in a forfeit, or the best player for the opposition being out. Sure he's dead, but then doesn't the wake of a man's life continue long after him? If my hands weren't filled with drinks I'd scratch my head.

We step out of the snug, my mother stands beside me, puts her arm around me, and we share a smile. The crowd joins in with the chorus and we add our voices as well, the swell of music surely carrying out into the street, across the Liffey and out across the land.

Ring a ring of rosy, as the light declines,
I remember Dublin City, in the rare 'oul times.

18

We had left Dublin by train in the early morning, the stillness of the new day and our walk to the station broken only by trucks carrying empty kegs, gaggles of school kids queuing for busses, and flights leaving Dublin Airport bound for the continent. My mother had driven only as far as Newry the previous day, catching the late afternoon train south and giving us this wonderful opportunity to ride north in the emerging dawn.

The Irish countryside passed before us like scenery out of a film. We were each of us lost in our own thoughts, the occasional meeting of eyes, a quiet smile, her hand lighting on mine. When the train would rise with the hills, there would be the occasional glimpse of the Irish Sea, framed forever by pastures, farms, and steeples. We drank tea, commented on the unraveling vista or on the upcoming funeral, mentioning this relative or that, would he be cremated, would there be a wake, how long would it last, but mostly we just stared at the green blur of bushes, the brown blur of stones, and let our thoughts sway with the rhythm and sound of the train.

It had been a week to the day since the bomb in Omagh went off. Splintered images from the nightmare that night appeared every so often in my mind's eye, blending disjointedly into Hooker's Hill, apple trees, and running through blackthorn. It all seemed like too much to me. The funeral was enough. I saw no sense in smelling the smoke, seeing the blackened buildings, reading the names. My mother had insisted, saying again and again that we have relations in Omagh. We owe it to them to stop by. I only wanted to get the funeral over with, find a pub, smell the sea through the windows, and wake up a week later.

My mother and I would fetch her car from the station in Newry and drive to Omagh. Our cousins lived just outside the town, but were meeting us at the Drumagh car park near the Strule River. A vigil had been scheduled there for the afternoon at three-ten, the same time that the car had exploded.

We stepped off from the train, wove our way through the Newry station and out into the car park to search for her old, blue Fiat. The sun had risen, it was nearly nine, and the low clouds of an approaching front scudded across a bright sky. I absentmindedly tapped a rolled-up *Irish Independent* against the palm of my left hand and followed mom to the car, my head swiveling to take in as much of the Northern scenery as possible.

"Jaysus, I can't believe this thing still runs."

"Hush yourself, you're in the presence of a miracle."

"I'll say. Why haven't ya gotten a newer one," I asked.

"Ack, it would be like cheating. Old Blue has been as faithful as that yorkie we had when you were a boy."

Luggage stowed, myself thinking fondly of the old lap dog, she left the car park and drove with the sort of disdain for other drivers only the elderly or very forward women can ever get away with. I looked over at her, a graying, black forelock falling over her face, her left hand shifting into fourth before brushing it aside. She had a cocky, half-sneer, half-smile on her face, eyes squinted as if this were the Grand Prix. She shifted into fifth and I finally felt my body relax.

"So, Wiley," she looked over at me from the corners of her eyes, "what's the name of your restaurant?"

"I don't own a restaurant." This was an old conversation.

"Twenty years a chef and you don't own a restaurant."

"I nearly had the money saved for opening back in Boston."

"Lost, huh."

"Aye," I conceded, "the divorce."

"You're better off, son. I never did like that one. What was her family name?"

"Hampton."

"Aye, that's it," she exclaimed, a wide smile brightening an already beautiful face, "Dora Hampton," I cringed at the memory, "sounds like a building. The Dora Hampton Hotel," she turned her face to me and leaned over conspiratorially, "and convention center."

We laughed our way from Newry to Omagh. The A28 led us to Armagh and then to the sleepy border village of Augh-nacloy where we picked up the A5. Our catching up was years in the making. We talked about everything: life's turning points, the mundane day-to-day stuff, work. It was one of those rare opportunities to sit with your mom without any other siblings or family members and just hang out.

"So Wiley."

"Yes, ma."

"How long has it been since you've been to Omagh?"

"I don't know, twenty years."

"Then you'll not recognize your cousins. I'll introduce ya all over, like."

"I remember Sean and Michael, and their wives, Kathleen and, shoot."

"Mary. None of their kids, though, aye?"

"No."

"Alright then, Wiley. Seriously now, I stopped for a night on the way to Newry. It's awful, the bombing. I don't want to look at the site again. I'll park off of Scarffe's. We'll walk to the High Street. I go left, you go right. I imagine you'll be skipping the Vigil. It's alright, son, I understand. Once you've seen the site, like, well, it's a bit staggering. There's one good pub, Gallagher's, off of High Street. Distant cousins. The only mixed pub in town."

I nodded. She sat up in her seat, downshifted for a corner, and I could tell that the conversation had ended. She was like that, hot and cold. Giving, giving, giving, and then boom, suddenly stoic, suddenly strong, letting us know that the fun must be set aside. I watched her from the corners of my eyes, admiring her determination, her strength. She had about her a sense of purpose, a feeling of miles walked, of hills climbed. There seemed nothing she couldn't do. If it hadn't been for her, well...

I turned to look out my window, the farms of Tyrone surrendering to the outskirts of Omagh. Rich, beautiful land. Land worth fighting for, and had been. The stark bluntness of that statement shocked me. Before I could figure out where or why I had thought it, she pulled over a curb, the car jostling, and into a car park.

"Now," was all she said, gathering her handbag and an umbrella, the door closing behind her.

I exited the Fiat, it so low to the ground that it seemed like I was rising from a sofa. Stretched and looked up to the city center. A gray sky closed in about the old stone buildings. Crows cawed flying from steeple to steeple, tree to tree, wheeling about above the town, and it was then that I truly felt I was in Ireland.

We walked up Scarffe's, turning near the top down an alley to a flower shop. We went in and she had me buy a dozen roses and a card.

"Now, you write something nice in that card. They're collecting them for a memorial. I'm taking the roundabout way to the Vigil. You'll find your way about. I'll meet you at Gallagher's." She leaned forward, gave me a kiss on the cheek, and more than that, a very serious look. "You mind yourself," and off she went, leaving me with a pen, a card, and red roses.

I paid the shop clerk, my eyes searching hers without realizing it, looking for some clue, some hint as to what might lie around the corner, how had she been affected. Her smile was wan, but genuine, and I found myself falling into that old trap of trying to guess which side of the fence she was on.

Out the door and back down the alley, up Scarffe's, the incline leveling off, and onto Market Street. I looked left down High Street in hopes of catching sight of my mother, saw the sign for Gallagher's on the left side of the street, and then felt the hairs on the back of my neck stand up, my skin begin to crawl. I turned my head, eyes resting on the roses in front of me, an acrid, charred odor prickling my nostrils, and then glanced to my right.

I was only half a block from where the bomb had detonated. Yellow police ribbon cordoned off the area. A number of emergency trucks and lorries blocked my view. I could see that the tops of the buildings on both sides of the street were demolished and burnt out. Looking to my left I caught the eyes of an RUC-man and felt suddenly absurd standing there, with flowers and a perplexed expression.

'Fucking awful, isn't it," he said. "Twas a beautiful town, it was. Peaceful town. Now it looks like fucking Belfast." He ducked under the ribbon and began to direct some of the workmen.

I turned back down Scarrfe's, left at the end of the block, left on the Dublin Road, and walked slowly toward the bottom of Market Street. As I came out into the intersection, I turned to my left and saw the hole. I saw the baked sidewalk. I saw the tumble of breezeway blocks and bricks. I saw the rubble that had once been a vibrant intersection in a market town. I stood there staring, my mouth agape at the brute destruction. A workman noticed me and with great kindness pointed me toward the bridge where the memorial was being placed. I stammered a thank you and walked in that direction, my eyes riveted to the hole.

There were dozens of people who milled about the memorial. Crying. Holding each other. Staring dumbly. Some placed flowers next to makeshift markers of poster board. Others walked in trances along the bridge or past the site. In hopes of discovering what to do or how to act, I joined them. Before me was a decorated poster board with pictures of one of the victims. Their life from birth to death, the smiles, hopes and dreams of one individual now erased from the planet. Names and dates streaked in red ink from the rain. I turned to the next, and the next and the next.

There were piles of wet flowers, hundreds of pictures of faces. A dozen wet, teddy bears beside pictures and names of children. The newsreel voice spun in my head: twenty-nine dead, nine children, two yet to be born. Two hundred and twenty injured. The sound of the river rose in my ears, the newsreel voice echoing on in an endless loop. It became a painful rush of noise, my hands going to my ears, my body flinching.

I staggered from memorial to memorial until I was on the bridge. The din of traffic on the Dublin Road was as constant as the stream below me and just as loud. There was no way to escape the faces, the faded flowers, the wet mocking teddy bears. The white noise of the river, the cars, the sudden roaring inside my head, it was all too much.

The sky pressed lower, opened, and a determined Irish rain fell for ten minutes, fell for an eternity. I looked past the rushing black water for a way out of any kind. The utter folly of my species becoming overwhelming, my tears mixed with the rain, my body racked with sobs until the rain stopped, the noise abruptly stopped and I winced my eyes open.

Pain. Sweet physical pain had brought me back. Sure it was that, and a sound, an unnerving, hard to place sound that had cut through the rush of noise. Over and over, sharp, metal on earth, it's echo bouncing from walls, flying out across the banks, this is what had snapped up the black shade. I looked over from the river to my hand and saw the blood running down my wrist. I had squeezed the clutch of roses so tight that the thorns had cut my palm. I raised my head toward the direction of the sound, my eyes reluctantly following, and realized it was a spade on wet earth, the smack of shovel on stones, on bricks, of digging out the debris. How many turns of dirt had been lifted and returned in Omagh the past week?

I laid the roses on the cement beside the countless others, the card unwritten inside my jacket pocket where it would stay, and crossed the bridge to find my mother, hear the Vigil, and escape the clouds of confused and terrified ghosts.

19

I took the coast road from Dungloe to Maghery, the sound of my favorite pair of boots hard against the pavement, the road itself undulating, broken and popped from heat and cold, wind and rain. I wondered how many times in the past I had walked this road, run this road, wanted to run away on this road. The rugged Donegal Mountains frame the two little villages and make it quite easy to believe there is nothing beyond those hills. It is as if this spit of land is all the world has to offer, and even the ocean covets that.

The close, pressing Irish sky is filled with rain. Sunlight illuminates fields surrounded by ancient stonewalls covered in ivy and moss. They suddenly become brilliant with light until a cloud once more covers the sun, and then return to gray.

I walk through this like an apparition, my mind trying to remove myself from the landscape. Trying to be so very small that I am unnoticed by even God. It is an old feeling from some distant past not well remembered. I cannot even place its source, but I know it is because of him.

His people had gathered around his casket, himself lying at rest in his only suit, and spoke of him highly. The reality of the event evading me, like the meaning of a very odd play. I could not believe it was really happening.

His sisters would throw me looks of reproach, their narrow eyes picking at my guilt, accusations lying just beneath the pleasantries. They wanted to hang me. They wanted me to know I had abandoned him, had turned my back on him; that I had been cut from the same yard of cloth as my mother and brother. He was a hero to them. He was their great man, their champion.

I hated him.

My cousin Padraig had come from New York for the funeral. His father Colm had drowned, so having been down this road before, he tried to keep me grounded. His sense of humor was as welcome as the whiskey, but his father had truly been a great man, the bravest fisherman in Donegal, so it was difficult for him to relate to my unease and black mood. He didn't quite know why I hurt, in fact, largely, neither did I, but he was an old friend who cared, and he did the best that he could.

"Sure Wiley," he would say, "do ya know why all his people are standing about with their hands in their pockets?"

"No, Padraig," I would answer, "I do not."

"Because they're trying to make more room in them for when they read the will."

We were the only two people laughing at the wake. Padraig said there would be more jocularity at Ian Paisley's funeral. He had told the wee children that my da had taped pennies to the inside of his eyelids. We were in stitches every time we could see a child craning their neck to see the coins.

My mother did not attend the wake. She had stood at the church in black, and alone. She wouldn't allow even me to attend the funeral beside her. She had faced his family alone through all the years, cast aside by his people, and she intended to see him off the same way. I have never seen a person's chin set as firm as hers. The priest had made a point to come over and take her hand. She refused.

The Mass, in Gaelic, swam about us with the incense, the mysteries of Grace and mercy and salvation as tongue-tied and brooding as the language. It was the first church I had been inside in quite some time, and the rush of parochial memories only added to my confusion.

When the funeral had ended, knots of us waiting for the casket to be carried out of the church for the ride to the yard, the sky had opened up in a deluge. Umbrellas were useless, parishioners ran for alcoves. Myself and Padraig ducked into a pub forgoing the burial.

There was a small gathering at his mother's house afterward, replete with ham sandwiches, whiskey and beer. Conversations in hushed tones as if we were still in church. The house was as stuffy and closed-up as I remembered it.

My cousin had left with a fair-haired young woman. He tried to get my attention as he went through the front door, but I pretended not to notice. The whiskey, the funeral, and all the bad blood had finally succeeded in dragging me down. I shot contemptuous, drunken glances at his family, poured a whiskey, and left out the back.

I needed to breathe fresh air. Smell the salt from the sea; feel the sting of sand on my cheeks. I wanted to throw myself off a cliff, let fate have a go. Just see what would happen.

I had started to run, the glass of whiskey falling from my hand and tumbling down a steep hill toward the harbor. No direction just yet, just running. I had taken the back trails, trails that had been there since before the town was a village, before the village was even peopled by us. I could not face one more human being. I could not answer one more question about Him.

The mountains of Donegal, guarding until not quite forever the land from the sea, watched me run along the small cliffs between Dungloe and Maghery. They watched as I cut across the fields, through copses of blackthorn, their needles as sharp as memories, sheep indifferent to the wild man jumping the rock walls. Their granite faces saw as I slowed, to marvel them, the fields, the ocean, briefly. And when I hung my head, exhausted in spirit, the body caving in, perhaps they felt the tears softly landing on the sod.

The weight of expectation and disappointment, guilt and hate, fear and self-loathing had consumed me. I thought about Omagh, the bridge and the river, the hole and the wee, wet bears, the sting of thorns and my inability to even write a card. I thought about all those good people wasted in their prime, in their youth, and how had God let my father live as long as he had. Where was justice, or fairness; where was balance? Behind my eyes, it felt like having all the lights in the world go out at once.

I ran down from the hill above Maghery, past the playing pitch and on to the strand. The surf pounded the beach, a reminder of the squall that had just passed through this morning.

I closed my eyes and ran out into the sea. The cold surf wrapped around my ankles, my knees. The pull of the tide began to press at my back, pull at my sternum as the water slapped my chest. My body began to sway violently back and forth; the rage in my head boiled over.

"Goddamn you!" I screamed at the top of my lungs.

"Goddamn you!" My fists pounded the waves.

"Goddamn you!" I roared at the sound of his feet on the stairs.

My footing was suddenly taken, the undertow pulling quickly, and my head dipped below the surface. I tried to turn over and scramble up the beach, but the rush of the incoming wave drove me into the sand. I tried to get to my knees, to raise my head above the water, but the wave was now going out to sea, and I with it.

I did not fight this. There was no more will to fight. There was no desire to live. I simply decided to drift, to let fate have its go.

At that instant, just before drawing in what would have been my terminal breath, I felt two strong hands lift me up above the surface. Hacking seawater, my lungs stinging in pain, I stumbled and fell onto the beach.

Doubled over, I wiped the sand from my eyes and looked up from the wellies to the face of the man who had just saved my life. It was our neighbor, old John Gallagher.

"I take it the funeral didn't go so well."

Dumbfounded, I stammered into a laugh.

"No," I coughed, "it was a fucking joke."

"You were never a strong swimmer, Wiley."

"I know, I know."

He stood there with a crafty smile upon his face, an odd look in his eyes, his arms hanging beside him like a wrestler's, the dirt of Ireland still lodged beneath his farmer's fingernails, and began to laugh. In response, the near-tragedy framing this particular moment in time, the waterfall of emotions leaving me as wracked as the ocean, I began to laugh as well.

"I've got some warm clothes in the boot of my car. Hurry on now, the pub opens in ten minutes and we haven't much time." He turned, his laughter becoming a low rumble, and began to walk up to the car park.

I stood there for a second, sweet Donegal air filling my lungs, my clothes matted to my body, the hills of Donegal standing by as indifferent as the sheep had been earlier, and just like that, without so much as a drum roll, I took the first step down the road we Irish affectionately call, 'going on the piss.'

20

Her name is Marie Rose, but to me, it may as well have been Maeve, or Helen of Troy or any other beauty of great renown. She is fair-haired, with a heart-shaped face and soft green eyes, the kind of eyes that dance, the kind of eyes you can lose yourself in like a summer's day.

Or lose yourself as I had the past week. How I ended up in this pub is a complete mystery to me. I was just trying to reconnect a series of staggered events when she turned the corner from the far side of the bar. At that moment, any train of thought I had was instantly derailed.

I recalled how somewhere in some pub over the course of the last fortnight, someone had told me of the beauty who ran the pub at Tir Conall's. However, being solely preoccupied by the funeral of my father and the resultant binge that came from all the hard feelings, I let the comment stray. Now, with my flight back to the States looming in front of me, I could kick myself squarely in the arse for not having come up here sooner.

She called over to me, shaking me from my daze, and asked if I wanted a pint and a wee one for last drinks. But of course, and it was then that I realized how I had ended up here in the first place.

My hometown of Dungloe is really a one-street town. That one street is a steep hill that runs parallel to the bay, the top affording a fine view of the bay, the sea, and the mountains. The island of Aranmore lies sitting in the distance like a sleeping bear. At the bottom of the street, before it goes back up around the bay and becomes the road to Burtonport, there is a wee little bridge with a wee little river flowing in a series of falls down to the ocean, the water both black and orange from the rock and mineral deposits it flows through.

After having spent the better part of four days lost in The Strand View Bar in Maghery, reliving my story of almost drowning a dozen times, I decided to branch out and go on a bit of a pub crawl through Dungloe. There are a good dozen pubs here, and I was determined to talk, eat and drink in each one of them. Hughey the Postman was kind enough to give me a lift from Maghery. The two of us trying to peel our eyes open from the night before.

The journey began at The Midway Bar, halfway down the hill, next to the road to Maghery. It was going to be one of those days. As I supped my pint of Guinness an older gent walked up to me, recognized me, and bought me a glass of whiskey.

"Wiley! Jaysus my boy, it is you. Tell me about The States, son. Finish those up, there's a better pub across the street."

And so it went.

Now when I say a pub-crawl, I'm talking ten or twelve pints over the course of an entire day. Pints so slow they grow warm because the conversation is too good, the papers are too interesting, and the ponies are too thrilling to watch. At the end of this sort of trek, you are just as sober as when you start out, but much richer from discourse.

Now, the leisurely sort of day I had been hoping for, where I could immerse myself in all things Dungloeian, was doomed from the start for three reasons. One, it was Thursday and that meant it was market day. So every gent and his wife were in town, the wife shopping and the gent doing what gents do. Secondly, the pension checks had arrived just the day before and so all these older gents had the odd bit of bob in their pocket. Finally, and most dooming of all, the Listowel Races were all this week and every betting shop and pub would be filled with punters trying to find the right combination of horses.

Everywhere I went someone hailed me, saluted me and bought me a drink. By three in the afternoon I was thoroughly pissed. By five I was stumbling into Sweeny's Hotel for a hot whiskey. By seven I was in Beedy's trying to convince three Yank girls that I really lived in Great Rapids, Mitch-e-gin and owned several eateries.

I was on my way down to The Bayview, or to simply stare at the falls, when one of the Boyle brothers waved to me and asked if I would hold onto my mother's butcher order, as he was closing for the day. Not wanting to be encumbered by a bag filled with rashers, pudding, and lamb cutlets, I asked if he could just leave it with his brother, who owned the only other butcher's shop across the street from his. He frowned, set his face, looked over at his brother's shop, back to me, reset his face, and then decided to cross the street and see the competition. This bit of diplomacy completed, I forgot about The Bayview and walked into The Bridge Inn.

It was a square sort of bar, with seats on two sides and the back bar on the other two sides. I called for a pint and did what I always do whilst waiting for the pint to be drawn, looking about the room, taking in the patrons and the decor. It is the bits of bric-a-brac that tell you about the people who own the place. Not the usual things every pub has on the walls: maps of the county, of Ireland, the family crests, but the personal effects they have taken from their home and set here in the public house.

The most interesting that I found was a plaster-of-Paris chef, about two feet high, set on a corner shelf at about shoulder height. It had a floppy, black chef hat, chef whites over its rotund belly, and was holding a small blackboard in one hand that said 'Today's Special.' The free hand pointed to the blackboard, a wry sort of smile painted on his face.

Market day had long since ended, and the pub was dark and quiet. The night crowd would not appear for another hour or two. I rubbed my face with my hands and suddenly felt the room begin to reel. The lights set into the shelves above the bar seemed to multiply, and the man on the telly was speaking Swahili. I decided to stand up and in so doing knocked my bar stool to the ground. Bending over to pick it up was a great mistake as the blood, and lots of drink, rushed into my head with the impact of a frying pan. I righted myself and felt the room swim and spin around me like a carnival ride. I couldn't help but smile.

In the midst of all this, a little voice seemed to be whispering my name, at first distant, then closer. I determined to step through the haze and see who was hailing me.

I leaned toward the voice, cocking an ear in that direction to get a better listen. There, on the corner shelf, the plaster-of-Paris chef had set down his blackboard, swiveled around on a fat hip, and was pointing at me.

"Wiley? Wiley? Are ya drunk yet?"

I stared at the impish chef in disbelief. My mind, a distant part of it anyway, trying to recall the voice in which the figure spoke.

"Wiley, you useless sot, are you gonna make love to me or has the drink dove to your purpose!"

I swayed, wide-eyed, staring at first at the brazen statue and then to behind the bar, searching for the barkeep to make this thing go away.

"Wiley, you drunk git, have ya no virility left at all!"

It was then, the room rushing away from me, the drink rushing up from my nether regions, and the shock rushing in, that I recognized who it was berating me.

It was the voice of my ex-wife.

I threw my hands up in horror, knocking over my pint, stumbled over the still fallen bar stool, and raced out the front door.

I ran up the street to the bridge, where the day's drink joined the black and orange water in its journey to the sea, then attempted to put as much distance between myself and the mocking fat little chef as possible. I stopped outside The Midway, the cool breeze from the bay stilling a throbbing temple, repairing frayed nerves, and gazed out toward Aranmore.

"Wow," was all I could muster, a border collie staring at me from across the street quickly tilting its head at the sound of this one word. The quiet Dungloe streets absorbing my voice, and me, as I walked slowly up the hill.

The last pub as you leave town, at the very top of the hill, is Tir Conall's. In my haste to sit down, I failed to notice the barmaid. That is, until she came over and asked what I'd like to drink. I don't know what I said, but she poured me a Guinness.

As I sat there, my belly empty and cold, her face warm in my heart, I felt something change inside of me. Subtle at first, but then very distinct, it sobered me. Had I reached the end of the line? Had I run long enough?

The lights dimmed on and off twice to let everyone know that the night was about to come to a close. She then brought over my last round, poured herself a pint of stout with a drop of blackberry currant in it, and took the stool beside me. She talked to her mates in that way that Irish girls do, where there doesn't seem to be time for even a pause. I tapped her on the shoulder. She turned.

"Are you off this Sunday."

"Yes, why?"

"Would you like dinner?"

She looked at me quizzically, weighing me up a bit.

"Sure. Half-Eight, here." Then turned back to her conversation.

And once again, for the second time that night, the room began to swim.

21

It had been years since I had stared into a mirror this long. Tonight would be the first date I'd had in even longer, and I wanted everything to be perfect. Not that I was putting on the Ritz, not by a long shot. In fact, as we would only be walking from the top of Dungloe to the bottom, a trip of ten minutes even by the most senior of our citizens, dressing to the nines would be pure foolishness. Still, even in blue jeans and my favorite pullover, it had to be perfect.

I really liked this girl. The past few evenings were spent at Tir Conall's where she worked, engaging in light conversation and laughter. I had even gone so far as to go to Sweeny's Hotel and once-over the menu and the wine list, asking for a specific table.

All of this made me especially nervous as I walked up to Tir Conall's on this fine October evening. A sliver of a moon hung off to the East, a few clouds lit up by the glow, and I couldn't help but see it as a grin. I stopped suddenly, the grin seeming almost a leer, the smile of someone possessing a cheeky secret.

I shook the thought from my head, opened the door to the pub, and any misgivings I had were evaporated by the sight of my date, Marie Rose.

She sat in a bar stool, a thin, black sweater covering a white blouse, a short, plaid skirt of dark green revealing long legs crossed and in dark green hose. The obligatory black shoes with the fat heels, toes pointing up and down as she spoke with her hands, making a point that brought laughter from her captive audience of men of all ages. As the door slammed behind me, all heads turned to see me staring at her legs.

"Wiley! Jaysus lad, my face is up here." More howls of laughter. "Have a drink with us before we go to dinner."

"That sounds like a solution to me. Evening, lads."

Nods and hellos followed, we made small talk and sipped at our drinks. The last wee bit of Irish sunlight slipped over the horizon and into the Atlantic, the windows of the pub no longer windows but mirrors. Seeing my reflection made me feel foolish, and I wondered if I was really ready for this, the sting of divorce now a dull ache, like a muscle recovering from a charley horse.

We finished our drinks at the same time, the simultaneous clunk of our empty glasses making us aware of this. We smiled at each other, prompting her to lean over and give me a kiss on the side of my face. I grew warm, reached for her hand, and we said so long on our way out the door.

The grinning moon still leered at me as we walked down to Sweeny's. She told me little quips about the different people we saw on the street. Sometimes as she leaned over telling a mock secret, her hair would brush my face, giving me a chill. Smitten? Yes. Infatuated? Maybe. But for some reason I could not shake the moon.

The table at Sweeny's was just how I wanted it. The waitress poured the Pouilly Fuisse, we each ordered a starter to share and the grilled salmon. As she pulled mussels from the shell and dabbed them in garlic butter, the conversation turned.

"O'Wary?"

"You can call me Wiley."

"Are you from the Dungloe O'Warys, or the Crohy O'Warys?"

"Dungloe. Why?"

"Ah, sure, I'm just curious like Yer ma, what was her maiden name?"

"Gallagher, like every bloody one else around here."

"Really?"

"Yes, why?"

She paused, wrinkling her nose in thought.

"Now, is it the Dungloe Gallaghers, or the Crohy, or the Maghery?"

"The Dungloe Gallaghers by way of Aranmore."

"Go on. From Illion, or Leabgarrow?"

"From Leabgarrow to be sure. What are you going on about?"

"My mother is a Gallagher from Leabgarrow. Only we didn't stay in Dungloe, after a bit we moved to Omagh."

"Hold on, yer ma is a Gallagher from Leabgarrow, who lived a short time in Dungloe and then moved to Omagh?"

She nodded, and with that I looked out the window and up at the laughing moon. "Her name wouldn't be Mary, would it?"

"To be sure. Wait a minute. Yer ma wouldn't be Eileen?"

I placed my head firmly in my hand and nodded, "Aye."

"Well then, what's that make us?"

As I spoke the words we both drew ever so slightly away from the table, "First cousins."

The rest of the evening was awkward at best. We toasted each other with cognac after the meal for having found a long-lost relative, and did our best to laugh off the romantic notions. As we walked back up the street to Tir Conall's, I couldn't help but shake my head over the whole thing. What dumb luck.

At the door to the pub, I declined the drink, gave her a wee hug, and said so long. She asked if I'd stay in touch and I promised I would. As she opened the door, the din of pub noise filtering out onto the street, she looked back over her shoulder and gave me a wink. The door closed and silence resumed, the street empty, save for one fat, yellow cat, a bit of mist, and that continually mocking moon.

I took a long, slow walk down to the pier. The soft surf lapping at the shore and breaking gently against the rocks was the only sound. Standing at the end of the pier, I turned around to see the lights of my hometown. The enveloping mist gave a halo around each light, and I couldn't help but smile.

Closing my eyes, I thought about everything that had happened to me in the last few weeks. The catharsis of my father's death, the awful feelings that welled up inside of me as a result, the near drowning I had experienced. All of these things had done something to me that I could not quite put a finger on. Something palpable had changed. It seemed that something had been awakened, be it benign or malignant.

Four weeks ago I could not have fallen in love. Yet in the past week, I nearly had. What was the catalyst? What was it that had changed? Breathing in deeply, the smell of the sea pulled at my heart and it was then that I simply let myself go.

In the darkness before me I could see Ireland unfold. The rugged mountains of Donegal giving way to the bogs of Mayo, and the rolling green hills of the midlands; the lush, lonely beauty of Connemara in contrast to the bustle of Dublin. But it wasn't this that pulled at my heart.

I turned around, completing the circle, and looked back out across the black ocean. I gazed out beyond the horizon, past that place where the sun seems to sink, and let my mind go from there. It took me out across the Atlantic, along the routes the coffin ships sailed, through the Grand Banks and to America. I realized then, that I am that wandering Irishman, and will continue to chase the setting sun. Was I running? And if I were, would I ever know what from? At this moment, the fog settling on my sweater in tiny drops, the wine and cognac kissing me gently, I didn't care.

I lingered a long moment, turned back to Dungloe, and made my way home to my mother's and a mug of hot tea. That same fat, yellow cat was now at the bottom of the street, continuing it's beat, finishing or beginning the rounds. Curtains were being pulled over lit pub windows, publican's eyes looking for the guards, the conversation inside a muffled mish-mash.

And the moon, well she had turned, resting above the western horizon, nudging America as a Cheshire smile, and winking at me just before the ocean swallowed her whole.

22

White knuckled and giddy, fingers curled over the edge, our chins resting on the rock while we lie as still as possible in the breeze, we stare into infinity. Far below, seabirds wheel and cry searching the cliff walls for nooks and nests, their flight effortless in the continual wind. I look over to my mom, bright eyes tearing, a wide smile of exhilaration, she looks back to me and shakes her head in disbelief.

Incredibly, neither of us had ever been to the Cliffs of Moher. My sister, who claims to have been to every county in Ireland, made precise arrangements for us on our way to Shannon Airport. Now, with one night left, I am eternally grateful she had.

It took better than half an hour for myself to talk herself into lying down on the cold rock and belly-crawl to the edge. After she had seen me do this without tumbling over three different times, she nervously agreed. As we peered over the edge and down eight hundred feet to the Atlantic, she laughed excitedly, saying thank God she hadn't worn a dress. It was a fine day and the views went out past the Aran Islands, white, fluffy clouds scattered like sheep, their shadows slowly scooting across the ocean between the Cliffs and the Islands.

We had driven down from Donegal, a much too early start for me, stopped for lunch in Galway and had taken the coast road at Kilcolgan. We felt a bit guilty, my sister insisting we should have lunch in Ballyvaughn at Monk's Pub, but our appetites drove us into a lovely bistro near Eyre Square.

At the cliffs, we had walked from one high point to the other before jumping down to this lower, flat area at the edge. A number of Americans from a coach had gotten down on their hands and knees, then their bellies, and inched their way to the precipice. When I had seen them do this, I turned to my mother who was already looking at me and shaking her head. Well, a son's insistence overcame any trepidation and so we lay there, the wind rushing up the walls of the cliff into our faces, our conversation as light as if we were at tea.

"So, Wiley," she looked over to me.

"Aye."

"Are ya dating any cousins I should know about?"

"Ah Jaysus, so ya heard of that, then."

"Sure it's a wee, small town. There's not much happens that we old ladies don't know about."

"How embarrassing. First date in years and it's my own kin."

"Don't trouble yourself son, she's a lovely girl. Sure you're not the first cousin that's had an eye for her."

We returned to the view, the autumn sun pouring through clouds and warming us. I looked closely at the stone in front of me, mere inches from the void, and thought of the cemetery.

"I'm very glad you took your sister to the grave. She didn't have the need for the funeral. She was away with your Aunt Maura for almost all of those troubled years, and too young to remember the rest. To her your father was more of a distant uncle. Someone she could ignore."

"I never understood why she got to go to London. I had always wanted to go, study abroad, get away."

"Ah, one day you might understand. It was for the best, and weren't those the crazy days. It's amazing any of us survived at all. Besides, it's water down the falls."

I looked over to her, my eyes and heart asking for answers, for whole sentences, the completion of her thoughts.

"Wiley, I hope and trust you buried the dead at that grave. Let the man and all the things about him lie in the cold ground where he belongs. You have a life to live, in a new place with new friends. Go to them. Show them the person I'm proud to call my son."

I smiled my best happy-son smile, still troubled, and returned to looking down. She started to inch away from the ledge, backed up a few feet, kneeled, turned and rose to her feet. I followed, as another coach-load of Americans gained inspiration from us and were belly-crawling to the edge. My mother walked up off the lower ledge and onto the grass. I trotted up beside and placed my arm around her.

"Where has my sister commissioned us to stay tonight?"

"Newmarket-on-Fergus. A place called The Huntsman. It's a short drive to Shannon from there. She says they pour a good pint, and the mussels are lovely." I shook my head in happy acceptance, a pint just beginning to sound good.

We walked up to O'Brien's Tower for one last look out at the sea, the Aran Islands, the horizon. She stood leaning against the stone of the keep, her hair blowing back in the wind, eyes squinted, a most set look on her face, a countenance of strength about her. I looked at her for a long time with an almost reverence.

"Mom," I said as she turned, "thank you." I had won a smile, her head turning back to the sea, her thoughts as far away as the coast of Greenland, until it dawned on me who was missing.

"I just thought of something."

"Yes," she said, not moving.

"My brother, have you ever heard from him?"

She dropped her gaze, brought a hand to her face, to her chin, to her breast.

"Only once since he left that Christmas day."

"How long ago?"

"Nineteen years, five months and six days."

I stared hard at her for a moment, a brief spike of jealousy.

"Did you see him?"

"No. A postcard."

"Really? I saw him in Dublin since then, maybe twelve years ago. You've had no word from him at all?"

"I'm surprised you got to see him. I would like to, just one last time."

"What did the card say?"

"There was a picture of the Sydney Opera House, and the harbor, *Greetings from Australia*. All he said was, 'Thinking of you and dear, old Donegal'. He spelled it the old way, a-u-l-d. 'Thinking of you, and dear, auld Donegal'."

"That was all he wrote?"

"No," she turned slightly, looked to the thin grass, "it also said, 'All the king's horses, and all the king's men, couldn't put old Billy back together again'."

There was a pause, time filled with wind and silence. She looked up to the sea. I could see her mist over.

"I don't get it. I mean you hadn't heard from him in almost two decades, and he writes to you a nursery rhyme. That just doesn't make sense."

"Wiley," she said, her eyes filled with tears, "it was written in crayon."

We walked back from the cliffs, through the car park and to the car. She had her arms about herself and was still shaking from crying. I volunteered to drive, but she stiffened, said 'thanks anyway,' and drove us silently through the Burren to Ennis.

The karst moonscape was a photographic negative of our train ride north not three weeks ago. Highlights slid past in silence: Mullaghmore, Poulnabrone, Loch Inchiquin. No matter what vista presented itself to our racing automobile, neither it nor I could get past her brooding. After an hour of this, along with the steep, hairpin curves of the roads slicing through the limestone hills, and the simple fact of two adults used to only their own company, resentment on both our parts began to emerge.

She pulled into a parking spot off Abbey Street in Ennis, saying she needed something sweet. I said I needed a pint, agreed to meet her in an hour, and walked past the monument to Daniel O'Connell. I was muttering beneath my breath, cursing her driving, her disproportionate love for her older son, and myself at the same time for being so childish. I truly hoped this would not be the way the holiday would end, another emotional page in the O'Wary annals, another rift two stubborn people would take years to cross.

The road carried me to a bridge overlooking the river Fergus. A number of banks lined the street on the other side, but it being long since banking hours had ended, the lane was empty. I was alone, half way across, leaning on the stone and staring down the river, past the swans and out toward a broad, grassy meadow. In the distance over the town, a single steeple pierced the sky and it was to this that I decided to walk.

I breathed in the smells of a county town: petrol fumes, the smell of slurry somewhere in the distance, a chippy doing happy after-school business. Beneath this, like that pulse in our music, lay the sweet smell of peat burning in a thousand hearths.

Through the collection of streets, meandering as they did from around the town square to all points of the compass, I eventually found the cathedral. My eyes followed the lines of the building from the courtyard in which I stood, up over the arched doorway and along the steeple into the dusk sky. Swallows flew with abandon through the dark purple of approaching night, and it was then that I realized again the void in my life.

"Dear brother, where are you? So many times you came to our rescue only to become a ghost, a memory," I said, to no one, to myself, to the empty courtyard, and then thought how hard it must be for my mother.

Looking down the road, I could see it rise through the close buildings toward the monument, and set off in that direction. I had only been gone a short time and decided to avail myself of the last few pints of true Guinness before flying back to America.

I stepped down an alley and into Brogan's. There was a crowd of people in clutches about the place that made it feel busy. One stool remained at the bar, I settled into it, called for a pint, and rubbed my temples, trying to clear my head.

"Well aren't we the pair."

I turned, my cloudy thoughts interrupted to see my mother standing before me, a hot whiskey in her hand.

"Something sweet," I said to her, motioning to her bright, gold drink.

"Go on yourself, a town of five thousand and we get away from each other in the same pub."

"We must be suited."

"Indeed. I watched you walk in. Couldn't believe it. I thought you'd still be reading the monument, or would have walked over to the Fergus."

"I did, but didn't linger long. Something in my head that's puzzling me."

"If you mention your father's name I'll clout you in front of all these people."

I laughed so hard I choked. "No, nothing of the sort. You've only had the one postcard from my brother?"

"Right."

"What about our sister? Has she heard anything?"

"You're a smart man Mister Wiley O'Wary. She has, but hasn't said a word of it. He made these arrangements. There hasn't been much now, but over the years she has heard more than you and I."

"Well then what has he said? Where is he? Why can't we talk to him?"

"There is a protocol that I am not privy to, although in the last ten years that may have changed. She has had only a letter or two in that time, and a promise."

"What sort of promise?"

"The only thing he let her tell me was that one day we could all be together again, but it may not be for a very long time."

She stopped, each of us in our own thoughts, absentmindedly looking at the faces around us. I finished my pint in short course, ordered another round, and took the car keys from my mother's hand.

After long moments, I asked, "What's a long time?"

She took up her new drink, stared into it a moment, lifted it to her lips, and then returned it to the palm of her left hand. A group of people in a booth in the corner began to sing *From Clare To Here*, at first off key, then quite lovely.

"Wiley," she said, her voice cracking, "His parole is in thirty years."

23

Squinting my eyes, the tears welling up in bunches, I look up from the cutting board and out into the late, autumnal Michigan sky. The dark, roiling clouds allowing enough light to filter through so you could call it daytime. I wipe my face with the sleeve of my shirt, pick up the knife, and return to the onions. It feels good to work again.

The weeks in Ireland are now a collection of memories like the quilted fields of that beautiful country. In my mind it is easy to be back there, easy to picture my mother sitting at the old bar of The Strand View, a forlorn glass of sherry beside her. My pint of stout, not quite so forlorn, nearly empty except the foam rings representing each time glass was brought to lips. Just outside the bar and down the road is the strand, the surf washing away the land a spoonful at a time. With having been back there, with the impressions it has left, Ireland pulls at my heart in the same way you remember an old friend, or a place you used to run to when you were scared. The longing has ebbed and been replaced with the warm glow of knowing that Ireland is always with me, in me, a part of me.

Today it is the simple rhythm of working. The security of routine is as pleasant as my mother's face when she saw me off at Shannon Airport. The familiarity of being in a kitchen, the kitchen I had left so many weeks ago, is nearly as reassuring as that last embrace.

Sweeping the onions into a bowl, I turn from the prep table and walk over to the line. My friend the Sous Chef, visibly bursting at the seams to tell me something, gives me a wink and a sideways nod. It is a Friday, my first day back, and the Chef has tasked me to prepare the night's special.

The restaurant feels charged, as if something tangible has happened while I was away, and no one is telling me about it. The looks on people's faces seem brighter, almost exaggerated. There is an underlying buzz like at the beginning of a rock concert. I try to pawn this off to jet lag and that misplaced feeling you get from having been abroad. Perhaps it is the fact that I haven't been here in a while or maybe it's just delirium tremens. As none of these explanations seems to satisfy, I go about my work, the undercurrent continuing to give me pause.

I have coated the cubed lamb with whiskey and flour. The flattop is hot, oil popping off the surface making a disjointed series of staccato snaps. Taking the hotel pan of meat, I dump it onto the grill, relishing the concussive sound and letting the whiskey steam stream past my face. This is one of those little things in life that makes it all worthwhile.

The smell of the lamb reminds me of the kitchen in Dungloe, those troubled years, and how it seemed that the mere act of cooking would bring any row to an end. It was as if preparing food was an act above the shallow violence of life, a ritual too sanctified to be demeaned, an event heightened further and rooted deeper by the famine. My mother would cook lamb once or twice a week, we were that fortunate. This smell and this recipe are really hers. The funny thing about time is that moments seem as if they happened yesterday, and yet those meals were well over thirty years ago.

"If you don't turn the meat, you're liable to burn it."

Startled from my fog, the Sous Chef standing beside me, arm draped over my shoulder, his smile way too broad for any human face.

"Sage advice, my friend."

"So," he said, eyebrow arching, looking at the ingredients spread before me, "whatcha making for tonight."

"An ancient alchemic brew that raises banshees, why?"

"You know, you could have left your sense of humor back in Ireland and no one would really have missed it. I've got some great news to tell you, but its got to wait 'till later. Coupla beers, after work?"

"Man doesn't live by bread alone."

"I don't think that's about beer." To which he smiled as broadly as before and walked away.

Shaking my head, I scooped the lamb off the flat top and dumped it into an enormous kettle. I added a broth made from the bones, garlic, thyme, bay leaf and a little sherry vinegar, looking over my shoulder and saying an apology to my mother for just slightly altering her recipe.

It just feels like something is going to happen. Something completely out of my control is going to upset the apple cart, and not only can't I do anything about it, I am having trouble even naming it. The feeling is like having someone ask you a trivia question, about a subject completely feckless, a topic you usually don't even have to think about, and suddenly you can't remember the answer. It plays at the edge of your consciousness, as if there were an imp running through the corridors of your mind placing the words on the tip of your tongue but removing them before you have a chance to say them.

"What now," shaking my head, "what bloody now."

The kettle covered and simmering, I walk outside to lean against the wall and smoke a cigarette. Gusts of wind pick up autumn leaves into unseen eddies, their whirling dances reminding me of the music that night in Dublin when I learned my father had died. The weave of traditional Irish music, patterns that are easily discernible but never fully understood, I thought again about my brother, looked up at the tumult of clouds and felt the first cold drops.

Walking back into the kitchen, my head turning quickly at a friendly slap on the butt to see the Waitress smiling, and return to the kettle. I stir the simmering mixture with the large wooden spoon that everyone, regardless of age, wields like Excalibur. With the lid off, the smell is starting to fill the kitchen. At this point it is time to add the parsnips, potatoes, onions, carrots and celery. Tasting beforehand tells me to add a bit more thyme, a touch of pepper, and a little marjoram, working it into the mixture along with a pound of butter.

This dish is very nearly a cliché, yet every time I make it, I can't help but think how perfect it is. It is a wonderful hodge podge of familiar and comforting flavors, a national dish that truly echoes the voice of a people. When we look back on our lives from safe places, we can trace how far we've come and how much we've been through. Always, it seems, in these memories there is food, not just as sustenance, but an anchor that centers us to our culture.

There is more simmering, another cigarette, and even more thinking. Standing out by the waste bins, one leg propped behind me against the brick wall, the sky not having yet decided to rain, I think back to Dungloe.

My mother's house, silhouetted against a different sky, the Atlantic brooding in the short distance, I remember returning to the upstairs. I had poked my head into my brother's room, virtually unchanged from when he had left us, only now housing the debris of a broken marriage. It hadn't seemed odd to me at the time that she hadn't cleared out the room. There were piles of old clothes, packages filled with string, thread, and yarn. A sewing machine sat on his desk beside his hurling stick, and an ancient copy of the *Donegal Democrat*. There was a layer of dust that with the vintage of the clothing lent an air of forgotten nostalgia. Time trapped in a bubble. It was as if she had tried to make the room useful, but had failed in the attempt.

The things she had said about my brother began to make sense to me. Her wistfulness all these years, his name never coming up in conversation, the way the room had been left, the pattern started to emerge. I had shut the door to his room, these misty ideas forming, looked down at the door to my room, and quickly retreated down the hall, down the stairs and away.

"Wiley, head honcho wants you to finish up," the pantry chef from the kitchen door.

"Thanks."

I walk back into the kitchen, my head down still sorting things out, and over to the kettle. I add a quart of cream, slowly stirring it in. Taste and adjust, seasoning with the last three things that can never be mentioned, and turn from the stove to a dozen smiling faces, who, in chorus, remind me why I'm being so reflective.

"Happy Birthday, Wiley!"

My face becomes red as apples. I return the smiles of the gathered staff, give them a wink, and nod to the Sous Chef who dishes up ramekins of Irish stew. We clink them like flutes, the appreciativeness of everyone's taste buds witnessed by closed eyes and soft smiles. I turn back to the kettle for one more ladle-full, wipe away a tear, and am jolted upright by the bellowing of the Chef. The moment is over, the service is set to start, the printer chatters out the first few orders, and the dance begins anew.

24

As I pull on what seems like every piece of clothing I own, I'm beginning to sense that the warmth of Indian summer has been swept away by late November's winds. The grind of life, waking, working and returning, made more of a challenge by the chill in the air, the darkness of the days, the brusqueness of a weary people. We toil through this time, which is *No Time* in the old Celtic calendar, basking in the oasis of a laugh or a moment shared that reminds us of the summer past.

Despite nearly five years in Boston, the quick change in Michigan weather has caught me off guard. An unannounced arctic blast sent everyone scrambling for the stowed box of winter clothing, and myself down to St. Vincent's to see what the bargain bins held. Because of this foray, as I set down my empty mug of tea on the dish line beside an equally empty bowl of Tuscan mushroom chowder, I resemble an overstuffed scarecrow walking out the kitchen door and into the cold dark.

Lights are glimmering on bare trees downtown, a reminder for me of what will again be holidays alone. The joy of the season tempered with too many hours of work, too much stress, and an empty apartment. Last year was like this also, the final stages of divorce etched upon my heart, I picked up every extra shift I could so as to not think about Christmas Eve, Christmas Day or New Years. My friends were gracious, but I had to decline each invitation, partly out of stubborn determination, more out of not wanting to afflict their joy with my downcast spirit.

So, I intend to rally my inner-troops by attending tonight's symphony. My favorite composer is Sergei Prokofiev, and his score to the film *Alexander Nevsky* is the highlight of this evening's performance. Fortified with soup, bread, and tea, I walk from work to the show.

As I march through the rows of empty trees, each one aglow with bobbing lights, the wind in my face reminds me of the music I soon will be hearing. The brave Russian people trying to eke out a living on the Thirteenth Century steppe, soon to be overrun by the Teutonic Knights. What's a little pre-holiday depression compared to what some people have had to endure?

The Mall is empty, save for a street person who slowly glides past me in the opposite direction. His kind face frosted, he turns to look at me and a moment of recognition passes between us. But the moment is so fleeting and distant, and the night so cold, that neither of us say anything at all.

My mind continues to mull over the words of the Sous Chef. When I first returned from Ireland, he was bursting to tell me something very important that had transpired while I was abroad. Then, fate having its usual way with me, he was switched to days while the Chef holidayed in Cancun. This was an important time for the Sous, as it was his first opportunity to run an entire kitchen by himself. His free time vanished, and with it the opportunity for us to digest the news he had mentioned only briefly. That is until today, when my request to swap night for day was granted, and he and I could talk for the first time in weeks.

He had mentioned it in the way that he always mentions things of importance, sandwiched between a myriad of useless topics. So, somewhere in the middle of Detroit Lions football, the top layer of the shallots are spoiled so dig to the bottom, and Thanksgiving dinner is at One-Thirty please bring a bottle of White Zinfandel for my mom, he told me about the Waitress.

It was all very puzzling, and as a person who has just moved here, only worked at the restaurant a short time, and is by nature quite shy, I wasn't sure what to make of it. But the gist of the thing was churning inside of me, and no matter what I tried to think of, my mind would not focus on anything other than this ball of confusion.

Once I was inside the auditorium, I noticed how much I smelled like a restaurant. I had worked all day, right up to the point where I could grab a bite to eat and then dash out the door. Not being in the kitchen, or outside with a frozen nose, I could tell that the smell of fryers and garlic were wafting from me in waves. A woman, luxuriantly adorned for tonight's show, gave me one of those scurrilous looks down her nose. I could, in return, only give her a wink and a sideways nod.

My seat is light years away from the stage, somewhere in the back of the mezzanine. It is a long hike up what seems like every stairway in the place, as if I were in a drawing by MC Esher. Soon enough though, the snug, cramped feeling of the passageways yields to the spaciousness of the Hall. I pause, as I always do, to let the feel of the room hit me.

Gazing out into the expanse, the first thing I notice is the low rumble of hushed conversation. Beneath this, there is an almost imperceptible throb that hums through the building, through each person, a mounting expectation that cannot possibly be any different than the stories told around cave fires. The room is opulent without being gaudy, rich without being a distraction from the event.

A kind attendant views my ticket and points me to the back wall up two more flights of stairs. As I locate my seat, noses crinkling as I brush past in a flurry of 'excuse me' and 'pardon me', I realize I am the only person attending alone. Not wanting to be a bother and already feeling out of place, I continue to ponder.

My friend the Sous Chef has been kind enough to invite me to his family's celebration of Thanksgiving. I can count on one finger how many Thanksgivings I have taken part in. There is no such holiday in Ireland, and when I lived in Boston I worked at a country club that held an enormous Thanksgiving buffet. It is something I'm not very familiar with, and his family being very Polish, I am still wondering if they'll stuff the bird with kapusta

The lights have dimmed, and my thoughts have returned to the pretty face of the Waitress. First chair violin takes his seat as I think about her asking the Sous where I was, how long I would be gone and if I was seeing anyone. The conductor enters, shakes hands with the first chair violin, and the orchestra begins playing. The opening piece is morose and serves only to stray my thoughts and sink my mood. I wonder if she is still going out with that big geezer, and if her asking of me while in Ireland was only small talk.

Bloody holidays. Last year when I called my mother, the weight of the divorce in my voice, she simply said to me, 'Jaysus Wiley, lighten up and have a whiskey. I told you to marry an Irish girl.' A mother's advice always comes in three parts: one for the head, one for the heart, and one to remind you who's still in charge.

The opening piece finished, the orchestra alights on Mozart's *Symphony No. 40*. Like a lot of Mozart, the melodies that you remember, those incredible hooks, are the sweet softness that covers a tremendous sadness. How anyone could write music that is both so uplifting and yet reveals so much melancholy is truly amazing.

While my head slowly bobs to the music, I think back to my first night in the kitchen upon my return, and the Waitress slapping my butt as I passed through the pantry to the line. Well, that all but seals it, right? The Sous said she had asked of me, not once, but twice, and that she had been carrying a copy of Leon Uris' *Trinity*. What further proof did one really need?

With intermission, I return to the stairs, dash down to the main lobby, and avail myself of a glass of red wine. There are scores of people, mostly in pairs, mingling and talking. I busy myself with the program and try to fade into the wallpaper.

The last piece of music has left me feeling a bit blue. I gaze up at the lofty ceilings inside the lobby and detect a heaviness growing within me Alone, over forty, the honeymoon of the Irish holiday having faded, I begin to see only the differences between herself and myself. And even though I realize how pointless it could turn out to be, I know I will not be able to steer my way clear. There is a need within the human animal for contact. Outside of work, outside of having a few jars with your mates, outside of whatever burning passions one has, we must grace ourselves with another who fires the mind, stirs the heart, and kindles the soul. In the end, with the last breath on our lips, it will be their name we speak.

The house lights dip three times and I wend my way back to the mezzanine. The wine has flushed my cheeks, softened my thoughts, given me hope. I arrive back at my seat, crinkle more noses, sit and await the piece I have heard live only once before, in London long ago.

I lean forward, elbows resting on the empty seat in front of me, and close my eyes as the Hall's lights fall. The score begins, percussion and strings creating an abrupt cacophony that is vintage Prokofiev, only to have tympani thunder a cadence that is the Teutonic Knights. I imagine the thundering hooves of the heavy horses, clumps of snow and sod thrown behind them, the roar of their weight pounding the earth. Atop each horse, clad in armor, is the deadliest soldier in the world at that time. Who will defend mother Russia? Who will protect the Russian children? Nevsky will.

I let the music wash over me. Invigorating, inspiring, the words are foreign, but all too familiar. At what cost, with what bravery, will one people defend their homeland from another? The piece moves from near chaos to quiet, almost quirky passages that test the limits of the listener. The volume of the orchestra and the chorus rising and falling as if the battle were still being fought.

When all is played and sung, the ovations falling away like the ghosts on that long-ago battlefield, echoes of instruments hanging in the air like smoke, I follow the audience to the exits. The din of hundreds of murmuring voices carries me as swiftly as my legs, the glow of the experience, of concert, as tangible as the rush of cold air upon leaving the theater. Then, almost instantly, the sound of the exiting crowd is replaced by silence. And I, alone, walk to the bar.

I watch as the couple ahead of me pause to kiss beneath a streetlight. As I pass by them, the wind blows her hair across their faces. I turn away from them to look into the wind, thoughts suddenly returning to the Waitress, to the last words the Sous had said to me before I left work for the show.

Walking into the pub, taking my usual seat at the bar, I stop the barmaid from pouring me a pint of stout. I ask her for a double Stolichnaya neat.

It is Saturday night, date night, and no matter how you look at it, or what you call it, be it as an excuse, as solace, as a quiet numbing of feelings I didn't know I still could have, the vodka is just another ticket to the lonely-hearts club.

Yet, beneath the aching emptiness, there is a spark.

'Wiley,' he had said to me, 'she was singing your name over and over again under her breath, while she was filling salad dressings. I didn't know what she was saying at first, and it seemed strange anyway, then as I heard her clearly she looked up, caught my eye and scampered off in that way only a waitress can. You know, like they're superior or something'.

I had nodded, as I am now, my glass of vodka held before my eyes refracting light, and said an off-hand joke at the time. Only now, with the subject fairly well preoccupying my mind, did I acknowledge this spark to myself.

I look out the window to the kissing couple slowly walking past, arms about one another, hands held and eyes locked.

"Well, Nevsky," I say to myself, snow flakes beginning to fall, the couple having stopped to kiss once more beside the window, "is it I who shall be led out onto the ice?"

25

I watch the flow of traffic drift past my window, the first breath of sunlight flitting across the asphalt, nearly blinding in its reflection from the metal of the cars and trucks. The rare December sun is warm upon my face, the glass panes enhancing the heat from our distant friend. I let the river that is rush hour soothe nerves wrought with too much work, and too many memories. A mug of steaming French Roast in place of butter-tea, I have the wonderful detachment of a monk in knowing I have the day off.

I arose this morning with nothing to do but a handful of errands. The weather is brilliant and I couldn't help but be drawn outside. Of late, old man winter has been loading up on West Michigan with bits of his entire arsenal: ice, sleet, snow, and freezing rain. It was difficult just getting to and from work, let alone stretching the legs. But today, a balmy and clear forty-plus, I intend to get the agenda over with as quickly as possible, leaving the rest of the day open for walking.

The town is dressed for the holidays. My heart falls with every wreath, darkens with each image of the great elf, the annual melancholy of the season as part and parcel as the holly and the candy canes. I had entertained the idea of going back to Boston for Christmas to see some old friends, but my workload and sheer practicality stand firmly in the way.

Thanksgiving was good. The Sous Chef was kind enough to invite me to his folk's house for poor old Tom Turkey and all the trimmings. Still, it felt as if I were intruding. The Sous' girlfriend had come up from university and I spent most of my time reading Polish cookbooks and trying to figure out American football.

The last half-cup of coffee drained, coat donned along with all the accoutrements of winter, a stop by the loo for the first cups of coffee, and then out the door. My neighbor across the hall pauses to wave from his car before checking traffic and pulling away from the curb. He no longer bothers to ask if I would like a ride, not with the weather this nice.

After a stop at the library to drop off the previous week's books, I headed the few blocks over to where I work. Walking into work on my day off always makes me feel a bit guilty. The restaurant business has a camaraderie that deepens from so many shifts where it seems as if all hell has broken loose. Staff tends to connect in a way not unlike the military or athletic teams. It is almost a siege mentality, so that when you're not on deck defending God, cuisine, and crew, you must certainly be a traitor. The Chef instills more of this here, but he his still missing in action, a culinary competition in New York keeping him away from the kitchen and out of our hair.

I sit down at the bar, after having fixed myself some tea and toast, taking in the quiet and empty dining room. Sun streams in through the windows giving the still white-clothed tables, the polished glass and silver, the blacks, gold and greens of the room, a hallowed hue.

The Sous is sitting there, pen, pad, and furrowed brow, costing specials, writing descriptions and placing orders.

"Good morning, General. Ain't it great to be in charge," I say, clapping him on the back.

"Hey."

"Hey? That's it? Where's the enthusiasm."

"It punched out last night at one and I couldn't find it when I punched back in at seven."

"As I've told ya, you should have stayed clear of the catering business and just become a rock star."

"You're awfully fucking chipper this morning."

"Day off."

"Well go bug someone else. On second thought, I'm short today. There's an extra set of whites in the office."

"Not on your life. Paddy's taking his day off. No matter shaggin' what."

He leaned back, stretched, rolled the pen between his palms, a series of clicks as it brushed his class ring. "Big plans, then. Maybe a date?" He grinned at me with that knowing look in his eye.

"I wouldn't know what to do. Wait a minute, you know something."

"On my honor, I don't know a thing. But, here's the day bartender with your check and she, most definitely, knows something. Have a good one."

"Have a better one," I said, stealing a line from a movie, as the Sous stood, gathered his work, and left for the kitchen.

"Wiley?" It was the barmaid.

"Yes, love."

"One of the waitresses was asking for your phone number last night."

This stopped everything.

"Go on."

"No, really. I don't work many nights, so I don't know her name. She's the one you four saved from that bridge during the big storm."

"Really. How odd. Thanks a million. Cheers."

I got up to leave, quickly retrieving my plate and mug.

She smiled back, "Cheers, Wiley. Hey! Your check."

"Oh yes," I said, trying not to look as anxious as I really was.

"Wiley."

"Yes, love?"

"Good luck," she smiled.

"Irish luck is rarely good, I'm afraid," I gave her a wink, "but we'll see if the gods fancy me today."

This put an entirely different spin on the day. As I walked to the bank to cash my check, I couldn't help but think about the Waitress and the night we had raced all over town to find her. What an adventure. Ever since then there had been a connection between us, but I never thought of it as anything

possibly romantic That is, until I had come back from Ireland
to find the rumor mill working overtime, and myself enter-
taining these notions with a warm glow.

I cashed my check, arriving at the bank long before the
noon lines would resemble those found at amusement parks,
and then went to the post to mail out Christmas letters to Ireland and Boston. My mind replayed bits of conversation the
Waitress and I had shared over the past months. Not paying
attention, I stepped off the curb at Michigan Street only to be
startled from thoughts by the shrill blast of a truck's horn.

From the post, I decided to walk down Monroe to Riverside Park. I had not been back there since the night of the
big storm and could think of no place better to idle away the
day. The sun in its low winter arc cast long shadows from the
factories and warehouses. These old buildings, crowded with
ghosts of Grand Rapids' past, shrouded the sidewalks and
brought on a chill. I shivered my way past them, occasionally
rubbernecking to admire the architecture or the brickwork.
Eventually this district gives way to middle class neighborhoods, and then to the north side of town and a gradual climb
up the real estate scale.

The park seems empty, the river nearly silent as it flows
toward downtown, toward Lake Michigan. I walk up to the
first bridge, shaking my head at the holes where once stood
giant trees. With barely a breeze, it is hard to imagine the
storm that swept through here, yet where once there were
trees, now there are only wood chips.

I find myself drawn to the north end of the park. Despite
the sunshine, there is a melancholy in the bare trees and

the quiet, still fields, the paths upset by only a handful of footprints in the new snow. As I walk past the place where the derelict bridge once stood, my thoughts return to that windswept night. The way she shivered, her hair blown straight back from the force of the gale, cheeks wet with tears, her arms locked around the steel cross-beam fifteen feet off the ground. But what I remember most was the look in her eyes. Defiant. Afraid. Angry.

Amazingly, the old bridge has been moved, buffed to a fare-thee-well, painted, and put back to work. It now assists in supporting the new bridge that connects the middle of the park to the north end, over a wee channel that lets the water of the Grand pool into a lagoon and run back into the river by another channel at the first bridge.

I walk slowly down the path toward the old bridge, an unknown trepidation in my steps, my boots matching stride for stride another set of prints. My gaze falls on a flock of Canadian geese working the not-quite-frozen ground. Over forty of them are strewn across the path and on either side. I tread lightly between them, unfamiliar with birds this size and in such numbers. When I pass them and reach the bridge, turning to look at the flock once more, it feels as if I've just walked through a scene in a Hitchcock film.

Upon setting foot on the bridge I turn my head to face forward, and there, inexplicably, as if out of a dream, stands the Waitress. The shocked look on my face is answered by her smile, a smile as disarming as the winter's sun.

"Wiley! Of all the luck, I've been trying to get a hold of you. Don't you answer your phone?"

I had turned the ringer off so as to sleep in undisturbed on this rare day off.

"No, no, not usually. I mean, sorry. This is all very confusing, I mean, I was just thinking about you."

She smiled, "The Park looks a lot different, doesn't it?"

"I'll say," and did.

"Have you ever seen so many geese?" She walked up beside me, placed small, wonderful hands on the railing, eyes looking out past the river, past the expressway, past the west side.

"That is a tremendous amount of paté."

"Disgusting," she crinkles up a perfect wee nose. "I'll have you know I'm a card-carrying member of PETA."

"Yes, who happens to eat prime rib, I've seen you."

"A girl is allowed an indulgence."

"Is that so. What shall be the next indulgence?"

"Guinness, Wiley. I think it's high time you and I had a pint together."

"Would you like to walk me to the bar?"

"I would love to." She reached into her coat pocket and pulled out a watch. She guarded it closely, seeming embarrassed by the cheap plastic band and glass so scratched I could not tell how she read the face. "But, I'm afraid that not only do I have to work tonight, but Lisa, you know Lisa who works nights, she's my ride and she'll be waiting for me by the first bridge."

"Well, there it is then. Another time."

"Oh, Wiley, there will be another time."

She turned to go, a smile, a wave of nothing more than the fingers of her left hand lifting slightly, stopped, turned back, and then stepped up to me. She placed her hands on my shoulders, tilted her head to one side, I to the other, and we kissed. For someone who in the past two years has kissed only his mother, his great aunt Fiona, and the odd whiskey bottle, the carnival had definitely come to town. When she opened her mouth, brought her arms around my neck, her fingers lightly touching my hair, I became convinced that we were ten feet off the ground.

She broke the kiss, smiled, turned with the same small wave, and walked away through the flock of geese. She paused, just before she had passed through them, looked up to the sky and then over her shoulder to me.

"Kissing on bridges, Wiley, I wonder if that's dangerous." Then she left, the stillness of the park crushed beneath the pounding of my heart.

26

On the top of my book shelf, covered by books and empty bottles with candle stubs, is my treasure chest. It is an old wood box that once held a Methuselah of champagne, a remnant of a celebration I catered many years ago. There is an improvised clasp and eye with a tiny lock that acts more as a reminder than security. Steadying myself by holding the book shelf with one hand, one foot on a chair, the other on the shelf itself, I reach past a nearly empty bottle of Jameson and catch hold of the box, carefully bringing it and myself to terra firma.

The lid of the box slides lengthways in thin tracks, the sound not unlike a tiny door opening, and reveals a world nearly as old as myself. Within are the doubloons of my history. Photos, scraps of newspaper, keepsakes, they are, in a word, memories. Those points in time that are both singular and profound, whether realized or not, that shape us.

Beneath layers of unorganized photographs, Wiley at ten next to Wiley just last year, old menus and special events handbills, is a layer of bric-a-brac that includes my three Christmas ornaments. These are the objects of my search, and like each year before at this time, they will pull in me a string of memories that I hold very close to my heart.

The first ornament is really the first, a gold claddagh that my mother had given me when I was only four years old. It has hung on a tree every year since. The second ornament I made in school when I was seven. A sort of diamond-shaped clay thing with red and green lines on a white background, the patterns as alien to me now as they were to everyone I proudly showed it to then. The third was made for me as I sat with my older brother in a pub on Dublin's north side. It was December Twenty-fourth, Nineteen Hundred and Eighty-three, and it was the last time I saw him.

My brother left the house when I was very young. On a Christmas morning, both he and my father drunk and angry, accusing each other over past injustices, it turned from shouting to fighting, a flurry of fists and epithets as they rolled across the living room. The crash of the tree, dozens of ornaments shattering on hard wood floor, deafened by the sound of the front door slamming. Standing in my underwear, my eyes closed and small hands covering my ears, all I could think of is what Santa would think when he saw what we had done to our tree.

My mother, the footfalls of her first child leaving forever still echoing in her head, looked holes through my father, who in turn, the object of so much hatred now missing, looked at me. Whatever shred of a family we had was left on the floor with the broken mangers, the fractured stars, and the twisted candy canes.

I ran up to my room, the sound of bellowing below, of giant boots taking the steps two at a time, and quickly locked the door behind me, pushing a chair under the doorknob as my brother had showed me. My window looked out upon the town, and I watched my brother as he walked toward Belfast and the silent brotherhood.

The civil rights marches having been crushed by the police, he, a young man filled with angst and ideals, anger and a need for vengeance, left Donegal to defend the North. After so many nights of watching my father pummel him with words and fists, his ghost of a figure walking down the deserted main street was the closest thing to a hero I had ever seen.

Years later in Dublin, myself a young man in my early twenties, I went shopping on Christmas Eve day. My mother had arrived from Donegal and I, the young chef, would fix Christmas dinner for her, my sister and myself. The wee breeze came in from the bay and brought with it the smell of the sea. Bits of sun filtered down through the thick, Irish clouds, which made the day feel a bit surreal. All the more so, because the night before the wind had come from the southwest, from the Wicklows, and had dusted Dublin with a rare snowstorm.

As the salt air slowly melted the snow, I walked up over the Liffey to my favorite butcher shop. I had ordered a Christmas goose, plus all the trimmings, as well as the best black pudding made anywhere in Ireland. There was nothing better than coming home after a few jars, heating up your best skillet, dropping in some rich Irish butter, and frying up the sausage. It was with this that my mind drifted, that wonderful glow of brandy and coffee further softening the edges of the day.

He stepped out from the crowd as if he was Puck and the street was his wood. I never saw him until he grabbed my shoulder, whisked me down an alley and into the back door of a pub. My protestations were useless against his strength. In my surprise I did not know who or what was happening. As we rolled in through the door of the tavern, the two of us hitting the floor, presents and parcels scattering, a shower of laughter and shouts from patrons, I looked up into the face of my brother.

"Wiley," he said, and all I could do was smile, as if I were staring at an angel. "Get off the floor you sod, you're embarrassing me."

"Jaysus, you eejit, you're liable to kill me."

"Awww, baby brother, not enough Christmas spirit for you? Donal!" he called out to the barman, "Pints of stout. And short ones as well. Come on Wiley, on yer feet. There's the good chef." I looked at him perplexed, how had he known I was a chef?

"Where have you been?" I asked, and the suddenness of the question threw him. He smiled, so softly, so slightly, that it wasn't even really a smile. His eyes, the indigo of deep-ocean, sparkled as if sunlight played across the water's surface, drifted, then clouded over. He didn't have to answer, he already had.

Sitting here at my kitchen table, the shoe box opened, ransacked, holding a picture of him, I can only wish for what

might have been but could never be. All those years without
him, how many times I had needed his counsel, had hoped
to see him walk through the door; had truly needed my big
brother. But it never happened. Even after my father left for
good, my brother never returned to Dungloe. We could only
pray that he wasn't in it too deep.

I stand up from the table, walk over to the counter, and
pour myself another brandy. Staring out the window above
the sink, I fill my mouth with the liquid, swallow hard, and
choke back tears.

I can still see his face smiling at me, his hands playing
with a ball of thin wire, eyes darting to the door, to a gentleman beside the door. We talked a little about what was
going on in Ireland, but never anything political. Just the
light, breezy stuff: who the top footballers were, did you see
that match between Meath and Donegal, what's topping the
charts?

In between the small talk, he would ask questions about
Dungloe, about me. Only when he felt very comfortable did
he ask about our mother. I could sense in him a great deal
of guilt over his decision to leave on that Christmas day. He
and my mother had been very close, and his choice had done
something to her that none of us could ever mention, but all
of us could feel. There were times when she would stare, eyes
hard and fixed, and you knew exactly about whom she was
thinking, as if willing that Christmas tree to right itself, the
ornaments to piece themselves back together.

As the afternoon wore on, a forest of pints, shot glasses
and empty Guinness bottles littering the table, I watched as

my brother worked with the wire. His hands were rough and scarred, as if hot liquid had spattered across them. I looked up at his face and saw the years on him for the first time. The worry lines stacked around his eyes like tiny cracks in a clay mask. He seemed to breathe in sighs.

I asked him if he would like to walk with me, as I had several last errands to run before the stores closed. He said yes, but only after another round. He got up from the table, reached inside his long, dark coat which hung on a hook on the wall, and then sidled back, a heavy hand falling on the back of his chair to catch his balance, a limp in his gait beginning from his hip. He looked at me for a very long time, silent, and I realized how hard it must be for him to surface like this. I wondered how many hours it had taken to plan running into me.

"Thank-you Wiley." And with those words, I knew I would never see him again.

We finished our last round and got up to leave. I remember the door opening, a blast of sunlight blinding us, and the smell of exhaust. His arm around my shoulder, we left the pub and I had the distinct feeling that I should turn and take one last look. As if, in my mind, I needed to know exactly where each chair was, how each barman looked, the way the light fell across the tables.

As I turned to look into his face, I saw the Garda car as it sat idling down the alley and across the street. My brother turned, patted my cheek, pressed something into my hands, and stepped back into the crowd. When I looked back to where he had been, after watching the police get out of their car, he was gone.

I opened my hands to look at the present he had given me. From the wire, three Guinness bottle caps, and a fifty pence coin, he had made a small bell. The wee clapper that hung from the middle was a nine-millimeter round. It was this, I'm sure, that he had retrieved from his coat. I stared at it for an eternity, turning it over in my fingers. A bell that could never make a sound, that would never peal or ring, not even in a whisper.

As I stood there in the alley, the bells of St. Mary's began to announce the hour, causing me to start. I looked around nervously, my temple throbbing, disoriented from the drink, from the encounter. The winter breeze lay cold upon my face, I looked up into the sky where patches of blue lay beyond the pressing Irish clouds, and my tears were salty on my lips as they ran down my cheeks. I closed a fist around the ornament, tucking it away as the police brushed past me and into the bar. I walked to the end of the alley, looked over my shoulder at the empty cobblestones, the bare brick walls, and then stepped back into the holiday crowd.

In this world and in this time, the phone begins to ring, yanking me from my Dublin euphoria. I snap my head around at it, as if it were an illusion, or an intruder, and let it go on, six, seven, eight times. The ringing ceases, silence resumes, and I have a desire to fill its void. I walk over to the cassette-radio that serves as a stereo and press play, not knowing which tape might be in the machine. There is a long gap of dead air, the cassette switching sides, whereupon I avail myself of yet another brandy, this time a double. Then, suddenly and a bit too loudly, there is a bodhran in an aptly martial air, and with a deep laugh I realize it is The Chieftains, *O'Sullivan's March.*

I hang the bell in the window, my finger flipping the bullet clapper in hopes of hearing more than a metal tick. Glass raised, back straight, at attention. "Well, big brother, maybe we'll see you again."

27

I am staring out the window at grim winter as it clenches its fist. The snow, driven mad by the wind, comes down in curtains. For hours it has fallen with its own determination, night and day offering no delineation, no point of respite. It simply falls. It has to. Each snowflake has surrendered to the howls of the wind, to eddies the wind creates, and to pursuit of the ground.

I close my eyes, the light of street lamps lingering on my retinas, falling snow peppering this vision. The glass in my hand is all too easily raised to my lips, the whiskey, providing eddies of its own, burns as it falls down my throat. I open my eyes to a picture of my brother taken a very long time ago. Today is his birthday, and I wonder where in the world he is.

When I had seen him last, all those Christmas Eve's ago, it had snowed that day as well. A blessing in Dublin, as it rarely snows there. His few hours with me not unlike the Dublin snow, appearing as if from nowhere and then just melting way. Looking back out into the whiteout of the blizzard, looking back to that one chance meeting, I begin to fathom the void in my life at his loss.

The restaurant is closed for the day, it being Sunday, and I did what work I could, turning older stock into soup, consolidating some product, cleaning up after the busy weekend. The holiday season has proved to be most successful, and the kitchen resembles more a castle under siege than the home to haute cuisine.

With daylight about to fade, the sun's light more of an afterthought, I left the restaurant to brave the walk back home, a friendly and unusual clap on the back from the Chef for coming in on Christmas Eve. There was really nothing else for me to do, and the orderly work of the kitchen had provided a welcome distraction from the annual holiday brooding.

I declined a ride from the bar manager, my flat being not too far from work, and the experience of a snowstorm of this size first hand was too alluring. Blizzards are still something of a mystery to me. In Donegal, living so close to the sea, most heavy snows would melt quickly. I can still remember as a child, running out the door of the wee pub in Maghery, the air filled with snowflakes, and us, a gaggle of children, heads spinning with amazement, joy, and soda, running about the street chasing snowflakes with our tongues. Our poor mothers, following us around like tops, hands pressed to their cheeks in worry, imploring us to put on our shoes. In the background, lined up against the window and spilling out the door, the men howled with laughter and slapped their legs.

Walking up Fountain Street towards Heritage Hill, the scene is almost surreal. Encased in white, the streets and yards are one. Houses loom like sleeping animals in the dim background, trees, standing naked, their warm blanket of leaves now buried beneath the snow, shiver in the wind. With each step comes the promise of warmth.

I stopped at the local store to buy a bottle of Irish whiskey, talked with the clerk, an amiable lad who always asks about Ireland and threatens me with a game of chess. This time he asked about my fondest, snowy memory from back home. I told him about the pub as a child, chasing snowflakes; but I lied, dodging my favorite memory in hopes of not having another Christmas Eve dwelling on my missing brother.

I trudged to my flat from the store, the storm still as persistent as it was this morning, and found the front door jammed shut by a drift four feet high. I clawed through it with one hand, the other holding Mr. John Jameson, and entered the empty building, my fellow tenants away for the holiday.

Fumbled for keys, opened the door and stood dripping snow and looking for the light switch. Outer layers peeled off, feeling a bit like a frozen onion, I doffed the cap on the bottle, rinsed out a glass, and stood at the window, inevitably thinking back many years and many miles.

When I was ten, my brother took me to Mount Errigal. It was a very cold December morning, the wind had all but died, and in the higher places it had snowed. He told me it was a magic place where fairies gathered on days like this, bowled with rocks and made poteen from snow by holding it in their hands. I couldn't wait to go.

We hitched rides in the early morning from Dungloe, the miles passed with my brother chatting like an adult and I staring out the window, all the way to the east side of the mountain. The double summit seems as one from the base, the path to the top not visible until you've gone round to the steep, north slope. We were told that on a fair day you could climb to the top in three hours. My brother, older and stronger, would effortlessly be yards ahead of me. He would stop, one hand forlornly at his side, the other cupped by his mouth, and shout Irish encouragement. "Jaysus, Wiley, would ya hurry up. We're liable to miss all the poteen."

My thin young legs were already sore with what seemed to me like great knots of angry muscles shaking their fists at me from within my skin. I would look up, thinking I had traversed leagues, only to see the peak of the mountain silently laughing. The only sound was the crunching of the frozen heather beneath my shoes.

When we had reached what I thought was the summit, I turned for the first time and looked back. In the distance I could see the ridges of mountains that ran from Poisoned Glen to Loch Veagh, a handful of clouds sitting on the peaks, while below me fell the better part of the mountain, a patch or two of snow, the brown of the heather, and a thin ribbon of road winding its way through the vale.

As I turned back, I saw my brother slip around the corner of a rocky outcropping. To my right, across a desolate valley of rocks and small lakes, is Muckish Mountain. We are higher than it at this point. This side of Errigal falls away sharply, leaving only a few feet of level ground on which to walk. Sheepishly I put one foot in front of the other, my gaze never leaving the path before me.

As I turned the corner, a clearing opens from amidst the giant boulders revealing a lunar landscape covered in snow. I couldn't possibly hide my smile. I look for my brother to share this moment with, but cannot find him anywhere. I run from one side of the clearing to the other, looking behind this boulder and that boulder to no avail. Just as I'm about to yell for him, my mouth open, the first syllable of his name on my lips, I am pelted with a snowball in the side of my face. In true brotherly fashion, I must reply in kind. We chased each other around the clearing for what seemed like hours, snowballs flying to and fro, our shouts and taunts echoing around the rocks and into the thin mountain air.

When we both stopped, exhausted, our breath coming in pants, he suggested we climb the last forty or so feet to the peak. Giddy, wet, and never happier, I followed him to the top of Mount Errigal. The view that day will always be with me, but more so will be what my brother did next.

I asked him about the fairies, the bowling and the poteen. He told me we had taken too long to climb the mountain and that all the fairies were now asleep. I looked at him with two sets of eyes, one filled with skepticism, the other still clinging to childhood. I think now that he noticed this, and being more in tune with those times and our family, he decided to appeal to the child. He took out from his pocket a small glass, and handed it to me.

"Now Wiley, this is what you do. Go over there to the very top, scoop up some snow into the glass. Sit down on that little rock, right at the top, certain it's the top of the mountain, close your eyes, and hold the glass very tight between your hands. Then, slowly count to ninety-nine. When you open your eyes, the snow will be gone, and in your glass will be poteen."

I did exactly as he said, not missing a step, not skipping a number. And when I opened my eyes, in my glass there was no longer snow, but a clear liquid, just like poteen. I drank it very slowly, savoring each drop, fibbing myself into thinking I could feel the alcohol. I gave the glass back to my brother as we returned to the mountain, to the road, to Dungloe.

Standing in my flat in Grand Rapids, the snow swirling outside mad as fairies, the storybook scene lit by streetlamps, dim reflection of candles in the glass, my cheeks holding still the flushed glow of cold air, I look at the whiskey in my hands and wish I could turn it into melted snow, for I know that no finer elixir exists. This memory, more satisfying than the golden liquid, tugs at my heart, and to no one but one in particular, a birthday wish falls from my lips.

28

The snow swirled around so thick and so fast that it was dizzying. The wind would push it up, then down, and it would wrap around me like a ghost, the banshee's howl in my ears. It seemed to be a living thing, cognizant, alive in the sense that it was aware, but certainly possessed. I fought at its accumulations with a grim determination that bordered on hysteria. It was after midnight, and I had decided to clean the walks in front of my apartment house come hell or high water.

I had spent the better part of the evening staring at a picture of my brother and sipping on Jameson. The melancholy of it being his birthday, and I having no way to contact him or even to know if he was alive, had driven me out the door and into the maelstrom, the blizzard calling my name as surely as that white whale had called the good captain. I battled the snow instead of my own heart, the whiskey nearly sweated out of my system, the futility of what I was doing so very evident. The wee parking area in back, and the drive itself, I had cleared not fifteen minutes earlier, yet it was already covered with a fresh layer.

As I finished up the bottom of the drive, which emptied onto the street, the city snowplow came by and erased all of that work in seconds. This was the third time he had come by, and this time I swear he was smiling. Mephistopheles himself, his horns protruding out the eyeholes of a black stocking cap, gnarled hands gripping the steering wheel, a Carhart cape over a hunched back, he laughed with glee from deep inside his hairy belly. All I could do was shake my head, turn with the passing truck, and shout a stream of curses in Gaelic.

While the snow continued to fall, the streetlights illuminating pyramids of chaotic white, I wiped sweat and water from my face. I felt a bit like that chap who had to push the rock up the hill for eternity. With every shovel full, the skies only opened up that much wider. The cold sank in despite the exertion, despite the layers, feet and hands, ears and nose, no longer recognizable as still being attached. The runner's high was fueling my will, my body doing its best to keep up.

Still, there is something very liberating in working a job that can never be finished. As if the mechanics of the task outweigh the task itself, the freedom lying in the act alone, and not in the outcome. A light-headed giddiness arising from the sheer lunacy of the expectations, like trying to bail out the ocean.

When I lived in London, I would volunteer each Sunday to work in a soup kitchen run by the Capuchins. It was as close to returning to church as I ever could. The monks who ran the kitchen were very lenient, very pleasant, and a joy to work with. They understood that whether the food tasted good or not was secondary to it being available and the doors being open.

There was an elderly man there from Northern India, and it was from him that I learned everything about curry and quite a bit about life. I was fresh out of a very prominent cooking school, and like many young men fresh out of school, I was filled with ideas and ideals on how the world, and in particular how kitchens, should run. But the real world is not a textbook, or a lecture, or nearly as organized as the academic world. So he became my mentor, teaching me a kernel of truth every Sunday.

Standing here enveloped in the wind and the snow, I can see his face. It is the color of light brown sugar with packs of wrinkles around his eyes, eyes that lit up when he laughed. His thinning gray hair and gray mustache gave away his age, but only slightly, for his complexion was as radiant as his smile. He had a way of working that seemed effortless, as if his body knew the motions before they happened and had planned accordingly.

It was him who taught me to find the purpose in work, that the work itself is the reward. That in life, the simplest of things generally held the most meaning. He believed that each of our lives is already determined from before we are born. Everything we do, create and destroy, love and lose, had been written long ago, and all we could do is play the part in as joyful a manner as possible.

In the way the mind works, surrounded by this blizzard, numb and wet, these memories reminded me of a Norse saying that is nearly identical, that it is all predestined. Standing under a streetlight, staring up into one of those pyramids of chaotic white, I decided to test this theory by lying down in the middle of this cone of light and making a snow angel. If the principle held, I was doing exactly what I was supposed to be doing, it having been willed long ago.

I lay down on my back in a fresh patch of snow, which was not terribly difficult to find, and with my arms and legs working to and fro from my body, made a snow angel. The stillness of this tableau, the peacefulness of lying at the bottom of the storm and staring up into the light, brought to my heart a calmness I had not felt in some time. I decided to further test the fate theory by lying here endlessly. I thought of that old man from India, and of Hesse's *Siddhartha*, and decided to try and connect with all things at once. I closed my eyes, the falling snow peppering the lids, and breathed in and out the one word. "Om."

Then, in the white noise of the winter wind, I swear I could hear my name being called. I intoned the word louder. "Om."

There it was again, my name. The voice became more clear, distinct, a woman's voice just beneath the storm, just under the wind. I answered louder. "Om."

I now had the feeling of being watched, of something having blocked a part of my light pyramid. My mind raced to conclusions that were, if not supernatural, then certainly far fetched. But, given the circumstances, didn't seem out of proportion to making snow angels in an empty city during a blizzard on what was now Christmas Day. I opened my eyes.

"Are you okay? I've been yelling your name for half the block. Jesus it's friggin' cold out here."

Like an apparition, the Waitress appeared from out of the storm. The snow on her hat, hair and shoulders blending in with the snow falling all around her, and with the light behind her, it merged into a sort of halo. I shook my head in disbelief, trying to piece this particular part of reality into what had transpired this evening so far. Since we talked and kissed on the bridge, we had not seen much of each other. I truly didn't know whether to date the lass or not. Fate, presumably already written, made its decision.

"I've got a bag full of stout, two pint glasses I stole from work, a cribbage board and a deck of cards. Let's get drunk," she said.

"Okay," I answered.

As we trudged up the drive and the walk to the building, I took a look over my work. It was covered with a layer of white, blending it in perfectly with the lawn, the street and the storm. The wind had died down a bit, and the snow simply fell in great sheets.

"So, this is your place," she said as we stomped our feet in unison. "Where's your cat?"

"That's not my cat."

"I thought you had a cat?"

"It's the Sous Chef's."

"Oh. Cool place. Kinda sparse, huh?"

"Yeah, well I move around a lot. Plus, you know, working in the restaurant bizz."

"Yeah, I'm never home either."

We took off the many winter layers of coats, sweaters and vests, unpacked her bag of goods and opened up a couple bottles of stout. I turned up the heat and cleared a place on the table for the cribbage board. We toasted, gave each other a wink, and then settled into cards, which meant civility was kept as a rule, but blood was certainly an option.

It was in the middle of our rubber game, myself only moments from pegging out, that she employed a very subtle yet effective gambit.

"Wiley?"

"Yes."

"What's the difference between a jig and a reel?"

"Well, one's a jig and the other's a reel. Now, these points should just about do it."

"No, seriously. Show me. Please."

I stood up, perplexed and slightly annoyed at not being able to have the closure of pegging out.

"Well, this is a jig. Jigs are easy. Reels are where the action is, for instance."

She gave me a look of complete confusion.

"Have you never danced?" I asked.

"My sister showed me the hustle when I was five. And this other dance called the tiger walk. But other than *Proud Mary* at receptions, no."

I walked over to my boom box and put in a tape of assorted Cajun music. Pushing away the chairs and the table, I cleared a dance floor.

"Get up. There's only one way to learn."

At first we waltzed with the grace of drunken bicyclists. Each person treading on the other's foot in what looked like a particularly bizarre game of *Twister*. After thirty minutes, numerous stoppages for breath, stout, and lessons, we arrived.

"This is cool as hell. I can't believe I'm dancing. One, two, three, one two three..." She was all smiles.

"Nothing to it, eh. Do you want to learn a reel?"

"No! I'm afraid we'd crash into the walls. Let's just do this a while longer."

We waltzed until the stout was gone. We waltzed until the whiskey was empty. We waltzed until dawn. Dancing in crazy circles like the snow in the wind, the howls of yesterday's storm now matched by the singing in my heart. I could not remember ever being so happy.

I walked her to the door and out into the still morning. She gave me a long kiss, followed by a smile that made me blush.

"Merry Christmas, Wiley," followed by another long kiss.

I watched her as she rounded the corner on her walk home.

My feet traced a jig in the snow as I spun halfway around, let out a whoop of Celtic joy, closed my eyes and fell backwards from the porch into the snow.

"Snow all bloody day," I yelled into the wintry sky, my own smile warming me, the thin light of dawn filling the air, and made another snow angel.

29

Sitting here on my friend's porch, numbed by the events of the day, I drain another meaningless glass of whiskey in hopes of dousing the pain, in hopes of smothering grief, of numbing feelings. Clouds cut across the full moon, the silence of a still city broods beyond these walls, the cold night air made colder by the empty void above. About me, lingering in the air in place of a breeze, is death.

Just inside the window I can hear the Sous Chef, all six foot three, sixteen stone of him, sobbing for the loss of his friend. That old bastard death has cheated us once again. Cheated us so quickly you can't believe he was here, but the emptiness of the house announces his presence as surely as a dirge.

The day truly began as the Waitress, the Sous Chef, and myself met at his flat. We all had the day off, and with the January thaw providing the spark we decided to spend the late morning and afternoon visiting shops, museums, and pubs downtown. The lightness in our step propelling us the scant mile or two to the city's center, where we began our day with Bloody Marys at a bar around the corner from the restaurant.

As I looked over at the Sous Chef, I couldn't help but smile. There he was, a big man with half a dozen tattoos, an earring, and the perpetual cigarette, gushing on about his cat. Before we left his apartment, he had made a point to search the flat over, finding the cat, scooping it up in his arms and kissing it between the ears, a gentle giant, indeed.

The three of us wandered about downtown, window-shopping and kicking the tires of everything from jewelry to holidays in Cancun. We stopped at a half dozen restaurants, never ordering any food, just looking at the menus and having a drink. Time whiling itself away in that way lazy afternoons only can, our conversation always turning to work despite our best efforts.

It was the first time either of them had been in the new museum. I thought this rather odd, as here I was from a very long way away and had been in the building on three occasions. I chastised them for not learning more about their city, to which they both replied that they were from Detroit, and who really cares how furniture was made in the nineteenth century?

While we were walking through the wildlife section, I couldn't help but notice how uneasy the Sous Chef was as he looked at the dioramas. I followed his line of sight to a pair of stuffed bobcats playing outside a den. I looked over to the Waitress, who was wearing the same pained expression. She caught my eye.

"I don't like this room."

"Me either," said the Sous, before she finished her sentence.

"Let's get out of here."

"Yeah, thanks Wiley for showing us all the dead animals."

I thought about protesting my innocence, telling them they were fake, that it was a museum, that as restaurant employees we personally saw to the demise of thousands of animals every year, but they were already ahead of me, racing down the broad steps, past the gift shop and out the revolving doors.

We stopped at the local for a pint of stout and to finish our afternoon. Shots of Jameson materialized before us, and the daylight ebbed away in what seemed a very short time. We ordered food to go, called a cab, and prepared to head back to the Sous Chef's for a bite to eat and to watch the film, *The Field*. After the experience in the museum, I wasn't sure how this film would go over, the opening scene a murdered donkey being dumped off a cliff.

When we walked in the door of the Sous Chef's apartment, the difference in the flat took each of us by surprise. The feeling of the home had changed from contentment to urgency. It was something you noticed right away.

On the floor of the kitchen were tiny pools of liquid with streaks of blood in them. We all noticed this at the same time, the Sous Chef stepping past us for a closer, more concerned look.

"Mata! Shit! Where is she, dammnit! Mata!"

The Waitress walked over to get some paper towel, the Sous Chef into the bathroom to look for the cat. I peered around the corner to the rest of the flat, hoping it was just an accident, too much tuna fish or milk or rich cat food.

She came around the corner from the bedroom, all four legs shaking as she wobbled toward the sound of the Sous Chef's voice. Her fur was matted and covered with dirt from her cat box. Her eyes both imploring for help and asking for forgiveness, she didn't understand what was happening to her, and yet she was sorry for not using the litter box.

The Sous Chef followed our gaze when we stopped calling her name. He was flattened by her appearance. Shock, confusion and pain brushed aside in a stroke, he ran over to her, engulfing her in his large arms.

"What do we do?" his voice breaking.

"Do you have a vet?" I asked.

"What about the Animal Emergency Clinic?"

"She trusts her vet. Call her vet. The number is on the fridge."

I went to the phone. The Waitress cleaned up the messes, and the Sous Chef held his wee friend, talking to her as only pet lovers can talk to their pet.

"They can take her now. The Vet's in other procedures at the moment, but they can see her after."

"Take her to the Emergency Clinic, I'm tellin' ya," the Waitress implored.

"She likes that vet. We've got to go there. Let's go."

We jumped into his car. He had her wrapped up in her favorite blanket. I drove. The ride there was quiet but for the Sous Chef rocking back and forth, talking to the kitten, asking her to be okay. At one moment, stopped at a traffic light,

I looked over to see the kitten reach her paw out to touch his face, nails digging in gently, looking up at him with mournful eyes.

When we got to the Vet's, we rushed her in the front door. They took the cat into the back, but we could see no doctors at all. The Sous Chef demanded she be looked at right now, and they reassured us that she would be taken care of as soon as possible. They then asked us to leave, saying they would call us when they had had a chance to examine her. Reluctantly, the confusion of the moment, the eyes of others in the waiting room boring in on us, the buzz from the drink, we agreed.

We drove back to the Sous Chef's, picking up a bottle of Jameson's and a dozen stout. Sitting around the kitchen table, we reminisced about how he and I had found her under the mulberry tree back in May on that stormy night. What a fit she had given us, running back and forth across the wet grass, ourselves covered in mulberries from falling trying to catch her.

When the Vets failed to call several hours later, I decided to ring their office while the Sous Chef was in the bathroom. Upon hearing their report, I told my two friends I would run up to the store for cigarettes and another bottle of Jameson. Instead, I drove to the Vet's.

They gave me her body, heavy and lifeless, wrapped up in her blanket. They had at least washed her fur. She had probably swallowed something that had tore her up inside, and bled to death. Their eyes would not meet mine and when they did, I could tell that they had never looked at Mata. She had died in her cage alone.

I brought her back to the house, wrapped up in that blanket. The Waitress opened the doors for me and I laid her down on the very table she had slept on the night she was found. The Sous Chef, as if sucker punched, face twisted with sorrow, fell to one knee. His hands reached out, clutching the fur of his dead friend, his face buried in his arm, tears pooling up on the table.

We consoled him as best we could. When his head cleared a bit, the spasms of mourning growing further apart, he asked us if it would be okay to bury her under the mulberry tree tomorrow. Of course, we would be honored to help.

Throughout the night he would stroke her fur, sip on whiskey and remember things she had done. His tears would fall every so often with the rhythm of rain in Ireland, his broad shoulders shaking. He asked us why this could happen to something so young, so innocent. We had no answers.

I sit here alone on his porch the cigarette smoke wraps around my face in the still night. The Waitress left hours ago, a hand-squeeze, a registering look, and a 'call me' in parting. There is no light save the flicker of candles through the blinds, the moon having set. The house feels so heavy it is as if it too is grieving. My glass is empty, but I do not wish to disturb the Sous Chef who has fallen asleep beside the body of his dead kitten. In my mind, forever, will be this one image: my friend rubbing the kitten's ear between his thumb and forefinger, murmuring her name as tears roll down his cheeks, his other hand in front of her lifeless mouth in hopes of one last kiss.

30

It had been one of those perfect mornings, the two of us falling into each other's arms and falling asleep until nearly noon. The late night at the local seeming ages ago, distant echoes of a jazz quintet like hearing music from a valley while sitting on a hill. There was a quick cab ride home, a flurry of passionate kisses and my waking up to the Waitress' hair bunched on my shoulder. The soft sounds of her breathing a languid solo just above the beating of our hearts.

The day unfolded in the same wonderfully lazy way, our hands clasped from morning until night, long sighs and slow words, mischievous smiles walking us back into the bedroom. We had spent the entire day in my flat, except to walk to the store for sodas, the Sunday paper, and to pick up a carry-out order of way-too-much Chinese .

I sit here at my kitchen counter looking out across the floor where a proper dining table would have been, to the Waitress who is now falling asleep on the sofa. I get up, turn the corner, cross the room, and take the nearly empty white container of moo goo gai pan from her hands before it topples. A gentle kiss on the forehead, a glance out the win-

dow as dusk settles, and return to moo shoo pork and fond
thoughts of today.

My flat is always disheveled with books and papers. Today
it is as quiet as a library, the soft padding of other tenants
feet just barely audible. Throughout the day she had browsed
through my stuff, what little there was, asking questions
about Ireland, my growing up, and all the places I had lived,
had worked, had loved. The wine box, that great Methuselah
of Wiley antiquities, had been discovered early on, and then
carefully gone through, looks of bewilderment and feigned
disapproval on her beautiful face. I indulged these whims
with a growing love. Her questions were easily answered or
easily brushed aside, her curiosity exciting my own as to why
she should be so interested. I felt I was involved in an inter-
view for a situation I did not understand, or hadn't known I
had applied for.

While I gaze at her, chopsticks rolling yet another moo
shoo pancake, I feel a sudden twist of jealousy, her having
lingered too long on a photograph of my brother. This would
normally have inspired nothing more than a jest, but she said
how handsome he was and how we looked nothing alike.

The tang of plum sauce causes this to vanish, the corners
of my mouth turning into a smile as the sauce dribbled down
my chin and onto the counter. I truly believe a nation is only
as civilized as it's best Cantonese restaurant.

She moves with a start, fidgeting in her sleep, eyes moving quickly beneath the lids, her small hands curling into
smaller fists, fighting or fleeing. My heart goes out to her, my
own dreams of Omagh, of the old English barracks and of that

hidden, horrible face causing endless nights of pacing about dark rooms, staring out empty windows, straightening the shadows. I wonder where she's at, whom she's fighting, who it could be she's running from. The depths within her reaching out in tendrils while she sleeps. It seems all the world, from beginning to end, lies teeming just beneath our brows. It's enough to make a man roll one more pancake, reheat one more egg roll, open one more *Jones* soda.

Again across the room, glancing out the side window at snow settling beneath the cold air, beneath the bird feeder and the evergreen bushes of the house next door, and return to the photograph of my brother.

No, we look nothing alike. I can see my mother's face at the cliffs, the longing within her to see him one more time even though I stood right there in front of her. She and he looked so much alike. The good genes, I thought to myself, handsome and pretty, tall and strong. I look at a recent photograph of myself and quickly set it back down. It wasn't her side that I favored.

I return to the kitchen, to the oven, and pull out a pie tin with three egg rolls. Turn off the heat, leaving the oven door ajar, cross the kitchen to the counter, and set the hot pie tin upon the classifieds. I choose an egg roll, my fingers playing across the top like fingering a recorder, its crispy dough skin too hot to hold onto, and walk over to the front window. Small absentminded nibbles, new snow falling in large flakes, a weariness settling in with the waning light.

I close my eyes to picture my brother as I saw him in Dublin, and add the intermittent years. When his face becomes clear to me, as it would look now, a slight graying at the temples, a full head of hair, laugh lines adding a distinguished worldliness, cheeks slightly fuller with middle-aged weight worn well, I realize I have just stepped ever so slightly off the path. I open my eyes to the egg roll and an understanding that 'go with the flow' is the polar opposite of infatuation.

Shaking off a shiver, once more across the room, I pick up what's left of the paper, and settle in on the floor against the sofa. She wakens, repositions herself closer to the edge, leans over to kiss the top of my thinning head, rests her hand on my shoulder beside my cheek, and falls back asleep. Laying the paper down, eyelids heavy, I begin to drift off, and let the day end.

There is a shout from upstairs that opens my eyes, the end of a row, strong footsteps crossing the ceiling and a slammed bedroom door. A moment passes and a softer set of steps retraces the space between anger and apology. I breathe out in a long sigh unconsciously remembering similar moments.

The shadows reach back out, caress, envelop and silence returns. My last thoughts are sensory: quiet, warmth, and hunger stirring from the smell of Chinese food.

31

I look up into the cold, clear February sky, the stars staring back at me, distant and removed. The branches of a horse chestnut tree splayed in a pattern that makes it seem as though I am gazing through a window's lattice. The stillness of the night broken by the muffled throb of Irish music, and the Waitress's heels walking away from me, my face still stinging from the slap. I shake my head at the ancient points of light searching for an answer, knowing full well that this woman is as much a mystery as they are.

It was a Saturday in which not only did she and I have the night off, but the Sous Chef was on his last two days of holiday as well. It also just so happened that two lads from Ireland whom I had met last summer were playing at a wee pub in a small town north of Grand Rapids. I talked my friends into surrendering their Saturday night for an evening of Irish music, standing them the tickets to help ease them along. We piled into the Sous Chef's car and sped off into the country after starters and stouts at the local.

The show was set to start at eight, and my mates were keen on getting there before the music started. I did my best to convince them that nothing Irish has ever started on time, citing *Bus Eireann* as an important case in point, but they insisted on driving like mad to get there.

In our haste we became hopelessly lost, every orchard and field looking eerily like every other orchard and field until it felt like Rod Serling had given us the directions. The natural roll of the hills, the long distances between crossroads, and the few sources of light only added to our confusion. We consulted the map over and over; we took innumerable wrong turns; and then by stroke of fortune we spotted a glow of lights just over the hill.

"That's got to be it."

"What if it's Alpine?"

"Alpine is over there. I think it's further north."

"Those lights are it, I swear to Christ they are."

"What if it's just some fruit-packing place?" the Sous Chef questioned, emphasizing his point by slowing up.

"Yeah, what if it is some fruit packing place."

"It's the bloody bar, I'm telling ya."

While we went on like this we drove in the direction of the lights, which after all turned out to be a fruit-packing place. Fortune again, always showing one hand and giving the other, provided us with the first road sign that actually told us the direction to go in. We pulled up to the pub fifteen minutes late, dying for a pint and quite happy to see the place brimming over with people. The gentleman at the door told us we weren't late at all, as the band had gotten lost coming back from a meal.

It was standing room only. Smiling faces greeted us as newcomers, there were claps on shoulders and hails of 'slainte', 'failte', 'bravo lads,' as if we had all survived a journey. The three of us found room to stand at the end of the bar, myself calling for three pints and three short ones above the shouts of the crowd. We toasted to a grand evening with the shots and supped on our pints, cheeks still flushed from the winter cold.

Jimmy and Pat made their way to the stage. They were stopped many times by people familiar with them to say hello and wish them good show. Jimmy remembered me from the Irish festival in Greenville and made a point to come over while his partner tuned up his uilleann pipes.

It just felt good to hear someone who speaks the same way I do. His Dublin brogue, however softened by years in Chicago, still rolled like the Liffey. We talked about nothing really, but in a handful of sentences I could feel my heart warm with the gentle tug of home.

It was in this air of melancholy, the Guinness and Jameson making my head a bit light, that I introduced Jimmy to my friend the Sous Chef, and my girlfriend, the Waitress. The look on her face made me realize my gaff. Though we had seen quite a lot of one another, this was a term we hadn't used yet. Jimmy shook hands with the two of them, gave me a sideways nod, and then left for the stage.

The woman of the house, a stout and stern matron with a smile she kept close to herself, hushed the crowd, announced upcoming events, and introduced the musicians. In those few moments of quiet, between pub noise and concert, I could see my friends trying to place themselves, trying to take in the environment. It was a very Irish crowd, as one would expect, or not expect, this far from Chicago or Boston or New York, and I could tell my friends felt out of place.

As the music started, a jig leading into a reel, the sounds of pipes and bouzouki chasing each other around the melody, the Waitress shot me a cold look, downed her shot and then the rest of her pint in one go. I tried to apologize, I tried to reason, but she would have none of this. She called for another round, Pandora's box yawning open, a dozen malicious sprites dancing about the bar.

It was a game of cat and mouse through the first set. Everything I said came out wrong, her silence versed in a language that only a woman could write and a man never understand. We had become the distance between Venus and Mars. I decided to just shut-up and listen to the music. We were plying down pints with reckless abandon. When I reached for her hand, she pulled it away.

I had to ask myself, 'what was I really doing? Why was I following this path? Hadn't I learned my lesson in this sort of venture many times before?' I shook my head as if to clear it and joined the queue for the gents.

As I stood in front of the urinal, staring at the bricks in front of me, it dawned on me that she too would be asking herself these same questions. When we had first started seeing one another, it was more about two people still shaking off bad relationships, having a few beers and playing cards. But there had always been something kinetic, some connection just below the surface drawing us closer. I decided that a few words of empathy and understanding would do the trick.

As I walked back into the pub, I saw the Sous Chef standing at the bar alone. He looked over at me, and then over to a group of young lads standing beside a table. In the middle of them stood the Waitress, looking altogether too cute and being way too familiar. When our eyes met, her talking stopped and she sheepishly, in a great show, sidled over to our place at the bar. Whatever I was going to say was lost now.

The second set started, once again with a jig leading into a reel. She and I drank our pints. The lads at the table made comments about us, and the Sous Chef didn't quite know what to make of any of this.

And then, of all things, Jimmy introduced the next song they were about to play by dedicating it to her and I. He gestured to our place at the end of the bar, the first notes immediately ringing out, as it seemed every face turned toward us. I cringed inwardly upon recognizing the song, a tune by Luka Bloom. She stood there as if stunned, until the chorus came and the oft-repeated refrain, *'you couldn't have come at a better time.'* At that point, she drank the rest of her pint, slamming the glass on the bar, exhaled a sharp cry of embarrassed angst, and went storming out the back of the pub and into the night.

The Sous Chef looked at me, the lads looked at me, and even Jimmy made a face of apology. I was dumbfounded and made the one choice that seemed to make sense, I followed her.

The mid-winter night was very crisp and very still, you could imagine the cold going all the way up to the stars. After some searching, I found her sitting beneath a horse chestnut tree in the snow, turning a fallen, odd-shaped leaf over in her small bare hands. When she looked up at me, I could see her eyes were red and puffy.

She stood, once more in a bit of a show, took the several steps it took to be right in front of me, and apologized. The male in me wanted an explanation. Was she afraid? Were things moving too fast? Did she care about me at all? But I was wise enough to know that some things are best left unsaid.

She wrapped her arms around me and we kissed. We kissed in that way that lovers do when they make up. Very hard, very deep, as if the kiss itself is the apology. And then, once more, without even realizing I spoke, I did. "I love you."

To which she cried out that same yell of angry disbelief, slapped me resoundingly on the face, pirouetted, and walked back in the direction of the pub.

I blinked. Wondered. And stared at the stars. My breath hung before me, slowly rising to the heavens. A dog barked to answer the sound of her heels, as she walked away upon the frozen pavement. I kicked lightly at the snow, looked down, bent, and picked up the leaf she had been holding. I pushed it and my cold hands into my pockets, turning to follow once more. About me, the snow holding all sound close to its bosom, the streets lay perfectly still. I stepped as slowly as possible, one befuddled man walking through a ghost town of empty houses and rusting elevators.

32

There had been the blistering of paint, the accusatory stab of the Chef's forefinger, the averted eyes of the entire kitchen staff, and in the moments after the meeting had ended, silence. We had all sat there, perplexed, shell shocked, trying to figure out where he was coming from and why he was so angry. The restaurant had been sailing along, our numbers crushing those of any previous staff, our cuisine creating a fat and happy clientele. So, when the Chef had announced this odd, Sunday morning meeting, we were all feeling pretty good about ourselves.

Now, as we sat there numb, the Sous Chef, who had been particularly singled out, broke the thousand-yard stares in his own special way, "Well, didn't that just suck."

Everyone exhaled in agreement, shook their heads, raised hands to the sky, and the pastry chef wiped her eyes and cheeks.

"I mean, he just called us out. Why? We're the best restaurant in town. That bezillion dollar seafood joint on the river is the only kitchen in town doing the numbers we're doing. And their food's pure vanilla. I don't get it. I just don't get it."

Heads around the table shook yeses and nos. The Sous Chef continued. "You know what it is? Awards. Those flippin' magazine awards. That's what it is. Like those bullshit framed plaques on the wall have anything to do with feeding people. Well happy Sunday, folks. Thanks for coming down. Fuck it, man, I'm going to the bar. Anyone in? I'm buying."

There was agreement up and down the table.

"Wiley?"

"I can't"

"What! You can't help provide some Irish wisdom to this mess?"

"Long night, lads. This pretty much topped off a bad weekend." I stood to go, gathering up an empty sheet of paper and a pen. "I'll sees ya on Monday."

"Aw c'mon, Wiley," the Sous Chef bemoaned, "Where's the European solidarity?"

"Sorry, lads. Bad timing. If we strike tomorrow, let me know. Good luck," and I left my befuddled compatriots that much more befuddled.

I walked up the street to my apartment in the Hill, trying to shelf the Chef's diatribe and clear my head. It had indeed been a long night, with a short night's sleep, this morning's meeting coming way too early. The Waitress and I had had a bad row, drank too much beforehand, and the end result of the catharsis had been some very disturbing revelations. Perhaps we have more in common than I had first realized. Maybe we truly are attracted to those who are similar, even if those similarities are deep inside.

Beneath all this, I was angry with myself. I had come here to get away from Boston and all the heartache my marriage had inflicted on me. I had come here to become obscure. Unconnected. Unknown. In hopes of finding time to read, to walk, to piecing myself back together once more. In Boston there were only endless weeks of overtime just to stay afloat. The continual struggle to keep up with a class I wasn't part of, and the unending fighting between my ex and myself. It had hollowed-out my soul, had injured me in a suffocating smother.

So, here I was again, working nearly as much as I had in Boston and drinking twice as much. Involved. Infatuated. It was enough to drive a man to religion.

I stopped to light a cigarette, a strong west wind pushing at my back, the February cold numbing my ears. The sun peeked through low scudding clouds, a minor miracle, as we hadn't seen it in weeks. I hunched my shoulders, cupped my hands, and inhaled deeply, my thoughts returning to the Waitress as I walked to the store before going home.

We had argued hard, not so much out of anger as out of frustration. I had known that something was wrong, but she wouldn't tell me what it was. I asked, I queried, I quizzed, all of this winding her up more and sending her hiding to that place behind her walls. Because I had meant well and wanted to help, I was hurt by her dismissal, by her not confiding in me.

In the end, the passion welled up inside her having been vented, and myself, through some sublime signal, having reached a place that she could be comfortable with, she then told me why this day was her second birthday. She told me why she hated this day.

Her home had not been a happy one. Her mother abused her badly and her father, trying to raise so many children on a shoestring, was always working. They lived in an industrial town south of Detroit, a town reeling from outsourcing. Families once secure were now living day to day with all the stress that involves. She described how her father would amble to the chained gate of the factory where he had once worked, meeting other fathers for a six-pack. The street was losing its pulse with each newly empty house and vacant lot.

On one evening, eight years past last night, her mother was in a particularly foul mood. She had been drinking cooking sherry and mixing it with prescriptions. The kids knew she was taking Valium, and had even tried to hide the pill bottles when their concerns had fell on the deaf ears of their father. The Waitress tried to describe how disheveled her mother looked. The distance in her eyes, the slur in her movement, a patchwork of ill-fitting clothes that gave her a clown-like appearance. She was going on again about how rich she had been when she was a kid, and how she had crossed the tracks to marry her father. 'The expectations,' she would shout at the ceiling, 'the dreams, the hopes. I rode ponies! I was somebody! We didn't want! If only I'd married that boy in the bright blue cardigan'.

The Waitress paused, the tears welling up in her eyes. She poured herself a glass of Jameson, and with hands shaking brought it to her lips. I told her she didn't have to tell me anymore, the male in me flinching both from the story and from having not been there to help her. But to this she was most indignant, only a look, however brief, and I realized she was sharing something she didn't share very often.

Her mother was trying to fix dinner, but was too incoherent to do so. She had boxes of Hamburger Helper opened all over the kitchen and had already dropped a casserole on the floor, the sound of the baking dish shattering bringing the children running.

She stood amongst the broken glass, swaying to a rusting metronome, her eyes trying to focus on her children who gaped at her from the doorway. She slurred a series of epithets at them, went on about the boy in the cardigan, cleared a lock of hair from her forehead leaving a smudge of raw hamburger, and turned to finish preparing dinner, her unshod feet stepping on the broken glass.

The Waitress implored her mother to sit down and let them finish making supper. With every staggered step she took, glass popped beneath her feet. The level of the kid's voices rose louder in pleading. In her confusion she thought they were screaming at her. She took their concern the wrong way, and then became very angry.

She picked up the frying pan she had been using to brown the meat. The Waitress had stepped into the kitchen, kneeling to pick-up the glass. Her mother spun around from the stove, a shower of hot grease spraying the counters, the walls, and held the frying pan like a sword. She began ranting at them, the pan thrust at them as she made her points. It was the same litany of lost youth, of how things should have been different, and how no one cared or understood. 'If it hadn't been for you little bloodsuckers,' she had screamed, plodding closer to them.

The Waitress had been through this one too many times. She got up from the floor and confronted her mother. They stood toe-to-toe, voices slamming into each other as the piercing wails of the little children added a chorus. Confronted, cornered, and unstable, the mother swung the pan across the Waitress' temple.

As I sat at my kitchen table, my brow furrowed, my attention rapt, I could only think of how my father had treated my brother. How on that Christmas Day it had come to a head and resolved itself the only way it could. It was the same lines being said by different actors. Their accents a little different, the set slightly altered, but the themes were the same I shook my head without realizing it, the words of the Sous Chef about the Chef jumping into my head, 'all it takes is one asshole to fuck everything up.'

She paused. Sipped a little water, lit a cigarette. Looked up at me to see if I was still paying attention. I reached out and squeezed her hand. She closed her eyes and continued.

The Waitress, dizzy from the blow, staggered and fell onto the floor and the glass. Her hand split open, blood flowing over worn yellow linoleum.

The mother, sensing victory in some primordial way, raised the frying pan to the ceiling and brought it down towards the Waitress' head. A copper and silver arc of metal whistled through the air. The Waitress regained her senses and ducked the blow, drugged-momentum sending her mother reeling onto the floor.

The Waitress stood, walked over to her mother who gaped up at her expecting to be struck, and simply said, 'good-bye'. She walked out the door, down the street, and away from that town forever, not unlike the way my brother had left home so many years ago.

My walk from the store, from the restaurant and the meeting seems as if it had happened long ago. Standing on my front porch, thinking about what she had told me, I light another cigarette and bounce from foot to foot to stay warm. In the lee of the porch, sheltered just so, the wind whistles through the trees like distant voices. Why can't the past just leave us alone and let us get on with our lives.

I slowly open the door to my flat, lay keys on the counter with my wallet and a bag from the store nearby. Ever so quietly, I walk into my bedroom. There, curled up, her small hands holding the blankets up to her chin, is the Waitress. All the tiredness, the anger, the frustration of work and of having fallen in love against my own wishes, ebbs away. She lay softly sleeping, and I could not fathom how anyone could hurt her.

On the nightstand, beside her, I set a piece of carrot cake and a birthday card. In the wee light that filters in through the closed blinds, I can see the scar running across her temple. I bend over, close my eyes, and gently kiss it, a wee prayer in Irish about mercy, about love, about hope, barely breaking the silence.

33

The sky was clear, the sun was shining, and my eyes were bright with hope as I walked to work this morning. The road wound down a hill to the city center, behaving much as roads do all over the world. The thin, bare trees just beginning to bud, the Ides of March embodied in a sharp, cold wind, all that separated me from St. Pat's proper and a day of leisurely supping pints was about eight hours of cooking corned beef and cabbage.

At the time, the way the day would unfold was as far removed from me as my mother back in Dungloe, County Donegal, Republic of Ireland. I had rung home earlier, her voice as soft as morning, bringing tears to my eyes as she told me the skinny on everything happening back in that tiny village by the sea.

Now, hours later, I chase after my heart, it being inconveniently stashed at the bottom of the Waitress's handbag. The sound of her heels, her sobs, her swearing,echoing around Calder Plaza as she runs away once more. The sound and fury of this woman blending inexplicably with the laughter of a street person. He has seen us at our worst and discovered the folly I can't see myself.

When, I arrived at work earlier today, the Chef, who hates St. Patrick's Day and indeed all things Irish, was on me right from the start. Asking if I was sober, if I could concentrate on my work, or if I felt the overwhelming urge to blow something up. I queried him as to how Mrs. Chef was doing and would she be kind enough to return me knickers. He then made several disparaging remarks about Catholics, wished Michael Flatley, U2, and the entire island would sink into the sea, or at the very least, hoped I would pick some other kitchen to 'dink around in.'

The entire staff had witnessed this, tension thick in the air already as it would prove to be a most busy day, and an uneasy silence fell over the kitchen. To my rescue, as I returned to the back prep table, the Waitress smuggled me a shot of Jameson in a coffee cup. Anger flushing out the better part of reason, I downed it and gave her a big kiss. The Chef, lying in wait around the corner, saw the entire scene transpire and went right off the deep end.

"Wiley! What do you think you're doing! Drinking on the job! To my office, right now!" He grabbed me by the sleeve, my astonishment knocking me off balance more than his grasp, and pushed me toward his office, a dozen pairs of eyes following us as we crossed his kitchen. The Waitress dashed back out to the dining room floor. My friend the Sous Chef gave me a look of support. I entered the Chef's office, sat down, and winced as the door slammed.

He screamed, he ridiculed, he pounded his desk. He told me how my work performance had dropped sharply since I had started going out with that trollop. At this point I realized that it wasn't me he was really after. As the General Manager was on holiday, the Chef had control over all aspects of the restaurant, and with this new power it seemed he had a score or two to settle. I did my best to apologize without wrapping it in an excuse. I told him it was a complete lack of responsibility on my part and that I was entirely to blame. This was not enough. He knew where the shot of whiskey had come from, he could easily presume the Waitress had brought it, but he wanted me to hand her over.

I refused. Instead I continued saying that it was my fault, she had only done what I had asked. He stormed about the office again, a coffee cup perishing in his tirade, stood over me yelling, his breath smelling not unlike mine, coffee and spirit. Finally he sat in his chair, wiped a red, sweaty brow, and dismissed me back to the kitchen to work.

The Waitress was then called into the office, the eyes of the staff sneaking looks at the door, ears craning to hear a single syllable. When their eyes met mine for an explanation, I could only shrug.

After only five minutes she flung herself out of the office, grabbed her stuff, punched out, and raced out the back door, shooting me an icy look on her way out. I walked to the door to follow her, but the Chef intercepted me.

"She's been suspended. You're on probation. Get back to work."

And that was that. I had no idea what had transpired, but I could guess that without my testimony he didn't have the authority to fire her, so he did as much as he could. Why he didn't fire me remains a mystery, unless it was to simply spite her more, or to try and drive a wedge between her and I.

When the day had finished I left the kitchen by the back door, his eyes drilling holes in my back. He had spent the entire day right beside me, questioning every single move I made, pushing me to quit. But I stood firm, thinking not about him, or even about her, but about St. Patrick sitting on the hills as a young man, staring out past his flocks of sheep and across the Irish Sea to his home in Wales.

I ran down to our local, packed to the gills because of the holiday, ordered two pints of Guinness and a shot of Jameson. I fished out the remains of my pack of Majors, struck a match, lit the short, fat cigarette, and inhaled deeply. Letting the smoke go, my eyes followed it as it wafted toward the ceiling, the tension in my neck and shoulders giving them knots as hard as the bar.

I drained the first pint, called for some phone change, and then downed the Jameson. The heat of the whiskey eased things a might. I squeezed my eyes shut hard, knocking back half of the second pint. The barmaid brought me the change, and I walked through the throngs of people and over to the phone.

As I stood there, my elbow resting on the top of the pay phone, the receiver pressed against the left side of my face, the Waitress's telephone ringing incessantly in my ear, I looked up as the crowd split to reveal the long corridor between the booths and the tables. There, not thirty feet away, was the Waitress wrapped up in the arms of another man.

With a very controlled and calculated manner, I replaced the hanger on the cradle, blinked hard, as if looking at six-foot rabbits, and then methodically closed the distance between them and me.

This day, which had started out so benign and peaceful, my mother's voice making her seem to be right beside me, had quickly devolved into a real pisser. Now, the icing stroked hard onto the cake, I would vent the day's injustices on someone other than myself.

When I was within a scant few paces of them, the Waitress jerked her shoulder to tear away from the fella, but for me, it was too late by far. As I drew back my arm, the Waitress shrieking my name, her cry causing heads to turn, I landed my right fist squarely on his chin. He fell over the table behind him, pint glasses scattering, his eyes wide with surprise. Before his mates could join the fray, the bouncers, who had watched the entire thing unfold, grabbed me by both armpits and dragged me to the door. The Waitress was already heading out of the pub, shock and embarrassment glowing on her face.

Picking myself up from the pavement, I looked up Pearl Street to see the Waitress in full sprint. I followed for a few feet, saw her turn left on Ottawa, and then ran through the parking lot to intercept her at Calder Plaza.

We arrived at the Plaza at the same time, our collision made manifest by the two of us screaming at the tops of our lungs.

"How could you, Wiley. How could you. I can fight my own battles. None of this is what it seems."

"How bloody stupid do you think I am?"

"It's not like that. And that thing today, don't protect me, Wiley. I'm a big girl. I can handle myself. You're just too controlling. Why the hell did you have to fall in love with me. Huh? Why!"

"Believe me, it was the last thing I wanted to do."

Her eyes filled with large tears, she drew her breath back sharply in a sob and shook her head in disbelief. She balled up her fists, turned slightly, and then gave me a great shove sending me to the ground. She screamed an incomprehensible expletive, took a step to stand over me, bellowing something that made my eyes go wide. The sound of her heels and her voice both berating me as she ran as fast as she could. I shook my head to clear it, noticing something completely incongruous behind the theatrics. I frantically looked about hoping no one had seen us, when it dawned on me that the other sound I heard was laughter.

There, sitting on a park bench was a street person. A tattered green coat as big as a tent draped over his skinny frame, his head tilted back in riotous glee, I recognized him but didn't. One gnarled old hand stroking a long gray beard, the other clutching the ubiquitous paper bag, his bright blue eyes out of place beside a once handsome, black face. A single streetlight lit him as well as any stagehand could.

"Well, son," he choked out to me, "I guess you've got a choice to make?"

Stunned and ashamed at having been caught in a less than perfect moment, I stammered a reply, "Well then, what would you do if you were me?"

"I'm doing it." And he burst into another fit of guffawing.

I turned, looked hard at him over my shoulder, and set off to follow her yet again, his taunting laughter ringing in my ears, chasing me from the Plaza, and echoing throughout the heart of the city.

34

For days it has felt like I was falling, the sensation that with each lifted foot the free fall begins, only to be caught by my next step. And I, living from footfall to footfall, from every empty street to empty street, from the unanswered phone calls, to the blank face staring back in the mirror, can only whisper her name in hopes she will suddenly reappear.

Since she ran away on St. Patrick's last, no one has seen nor heard a thing about her. I feel as if I am chasing a ghost. I have to remind myself of all the times we spent together, painstakingly run through the files of my own mind to find even the most simple of memories. Her face recedes. Her voice fades, and all I can do is wait.

It is Palm Sunday today, a fortnight or so from that violent night when she left me, the haunting laughter of a street person chasing me from Calder Plaza as I ran after the Waitress. The sky is a far-away blue, distant and cold, the air seeming to crackle as I move through it. The sun, lingering above the horizon, looks down upon us and yawns, Spring is still around an imaginary corner.

At the restaurant, my work helps to keep me focused. The food, so long a part of my life, is simple and does what I ask of it. There are few mysteries. The new dishes I encounter are really older dishes garnished differently and called something else. 'Mutton dressed as lamb,' we would say back in Ireland.

The Waitress's friends here have had no contact with her as well. Not quite knowing what to do, the General Manager has left her name on the schedule, but left all the hours open. She has no relatives in the area and the few in Detroit have not heard from her either. The police have been contacted, but in truth, if someone does not want to be found, then they need not be.

When I am not working, I walk. Steeled against the worst, I walk for miles each day. The city has become my Church. The points of the compass are its Cardinals, the neighborhoods Bishops. Each few blocks is a Parrish, each street a Priest, and I make my ecclesiastic way through all of them. I have no plan, I simply wander until I am too tired to walk any further, turn, and make my way back home.

In the wee hours I ring my mother back home. I ask her for advice, but really it is just hearing her voice that makes me feel so much better. Tonight, somewhere on the west side, her sage words from this morning come back to me, the lilt of her accent making even the simplest of phrases seem soothing and perfectly apt. "Wiley, my boy, it troubles me to hear how heavy your heart is. You give your heart away so easily, and then chastise yourself when it comes back broken. I wish you could come home for just a wee bit. We could walk the strand down to the pub at Maghery, and join John Gallagher for hot whiskeys and laughs. You know, son, you've always been happiest on the road. Whenever you've settled, it seems then that the sadness comes knocking at your door. Do you know, son?"

"Aye," is all I could muster in the face of the truth and let her carry on with what I needed to hear.

"Someday, Wiley, you'll be back. You know, Wiley, all roads eventually find their way back home. I have to go now, call me tomorrow, please."

I wiped a tear from my cheek, stepped into a bar on Bridge Street, and asked for a Jameson. I downed the whiskey, turned from the bar, and resumed my journey. I headed for downtown in the waning light of evening. The wind had picked-up, causing the temperature to drop noticeably, and I thought it would be nice to wander among the tall buildings and the empty streets surrounding them.

As I crossed the river, I felt pulled toward the Plaza. I had not been there since St. Pat's and for some reason it seemed a good idea to finish Palm Sunday with a small prayer. I chided myself that she would be standing there, a tearful reunion highlighted by a warm embrace. I walked down the middle of Monroe to the stairs that lead up to the Plaza, empty iron and concrete, wind-strewn paper, the wind whistling through the aperture. The sun all but a memory, the streetlights flicker on as dutifully as soldiers, a solemnity in that I am the only soul who sees this.

My boots make echoes in Calder Plaza that sound like the footsteps of phantoms. The scratch of steel toes on worn pavement raises the hairs on my neck. I can see her face; I can hear her angry words, and it eats at my heart. I cannot leave the place fast enough, my walk becoming a run, the prayer left unsaid.

I cut across the street to a parking structure, to another set of stairs and make the turn for home. As I do so, I come across an older gentleman who is being overwhelmed by a throng of people leaving Mass. He is handing out candies for some cause or another and is having a go of it.

"Hey fella," he calls to me, "could you lend me a hand. On the back of my car are a vest and a can of Tootsie Rolls. Please, it would be very kind of ya."

I don the vest, pick-up the can of candies and step beside him to follow his lead. The congregation has pushed him to the edge of the curb, and just before he is about to lose his footing I catch him in the small of the back.

"Hey, thanks. That was a close one," he laughed in an off-handed way.

"No worries, man. Think nothing of it."

"You're Irish!" He all but yelled, his eyes lighting-up even more.

"Aye."

"From where?"

"Donegal."

"I've spent some time in Donegal. I love Donegal. The cliffs are magnificent."

"Aye. I grew up a bit north of there. You should see them from the water, it'll take your breath away."

He smiled. A genuine smile, and I knew I had met a friend. We waited for the rest of those who were milling about in the back of the Catholic Social Center to come out. Some made excuses, some gave begrudgingly, and others were quite willing to give what little they had. When it was over I leaned against his car as he put the money in a collection bag and said good-bye 'till next year to the rest of the candy.

"By the by, you look Irish yourself," I said.

"My folks came over in the Twenties from County Louth. Have you been to Louth?"

"Only on the way to Dublin. They always field a tough football team."

"Do you, what was your name again?"

"Wiley. Wiley O'Wary."

"Wiley, do you get back to Donegal often?"

"Not often enough."

"You miss home, huh?"

"Most times not too much, too busy. But tonight, more than you can ever know."

"I was in the Ardennes. I remember how much I missed my home town."

There was a pause, and we both looked up into the evening sky. Thin wisps of clouds illuminated by the last light, the contrails of a jet cutting across the sky to the east lit by a moon that hadn't broke the tops of the buildings.

"Ardennes! My God, what did ya do to deserve that," I exclaimed, having read at length about the Bulge.

"I got drafted!" he said, and laughed in that same easy way. "Say, Wiley, how about a round or two to take the chill off. There's a bar around the corner that's almost always open."

"The Irish bar on the corner?"

"Sure, what other kind is there," another wee laugh.

"That's me local. A drink sounds grand."

"Jump in," he said, pointing at his car.

"It's only four blocks."

He bent down and tapped his right shin making a dull wood sound. "Too far for me. Now jump in."

We drove to the local, himself explaining the candies and the cause and how long he had belonged to such and such. He parked the car across the street from the bar and in we went, the local completely empty save Jimbo the barman. I called for two pints of stout.

"No stout for me," he said, "too heavy."

"Too heavy?"

"Jameson and water," he nodded to Jimbo and set a twenty on the bar. "Yes, too heavy. My father always said, 'you can't bale hay on a stomach full of beer'."

"Jaysus, you *are* from Louth."

"So, Wiley, are ya long in Grand Rapids?"

"Just over a year. Five years in Boston before this. Then London, Dublin, Donegal before that, you know, the usual progression."

"Are ya interested in joining an Irish fraternity?" he asked.

"Only if there's an Irish sorority across the street." We laughed and Jimbo took the opportunity to return to the television and some paperwork.

"So," I asked, "is there a Mrs. Louth back home?"

He smiled, the beginning of a small laugh disappeared on his lips, looked out the window, "No. No, never married. Too busy." He reached down without realizing it and scratched at a leg that wasn't there. I nodded, looking away to the back bar and the perfect rows of bottles.

"You think this is cold," he said, his head motioning toward the window, the late March Midwestern evening.

"Bastogne?"

"Yeah," he said, finishing his drink. I could see his eyes moving quickly from side to side, a flood of memories building behind them from images they had seen fifty years ago. "Bartender?. Two more please."

"Were you in the woods?"

"Yeah, dug right in. Couldn't move back, couldn't move forward. Freezing cold. Coldest winter on record. They caught us completely by surprise. They said they didn't have any artillery within range. And then," he trailed off, accepted the new drink, paid for the round, pushing my money aside. Jimbo leaned against the back bar by the till, eyes intent on the old gent.

"Were you there the whole month?" I asked.

"No, no, no. They shipped me out about two and a half weeks into it, back to Paris, then to the coast to a hospital ship and then back to England. The usual progression," he smiled and winked at me.

"You weren't hit that whole time, were ya?" Jimbo asked, stepping closer to the bar, to the conversation.

"No, I had a healthy week in first."

I did the loose math in my head, "So you were injured for ten days before they could get you to a field hospital?"

"'Bout a week. Anyway, how do ya think the Tigers are going to do this year?"

"About as well as the Germans," Jimbo joked. "Do you remember when it happened?"

He set his drink down, held up his hands as if to ward off the inevitable questions, and set his face. "It was just like they say, it's the one you don't hear. After that, I don't really remember anything at all. The bumps in the road, the way the truck rocked back and forth, that's about it. I wish, to this day I wish, that I could shake the hand of the medic. Those were the bravest of the brave. Running from hole to hole during the fire. But it wasn't one of our guys. It was a guy from an outfit that had been wiped-out. We sort of absorbed them." He shook his head. "Never did find out who that guy was. Wiley!" he said, clapping me on the shoulder, "it was great to meet you. Here's my card. Call me if you'd like to join that fraternity or if you'd just like a drink sometime," he finished his drink, left a tip. "I hope the two of you have a great Easter," and then he walked out the door, across the street, and into his car.

There was a moment of silence, unusual in that it took place in so large an empty room that was normally filled with sound. We watched the gent drive off after carefully buckling his seatbelt on.

"Wow," Jimbo said, shaking his head, "that's one cool old dude you found there. I would not want to walk a mile in his shoes."

"No, neither would I," I answered, letting the room fall quiet again, and then on second thought, "I don't think we could fill the shoes."

"Not a chance, buddy, not a chance. Another?" he asked, pointing at my empty pint.

"No."

"Have a great rest of your day, Wiley," he said, shaking my hand.

"You too," I said, turning to make my way out the door, into the night, and up the hill.

A cold wind from out of the east made the going just that much tougher. "Ten days," I said out loud to myself, "damn." Then it dawned on me, with thoughts of the Waitress always just over the hill of my focus, I wondered if there was someone he was thinking of A potential Mrs? A face that haunts him? A ring purchased in London?

I stopped at the top of the hill and looked back out across the city, dusk settling like a wool blanket over a sleepy town. Before I realized it, I crossed myself and said a blessing in Irish for the old gent, turned back into the wind, and walked home. Staring at my boots, walking a mile, trying to ignore the face that keeps haunting my thoughts.

35

It has been my way for as long as I can remember. Walking. Foot following foot, the day measured out a yard at a time, until the road winds behind me as far as it rises in front. The worries of the day become as distant as whistle-stops on railroads, my boots on the sidewalk a poor man's version of iron wheels on iron tracks.

Today, I ramble north. The late spring clouds rush by as fast as the motorists. Division melts into Plainfield, the morning traffic steady both to and from the city center, and the sky has decided to shower. The perspiration on my brow meets the cool rain upon my face. I pull the hood of my jacket over a steaming head, a sudden nylon blanket smothering the road noise.

Things are not going all too well these days, as my head swims over the Waitress who is still missing. No one, not even her family, has heard a word from her in over a month. Her name has been removed from the schedule at the restaurant, and her position filled. So, as the shower abates and sunlight trickles through the cumulus, I wander ever north in search of a diversion, a gnawing feeling telling me that things may get a whole lot worse before they get any better.

Still, as I cross a bridge over a motorway, the sound of speeding tires on wet pavement rising with the spray, I recognize that an Irishman's sense of doom is only eight hundred years of bad memories. Hope is always there. Despite the greatest of odds and the most humiliating of defeats, the clouds continue to have a silver lining. We dream of *Dun Forgall*, of *Lochlann* and of *Tir na Og*, and in the ever-present tears, joy remains. Deep in our blood we know that once we were in each of these places, and to them we shall return.

As you walk, the horizon has a way of showing you something and then taking it away. It is the same as walking toward a mountain. Just when you think you've reached the foothills, a rise in the road reveals a disheartening expanse The mountain itself, not having to go anywhere, seems taller and further away.

It is in this way that the horizon has begun to reveal what looks like a Ferris wheel. The limited rationality I have says that this just cannot be, having walked upon this road many times. However, upon reaching the rise in the road, dotting the expanse between me and there, flags and banners fluttering in the wind, is a carnival. What luck. Diversion requested; diversion found.

It is one of those small, traveling carnivals. Ten days in this town, ten days in that town, until the entire year is filled with a sea of smiling faces, the din of children, the shrill screams of young girls and boys. The bright colors of the rides, the calliope music warbling in the air sounding both cheerful and haunting, these fairs seem to be more apparition than entity.

I wander across the parking lot and into the midst of it, letting the late morning sun, reflected on a thousand chrome surfaces, soak and blind me. I circle the carnival's grounds, empty but for a few souls, taking in the carefree spirit of the workers and the machines. Memories of similar scenes skit across my mind: a fair in Donegal town as a child, kissing that Protestant girl behind the side-show tent near Portrush, taking a girlfriend and her child to the seaside in Brighton.

As I walk past a game booth, the one where you toss a ball into a glass bowl in hopes of winning the goldfish swimming within, I hear a disembodied voice calling out to me.

"Hey Joe. Hey Joe. Yeah, you. You there, looking like you're hearing the voice of ghosts. Down here. What're ya, blind. Right down here."

I lean up against the bunting and crane my head to peer over the table. There, staring up at me, dressed in a patchwork of colors and bits of clothes, is a little person, his outfit blending him in perfectly with the riot of color that the booth is painted in.

"Are you as stupid as you look. You've been staring at me for nearly an hour with that perplexed, dumb look on your face. Wanna try at a fish?"

"From the likes of you," I said, noting his Lancashire-North England accent.

"No, from the bleeding fish, of course from me. Go on, give it a chance."

"Shag off," I reply, and pull out a pack of Dunhill's.

"Jesus, who d'ya think you are, the Lord Mayor hisself, smoking Dunhill's. Go on, give us one of dose fine cigarettes."

I said nothing at first, but lit the cigarette and exhaled in obvious pleasure. "Without a doubt, next to Major's, the finest smoke in the world."

"You're Irish."

"You're English."

"Then we agree to disagree. How's about a smoke, pal."

I gave him a wink and a sideways nod to which he ducks under the table, through the bunting, and is by my side as quick as can be.

"My name's Freddy, but you can call me Freddy. There it is, oh yes, haven't had one of dese in a long, long time. What's your name, Mick or Pat," he looked up to me, his walk more of a bob from side to side.

"Wiley."

"Wiley. What kind of name is Wiley. Is that Irish for something magic?" he asked, rubbing his hands together in a conspiratorial way.

"Something like that."

"Where do you hail from," he asked, as he guided me over to a maintenance truck where we sat on the old wooden steps leading up to the door.

He seemed about three and a half feet tall, with an unruly pile of red hair atop too large a head. His dark eyes darted around like a lizard's, but for all his nervous energy, he had an easy-going manner to him.

"Donegal. And you? Newcastle?"

"Lancaster. Lived there all me life, 'cept when traveling. Lots of us in Lancaster. Carnies that is. Loads of games, fair rides, amusements. Bit depressing really." He pulled out a wooden match from his pocket and struck it on the sole of his shoe.

"That doesn't make any sense."

"Not much does, these days. Wow! What a smoke. You know smoking dese things is what stunted my growth."

"I don't believe you."

"Then we agree to disagree." The sky opened up again, a small shower acting as a mist in the sunlight. He continued without missing a beat. "It's raining while the sun is shining, you know what that means, somewhere, the devil is beating his wife."

I gave him a long look. "Are ya going to give me a pull off dat bottle or are you going to hog the whole ting yerself." He laughed so hard he lost his balance and fell off the step.

"Ah it's good to hear the brogue. Not drunk, you silly MickorPatorWiley, that's an old Welsh saying."

"I never spent much time in Wales."

"Good thing cause you'd be likely to drown." And once more he lost his balance in laughter.

"Freddy!" A sharp woman's soprano cut the air. "Are you smoking over there," she continued, her voice having gone up an impossible octave.

Freddy thrust the cigarette into my hand, which I began juggling so as not to get burned, the hot end singeing my palms as I wrestled with it for control.

"No dear, just talking to this poor lost Irishman."

She turned the corner, a little person with her hands on her hips and a scowl on her face. She was about six inches taller than Freddy, dressed similar but in a skirt instead of trousers. She stabbed a finger at Freddy, "You get back to that booth, little man. We've got work to do." And with that, spun around on her heels with the precision of a Scot's Guard.

Freddy looked up at me, a sheepish smile flitting across his face.

"Well Mick or Pat or Wiley, here's some tickets for the rides."

"Ah, no. I can't take those."

"Ah, go on. But I'll tell you what, for a couple of extra Dunhill's, I'll read your palm."

"You're having me on, just take the cigarettes."

"No, really," he said, and grabbed my right hand.

As he looked at the lines crossing my palm like so many roads on a map, I glanced up to see a small child crying and being consoled next to the carousel. The wee boy pointed up to the frozen faces of the horses shaking his head no. In an instant, I took in the hooves clawing air in vain to touch the ground, the whirl of music both dizzying and disconnected, the small face turning red in panic. The mother insisting that the child try the ride, and placed him upon a charger. The carousel started with a jerk and the mother, distracted by a stuffed animal that had fallen, let go her grip at the same time. The child, too small to hang on, hands wet with tears, fell over backwards, striking his head on the hoof of the charger behind. There was an instantaneous wail from the now bleeding child, and a shriek from the mother as well. At that moment Freddy looked up at me and read me my fortune.

"You sir, have been running a very long time, and you're not anywhere near done. I think, now I'm not as good at this as my wife, but I think that your life is in for a terrible change. I think you may be in grave danger."

He looked up at me with sincere concern, his black eyes looking right through me, inside me. The carnival, the hum of motors, the disjointed music, the crying child being tended to, it all slipped away.

"Don't go to England," he said. "There's someone there, waiting for you. Someone big. Someone mean. Someone not right in the head." He paused, "there's a bright, bright light after a lot of blackness, but I don't know why or what that is?" He made a sharp nod as if this statement was certain, and then released my hand. He slapped me lightly on the face, took a couple of cigarettes, and walked back to his booth.

I stared after him, hoping for an explanation, or some words of reassurance, but there was only the hum of motors, the whirl of music, and the screams of a child.

I passed on the rest of the carnival, except the Ferris wheel, which I rode three times for luck. The sky opened up once more as I was leaving, the calliope music fading, the sound of flags fluttering being lost to distance. I looked back at the booth where Freddy worked, but of course I could not see him. So, turning to the south, I made my way warily back home, foot following foot, time measured out in three-foot intervals, the road winding behind me as far as it rises in front of me.

In my head, Freddy's prophesy stalked around my thoughts, coiling and uncoiling like an addict in a closed room. I did my best to unravel it's meaning, but in the same way the child would not ride the charger, I stayed ever so slightly clear of where this fortune was taking me. The faces of the horses, the clowns and harlequins, Freddy and his wife, the calliope music, these would haunt my dreams for nights, the images blurring into each other like a drunk on a carousel.

36

She had those far away eyes. Distant and removed, staring holes into the middle distance. The light in them had gone, replaced by a cloudy emptiness. They were the eyes of a child who has been through war, or been terribly abused.

I stared at her with a mix of pity, anger, confusion, and love. Her left eye was blackened, misshapen and swollen above a purple cheek that seemed as if it would rend itself open from its own pressure. Her lower lip, split up and down, protruded disjointedly from her face. She had a knot above her right temple, bruises along her neck, and a deep gash on her chin that nearly met the split in her lip. Her nose was cocked at an absurd angle, colored a blackish-yellow, dried blood caking her nostrils.

I wanted to smash everything around me to pieces. I wanted to find out who had done this and tear them into shreds. I felt at once stunned, shocked, and ashamed that I could not have been there to protect her. My mind staggered to think, numbed senseless by such an affront to someone so beautiful.

When I had come home from my walk, the light in my apartment telling me something was not right, her back was to me as I came in the door. I had reached out to touch her, to affirm the existence of this apparition, and when I did, she had chilled over so completely that I recoiled my hand. She then turned toward me, and in that instant upon seeing her battered face, the lifelessness in her eyes, I drew in a sharp breath. She was the last person I ever expected to see again, and certainly not like this.

In the nearly two months since she had left, my life had taken on a rote that helped me deal with the loss. The simple familiarity of pattern, having etched itself across the days and weeks, numbed myself to the pain. Rising in the morning. Going to work. Walking all evening long. A drop of whiskey, a bit of stout, then off to bed. Sleep fitfully, and then repeat. This was my recipe for coping.

In the midst of this, walking one wet and rainy Friday evening, my mind distracted by the words of the English dwarf at the carnival, I had realized that the fire in my heart for the Waitress was now reduced to so many embers and ashes. I no longer held out any hope that she would return. The not knowing where, or how she was, filed away with the other mysteries in one's life that can never be solved, like an overstuffed file cabinet in a police station that has been pushed to the back of the squad room, occasioning only sideways glances and 'I wonders'.

The rhythm of my boots on pavement, the different sounds they make on different surfaces, this has been the music of my heart. My tears for her seemed long since dry.

In order to move on, you must kill that part of your heart by watching it slowly die. The cancer patient, terminal, withering, is that last corner of your heart where you keep her smile, her last kiss, the essence of what the two of you had. Once this is accomplished, life, the fullness of life, returns.

In the spring shower that soaked me, the raindrops large and fat, with each step I felt this process finally come to its conclusion. I took a minute to stop my walk, somewhere in the very same park where we had rescued her from the storm nearly a year ago, and let this fully dawn on me. The twisted trees, the shattered debris of timber, the aftermath of the big wind now long gone, in this park where we had shared our first kiss, I felt that snap of letting go.

With a drop of melancholy, not quite believing that something I had held on to so tightly was now gone, I turned, looked long at the river, and began to walk home. The day's last light seeping through the clouds had begun to fully wane. Streetlights flickered on to shroud the city from the gloom, but their light seemed more in jest. A heavy silence hung over the town. To me, it felt like a pause, like finally catching one's breath after a bout of sneezes, apprehension at breathing in, wary of another sneeze, there is that frozen moment where one stops, and hopes, and then slowly exhales.

The pace of my walking now no longer driven, I let the rain soak into my skin. There is that wonderful feeling of having no direction at all. The tempest passed, scud clouds floating just above the surface, the quiet lull between fronts.

My feet felt lighter, my posture more easy-going, my gait became more of a wander.

I decided to step into a restaurant off Monroe, an older place with dark booths, no windows and a great reputation. I had begun having a 'pick-me-up' there during these weeks of walking and recovery, its rectangular bar becoming a halfway point for the homeward stretch. A celebration seemed in order, a dinner to help mark that point of finally turning, of finally moving on. A ribeye that was grilled to a perfect medium-rare, a bottle of cabernet, and a vodka martini the size of a fishbowl brought a smile to my face. I even began making out a list of books to pick-up.

I rounded the corner of my street, looked up the block to my two front windows, and saw a light in them that I had not left on. I stopped suddenly, a man with a grocery bag cursing as he ran into me, my mind racking itself to remember exactly what I had done before I had left. Remembering full well that I had turned-off all the lights, I cautiously walked toward my flat.

Who could it be? Who would have access to my apartment? I thought of as many solutions as possible: the landlord, the Sous Chef, my mother come to surprise me from Ireland, my sister from London, some petty thief come to take what little I own. None of it made sense, no one had a key.

The closer I got to the front porch, the stronger my heart pounded in my chest. Pausing, I stood staring at the outer door before opening it a crack to peer into the hallway. Only the security-light, the stairs, the hall, the mailboxes, it was empty save the light beneath my door. I entered, looked back over my shoulder, the click of the large outer door settling into its jamb echoing up the stairs. My hands shook as I fumbled with the keys, soft scraping of key on door and lock, the sound of the tumblers as they gave way, and the yawn of the opening.

Inside, across the room from the light, sat the Waitress. I stood staring in disbelief for what seemed like forever. She never moved, nor uttered a sound. There were no bags, none of her belongings, it was only herself dressed as she had been on St. Pat's night. Nothing in the flat had been moved, not a chair, or a paper, or even a cup. Nothing. I felt as if I had walked into someone's grave.

I whispered her name, but the silence in the room sucked it up. I couldn't tell if she was even breathing, my heart beating in my ears like a lambeg drum. The lamp beside my armchair, next to the windows, seemed to flicker, as if the darkness was waiting to expel it like the last bit of candle just before its own melted wax envelopes the wick. I crossed the room and reached out to touch her, the chill freezing me to the bone, my hand withdrew instinctively.

Slowly, she turned toward me and I saw her face, my hand going to my mouth to cover the gasp. I pulled away, another instinct, and felt shame in doing so, the steak dinner feeling heavy, excessive. I knelt down to be closer to her, to not seem threatening, a sob catching in my chest.

Then, as upon a still body of water a ripple breaks the surface, her eyes focused. She looked up at me, "Wiley," and a single tear ran down from a blackened eye, across a purple, swollen cheek, and fell like a raindrop into oblivion.

37

She sat in front of the easel as rapt as a child, hair falling in jagged lines across her face casting shadows that concealed her eyes, small hands demurely selecting crayons in a way that seemed more than simply drawing. Only purples and greens, she draws flowers on the wide, white pages. This is what she does. This is the medicine that heals her heart.

I watched her from across the room, the early morning light creeping through the blinds, the clock ticking too loudly from the kitchen, my hands cupping a steaming mug of coffee. A cup of tea rests beside her, long since cold, the same disheveled clothes hanging limp from her body like a suit tossed drunkenly onto a chair. This has become our tableau.

When I am not working, I spend my time with her. I tend to her as if she were my patient. The wounds on her face have finally mended, but the look in her eyes is still as hollow as when she came back. She has spoken nothing of what happened. She speaks little at all.

The drawing of purple flowers has consumed her, page after page. Some are as simple as a child's rendering, others as intricate as a mosaic, the lines at times carefully placed upon the page or sometimes cut deep. She spends hours each day at this, the easel beside the couch where she sleeps.

I told her the story of the petunias in the sidewalk. How a year or so ago I had found a hole in the sidewalk near an apartment building, and that someone had planted purple petunias in the hole. Though they had been picked not an hour after my discovering them, throughout the summer they continued to bloom. In a surprise, she wanted to see where the hole was and if we could go there now. I trundled us up against the rain, finished coffee, poured out tea, and off we went.

When we arrived at the spot where the flowers had been last summer, we found nothing in the hole except weeds. She nudged at them with her foot, her hands buried deep in one of my jackets, the rain spattering her face. In the day-light you could still see the fading bruises, where the cuts had been, damaged skin yielding to scar. She looked up at me, rivulets of rainwater running down her forehead, along her eyes, and down her cheeks, and asked if we could plant some flowers in the hole. In her eyes I could see a flicker, a light as small as a votive, the only brightness in a dark cathedral. I smiled, took up her hand and whispered yes.

In all the walking that I had done while she was away, I had come across a produce stand near Riverside Park that sold planting flowers. We spent the morning walking there, storm clouds building in the west, the on-again, off-again spring showers greening the world around us. Our feet splashing in puddles, the occasional swish of our sleeves brushing against each other, these were the only sounds we made.

When we arrived at the market, the Waitress stopped short of the tables of young flowers and vegetables, and looked down Monroe to the park. I asked her if she wanted to keep walking. She nodded and we set off in that direction.

It was almost a year ago that she had run into that savage storm. I could still see her atop that rusty bridge, crying and afraid. Our lives seemed to have become entwined from that very moment. It would be not six months later that we would stand not far from the very same bridge, talking and kissing, the world a much safer place.

Upon seeing the bridge, she broke into a run. My heart leapt in my chest, the worst fear being she would just keep running, that one day she would be gone again, no explanation, no note. With each step I winced. Every morning when I awoke, I would peek around the corner from the hallway, hoping she would still be there on the couch, drawing away after another sleepless night.

She stopped at the bridge, fingers tracing the railing like greeting an old friend. She walked from one end to the other, turned, walked half way back, and jumped up onto the side. She clambered up to the top, spinning her body so her feet dangled into the emptiness. She became as still as the surface of the pond, as quiet as the empty park, once more facing west across the Grand.

After some time, concern at first rooting me to the spot, I turned and walked down to the river. The sky had opened again, raindrops dappling the surface in a way both random and yet with pattern, and sat down to let the water flow to sea.

I thought about how odd life is, the sheer randomness of it. Had I not come to this town, had I not accepted a chef's position at that particular restaurant, had the wind storm not occurred, then what would be the likelihood that the Waitress and I would be here now, or have gone through any of the things we had. The rain on the water seemed to have more direction.

Time passed as only it can on a wet, dark Sunday. I left the river to its business and returned to the bridge, only to find it empty. My heart did not leap, nor sink. I sighed, thinking there must exist some things that have to be free, and perhaps she was one of them.

However, as I turned to walk home, I saw her sitting beneath a tree. She arose with her hands still thrust into pockets, her hair a tangled wet nest, and joined me as I walked out of the park and up the short blocks to the market.

There were several long tables covered with flats of flowers. She busied herself among them, fingers going through the petunias, sometimes lifting a single planter up to have a closer look. Her eyes squinted, her lips moving as if talking to herself or the plants, the intensity of someone who has drawn one thousand purple flowers now faced for the first time with the real thing. She seemed to catalog each plant before setting it down and moving on to the next.

After nearly thirty minutes she walked back to the third table she had been through, stopped for a moment, and reached out for a single planter. I was mystified at how she remembered which one it was.

She pulled out a wet dollar and paid for the purple petunia, the clerk shooting me an odd look. I said nothing. The Waitress held the plant up to the light, her fingertips touching the leaves as a child strokes the hair of her favorite doll. When the wind and rain came again she hid it beneath her jacket, carefully cradling it with both hands.

The walk back to the apartment building was much quicker, the task at hand having lent renewed purpose to her stride. We still walked in silence, me wondering if she would ever get better, would we fall in love again, could everything ever be the same once more. Her thoughts, if of past misdeeds, of terrible wrongs, or of purple flowers, I could only guess.

We stopped just short of the hole in the sidewalk. She knelt before it, set her plant down, and began to take up the weeds with her hands. The more they resisted, tap roots deep beneath the concrete, the angrier she became. In a fury, her fingers tore at their leaves, stems, and roots rending them from the ground.

She closed her eyes and took several long, even breaths. She then began digging a hole, carefully setting the dirt to one side. As she picked up the petunia, she began to sob. Great shudders racking her body, a spasm of tears showering the now bare earth, she pulled the flower from the planter, placed it in the hole, and began replacing the dirt around the plant.

As she did this I could hear her voice murmuring. Rocking back and forth, the petunia itself also swaying in the slight wind, she watered it with her tears. I leaned forward, cocking my head to one side to better hear what seemed like a prayer. Then, in a moment both simple and profound, I could hear what it was she sang, the first real words she had spoken in over a week.

"Hush little baby, don't say a word, mama's gonna buy you a mocking bird."

After a moment, eyes lingering over the flower with satisfaction, the verse having ended, she stood, took my hand in hers, and turned to walk back to my flat. I stared at my feet upon the sidewalk, few thoughts forming in an exhausted mind.

Once home, she laid down on the couch after putting the crayons away, folding the tablet closed, and pushing the easel to a far wall. I made us tea and toast, but by the time I had set them on the coffee table beside her, she was fast asleep. I drew the drapes, pulled an afghan over her shoulders, kissed her forehead, and went to bed, where, not one paragraph read, I fell off myself, the day slipping away with images of raindrops on the river, the water falling, flowing, returning.

38

It was later than I'd hoped, later than I wanted it to be, and later than we had finished cooking in a very long time. An altogether brutal night for those of us behind the line, a night replete with injuries, no-shows and what seemed like three hundred walk-ins. Even the suds looked spent, as we methodically wiped down our stations, skinned the pans and tried to snap the lids on the ancient cambros.

I wiped my face with what I thought was a clean towel, only noticing too late that it was the same one I had used on the flat top. Blackish-brown smudges streaked my cheeks and brow, a rancid, thick blotch ending up on my bottom lip. The staff, too tired to laugh, simply shook their heads as we all queued up to punch out.

"Wiley, here," the Sous said, tossing me a clean towel, damp with sudsy water.

"Thanks, lad. Jaysus, what a night."

"You going to the pub?" He asked.

"Too tired, man. I couldn't lift a pint to my lips with the help of forty virgins, block, tackle and one hundred camels."

"I have no idea what you just said."

"Going home," I simplified.

"Yeah, me too. Tomorrow's another day." He clocked out, clapped me on the shoulder and left the building.

I wiped the night's collective gristle and grease from my face, ran my card through the clock, the oh-so-satisfying double click announcing the end of the shift, and followed in his footsteps.

An unusually crisp breeze slapped me in the face. I turned towards the hill, a sigh issuing from my parched lips as I counted the streetlights going up to the top.

"Bloody hell," I said to no one in particular.

It wasn't until near the top that my destination, or rather, what lay in wait for me, came to mind. The Waitress and another night of my playing cook, nurse maid, counselor and gofer. It had been like this for quite some time.

"Fuck's sake," I said to no one in particular.

How nice it would be, I thought to myself, to be in love with someone normal. But then, what's normal? And was I really in love?

"Fuck-all," I said to myself in particular.

One foot in front of the other, the hill leveling off, I dismally wondered what would be the issues tonight. How many trips to the store? How many trips to the bedroom with this or that? How many tears or shrieks or rotten looks would there be tonight?

Then it dawned on me. It's too bloody late for her to be up at all. There's no possible way she could be awake. Suddenly, things looked better. That is, until I turned the corner and saw the light on in my flat.

"Ah, for the love of Michael."

Well, who knows? Maybe she has a grand dinner prepared, a little wine uncorked, something lacy on and a fire in the nonexistent fireplace beside the not-there-bearskin rug. Ah, sure. And some day Ireland will win the World Cup.

I trudged up the walk to the porch steps, the theme from *The Odd Couple* roiling around in my head, and mounted the steps. It seems in life that it's always uphill.

On opening the front door, a massive whiff of baked turkey slammed me in the face. I stood there, stupefied, wondering from which lucky flat the wonderful aroma was coming from.

The door to my apartment slowly opened revealing the Waitress, clad in nothing more than an unbuttoned peppermint-striped flannel nightshirt and holding two glasses of champagne, the tiny bubbles climbing to the rims like amazing lava lamps.

My mouth agape, I stood there speechless.

"You seem a bit speechless, Wiley. Thought it might be a nice surprise for you." To which she sauntered over and kissed my mouth, agape and all.

"This was not what I expected at all," I said, accepting the champagne, inhaling the savory smell of bird, and peeking at her bare bottom as she led me back into the flat.

"You've been great with me, Wiley. It was really the least I could do." She set her glass down and again came close. "I'm so very sorry for all the drama." She composed herself, "Thank-you, Wiley, for all your tenderness and all your patience."

What does one say? I felt more than a little guilty for having precious little patience and tenderness left. Maybe it was simply exhaustion, maybe it was time to do some soul searching or maybe it was high time to go on a right proper drunk. In my tiredness, I could only express those words all men say at a time like this, "It was nothing, really."

A warm and wonderful kiss ensued, the first one in a long time. My knees were half-buckled from an eleven-hour shift and this kiss nearly caved them in altogether. The taste of champagne in her mouth and the smell of food kept me from swooning. We broke the kiss as she picked up my hand and led me to the table. Another kiss and she went into the kitchen. In moments a feast was served.

As I tucked into the turkey, mashers, peas & carrots and the odd nip of wine, my hunger was racing my tiredness for control. Both of them would undoubtedly dovetail, it was really only a matter of when.

"My god, Wiley, you seem famished!"

"I had no idea how hungry I was. This is brilliant. Thank-you so much. In Ireland, there's a saying, 'hunger makes the best sauce'."

"Must be a pretty good sauce. More?"

"Yes, please. How about some more of the Pinot, too."

We ate, her precious little, and myself like a starved tiger. Glass after glass of white, red and champagne, and to her credit she only had a couple.

"I have a pumpkin pie for dessert," she offered.

"You must be joking. Where are we going to put it?"

"I'll let you think about that while I do up some dishes," she gave me a wink and a wonderful smile, tidying up the table and disappearing into the kitchen.

I poured a glass of port into my wine glass and quaffed it. Poured another and did the same. The effect being nearly instantaneous, the alcohol was now spiraling in on the food and the tiredness. I sat there for a minute then decided I should be chivalrous and help with the wash-up.

Standing was not a good idea. The turkey dinner, various wines and the long day now felt like a Mike Tyson uppercut. I sank back into my chair with a slam, nearly falling off of it. The room began to reel and just as I managed some control, she came back into the room.

She set the entire pie in front of me, produced a can of whip cream and said something suggestive as she sauntered into the bedroom. I think I leered. Then, the world went black.

I remember dreaming about quicksand. It seemed that I was thrashing about, not getting anywhere, when I remembered that if you lie perfectly still you will float on top of the quicksand and can then sort of quietly paddle over to the edge and grab hold of a root.

I was attempting this sort of thing when it dawned on me that I must be lying facedown as there seemed to be a significant amount of gurgling, spitting, wheezing and bubbles. Yes, loads of bubbles.

With tremendous effort I not only pulled myself from the quicksand, but also succeeded in waking myself up and lifting my head out of the pumpkin pie. Disoriented and blinking, my eyes caked with goo, I tried to figure out why I had done a half-gainer into the pumpkin pie.

Then, it sank in. I shot a glance at the bedroom door. Shut. I could feel the icy draft sweeping out from the space between the door and the floor.

"Damn it," I said to the pie, and myself for that matter.

They say timing is everything and her and I don't seem to have any at all. Of all the feckin' times to pass out, though I suppose it could have been worse.

I wiped my face clean of pie, my nostrils singing with pumpkin pie spice, and stood up. As quietly as possible, with the greatest of care not to make a sound as only the guilty can muster, I opened the bedroom door. I paused, letting my eyes adjust to the dark, and entered.

She lay buried under the covers, only her sweet, little face sticking out, snuggled deep into the pillow. There was a frown on her face, her brow was furrowed and I felt even worse. What to do now other than stick my head in the oven and blow out the pilot?

I disrobed slowly and quietly, went to the other side of the bed, lifted the covers what seemed like a scant few inches above the bottom sheet, and climbed in. Which is when one cold foot met up with one warm tush, prompting a boatload of screaming and swearing.

"Sorry," was all I could manage and really all one can say.

My eyelids grew heavy, the room fell far away and I drifted off into a dreamless sleep, far from kitchens and waitresses, far from anxiety and even farther from her.

In the middle of the night, thirst and the end result of thirst waking me, I left the empty bed and made my way quietly to the kitchen. The lamp at my desk, the Waitress beside it, intent, didn't really seem odd at all to my fuzzy brain.

The glass being pulled from the cupboard, the water being turned on, none of this drew her attention from whatever it was she was rapt over. I noticed the great, wine box of Wiley pulled down and opened and thought, 'how sweet', herself immersing herself in myself.

I gently set the glass down, returned to the bedroom by way of the bathroom, coin-tossing the flush between being quiet or being polite in favor of polite, which probably pulled the attention of the Waitress away from her study. The creak of floorboards now seeming quite loud, I went back to bed only to be joined by her and a wonderfully, mischievous smile.

"I think you're going to be as happy as I am that you're awake," whereupon she disappeared below the covers.

I awoke many hours later, the flat empty, coffee filling the air, a lovely letter letting me know breakfast was warm in the oven, and a big, fat red lipstick print beside her name.

"Well," I said to myself, "I'll be damned."

The 'Life of Wiley' wine box had been replaced to its spot atop the bookcase, the apartment was perfect and perfectly still, the coffee delicious, and for one of those rare moments in life, things seemed oddly in place.

I hesitated, being Irish and having been raised Catholic, waiting for something horrible to beat down the door and drag me away, but the moment passed and I settled into the couch visited by only silence, a novel and coffee.

My eyes, though, would stray from the page every so often, and look warily up at the wine box, a niggling feeling settling on the back of my neck. This yielded another cointoss, trust and love or suspicion and longevity? I decided I was too comfortable to get up, too in love to care and too old to worry.

And so the day wound its way away, until the shower, the cold air on the way to work, and the single click of the time clock made life less rapturous and a whole lot more singular.

39

It is the ability to save enough broken yolk to cover the last bits of toast. That wonderful, gooey goldenness provides the glue that binds the separate entities together. I eat breakfasts such as this in a very Irish way: loads of toast as a vehicle for all the other stuff on the plates. Bacon, sausage, egg and even potatoes, are cut into bite-sized morsels, dipped in yolk, and placed on an equal-sized cut of toast. Every fourth or fifth bite nudged into orange marmalade prior to placement in the mouth. Set the utensils down, sip coffee, tea or water, scan the page of newsprint making sure all is read. In a country that's so busy being a nation, one must step out of the river, pause, and dine.

A scant six blocks from my flat is one of the finest breakfast spots I've ever been to. If you don't get here early, no matter what day of the week, you'll be waiting by the coat rack, waiting in the breezeway, waiting in your car, or making other plans. I had gotten here early, the Waitress groaning me away, the night's revelry having been too much for her, and made my way through empty streets to a busy corridor that acted as a north boundary for The Hill.

The power of aroma, coffee, bacon, butter, the sharp smell of toast or batter just slightly burned, these are the smells that hit your nose upon entering. Intoxicating. This is the stuff we live for.

It was so early that there weren't any used newspapers stacked on the table beside the host stand. Dollar broke. Coins dropped into slot. Information and entertainment received.

I ordered three of everything, arranged the newspaper just so, sipped fresh ground, black coffee, and then let the world fall perfectly into place.

The headlines can be rather numbing, and it was the morning after a session, so my mind wandered as it tends to, wending away over hills of memories and dales of whatevers, the politicians, movie stars and athletes staring up at me from the paper as if from another world. In this life, it is that which surrounds ourselves day-to-day that preoccupies us.

For myself, this would be the Waitress. Her words of the night before, sometimes so careless, sometimes carefully aimed, always seem to sink a little deeper, and her saying how much she would like to meet my brother left me slightly disarmed. It wasn't that she went on and on. It's just that over the course of some time, this subject always seems to come up.

Jealous? Me? Of course, aren't we all?

Knife and fork placed on B&B. Newspaper held up, shook slightly, and page turned. Resume dining.

It's just that it's impossible to read people. You never really know what's lurking about in their heart. And this girl!

Obviously, she's been through a lot. But, when does that become an excuse, a crutch. When does one throw in the towel and say, 'that's it, good luck I've had e-bloody-nough!' I'm not sure when that is. Love clouds everything. Just when you're absolutely certain you've got life right sussed, cupid shows up and the next thing you know you're lying in a pool of blood with a dart stuck between your ribs.

Sausage, toast, yolk and a right good push into the marmalade.

"I'm really looking forward to meeting your brother." "He sounds so interesting. So mysterious." "Life is so boring here in G.R. Restaurants and churches. Haven't you ever just wanted to blow something up?"

Some birds cannot be caged. Some birds should just fly free. Some birds should be run from as if one was an extra in a film by Hitchcock, while others should be allowed to sit on a branch and sing all day. This one might need her own nature preserve.

And then, just as I begin to lean toward the side of e-bloody-nough! This bird sits on my heart's string and pitches a melody that melts me.

Bacon, spud, toast, yolk, hazard a quick glance over my shoulder for any armed cherubs, and into my mouth.

Breakfast shouldn't be this taxing. I remember this couple from Norway, years ago. They were in Donegal town studying some ancient something or other, staying in the same hostel that I was in. They would run up to the market, purchase four or five newspapers, everything you could imagine for breakfast and then would eat and read for hours. Perfect.

Soon, they invited me to join them at the table. It was winter, the hostel was empty save us, and we had the entire kitchen to ourselves. It was there that I truly learned to relax and dine.

I lift my head up and am rewarded with a fresh cup of coffee. Who ever invented the bottomless coffee cup in America was a right genius.

We are now at a critical point in the breakfast: eying up the amount of yolk left on the plate with the amount of toast and the amount of everything else. This is crucial. Here is where you earn the extra points, the higher pay scale. This is where the professionals separate themselves from the pack. Intuitively, I already know how much yolk for each remaining bite. It's just a matter of bringing that knowledge from the brain stem to the cerebral cortex while not forgetting the all-important motor skills that will give us perfect morsels and yummy sounds.

And then, I stop. Set down the utensils, pause and close my eyes.

"I think I've seen his face in a dream," she said to me. "But, I can't be sure. My dreams are so distorted. So out there. They gallop from one thing to the next and I can't ever be sure if they're trying to tell me something or if they're just a ride at a carnival. Wiley, do you have dreams?"

"Wiley? You all right?" It's the waitress, the one here in front of me at the counter in the breakfast joint, not the one whose words just thundered to the front of my memory, the one who is sleeping in my bed.

"Yeah. Yeah. Sorry, just drifted off for a moment."

"Can't imagine why, you've just eaten enough food to feed a football team. Check?"

"Sure. Yeah, thanks."

Dreams. How did the rest of that conversation go? Destiny. How the night of the windstorm had brought us together. Fort Wiley, the refuge from all storms, the place and fella you can always count on. Learning to dance. Learning to love books. Growing closer, but not too close.

That's the one! Growing closer, but not too close. I couldn't quite figure that one out. Isn't that the point? You fall in love, you grow closer and then you keep growing closer. Right?

Last bit of sausage, last bit of toast, the last of the yolk with the last of the marmalade, combined into the last bite and tucked into mouth.

Dreams. Destiny. Carnivals. If this woman came in a box from *Parker Brothers* she'd be a Ouija board.

I was beginning to wonder if I was merely a waypoint, a stop along her destined path. That bloke who saves the girl from herself so she can end up with the man of her dreams. Or worse, maybe I was just convenient.

I retrieved my wallet from inside my jacket, paid the bill leaving nearly thirty percent as a tip, finished coffee and rose to depart. I wondered if the object of so much thought was stirring, wondered what she was wondering about, and then shook it off. In absolute Irish-ness I spoke those essential words of survival, "fuck it."

Paper placed on the table beside the host stand, a smile for the folks stuck waiting for a place to sit and wonderful fresh air hitting me in the face like God's palm on my forehead.

40

We had made love the night before, a pile of sheets as rumpled as our hair, the heat making even the most languid of movements exhausting. A solitary fan sat in the corner pushing stale air about the room, pre-dawn light falling through the slats of the blinds, a grayish-pink of city-summer morning pulling the night's cloak away.

Our backs to one another, the looks on our faces carnival mirrors of emotions, I could feel the gulf between us widening. Even in the closeness of the act, we were miles apart. Drifting from thought to thought, trying vainly to be consumed by passions that were not connecting, we turned from each other to face ourselves alone. The simple questions of life, of being here now, of love and trust and building a life together, now as complex as logarithms. We were confronting each other with logic that the other could not understand. Two tourists from different cultures screaming at each other over a traffic accident in front of the sphinx.

At some point I had passed-out, a tangle of dreams that made no sense, until the all-too-familiar stairs appeared. Once again I was running through blackthorn, running toward Hooker's Hill, running away from something that seemed to engulf me. The rain, the ancient stones, the moss upon them and the spell of the apple tree, they all lined up once more, a constellation as old as myself.

I awoke, a gargled word on my lips sounding vaguely like a name, drenched in more sweat than before, hangover rising like an expectant tide. I turned quickly to see if I had disturbed the Waitress, but she was not there, and in my confusion I think I had wished her away, the folly of last night still dogging me.

When I turned the corner from the bedroom into the hallway, I could see her in the front room through the kitchen. She didn't realize I was about, her attention rapt upon something in her hands. She stood by what had been a fireplace, long since bricked over, now only a mantel. I decided to remain quiet, padding off to the bathroom to begin the day properly. In the course of this it dawned upon me what she might have in her hands. I mulled this over while dressing, remembering to grab my wallet, my keys and cigarettes, somehow sensing that everything had changed.

Returning to the kitchen, through the opening at the counter I could see that the great old wine box had been pulled down from its roost. A small pile of Wiley contents had been hastily piled beside it until the object of her desire had been found. She was leaning against the wall beside the mantel with her back to me, focus so intent she had no idea I was there. In her hands, not six inches from her face, was the picture of my brother.

I did not linger. I did not want to bother her, I did not want to cause an uncomfortable scene or start a fight. In fact, all I wanted to do was leave, leave without a trace. My first instinct, as old as that bad dream, was to run. So, I backed away, out of the kitchen, across the hall to my bedroom, opened the window, slid out the screen, and left my house like a thief.

It is hot, it is bright, it is Sunday and it is late-morning. If I had felt like shite before, I am the whole dung heap now.I made straight for the local, knowing it would not be open but hoping that maybe I would see Jimbo and he would let me in.

In Grand Rapids, the first weekend of June is reserved for Festival. Blocks of the city's center are cordoned off, tents and stages erected, and tens of thousands of people descend to partake in food, music, theater, and art.

I had tried to take her downtown for this yesterday, but it was only to be a lesson in futility. Upon seeing the throngs of people, she would panic, and bolt the other way. We went from street to street, circling the Festival like moths trying to get inside a porch light. Each time, no matter from what direction, we could never get more than a dozen feet into the event before the fear overwhelmed her and we were retreating. The press of people was simply too much for her, the riot of colors, sounds, and smells an overload to a woman who had spent weeks never venturing far from my couch and her easel.

I had so hoped that the liveliness of the event would draw her out of her shell, but in the end we walked back up the hill, an unsatisfying feeling of having accomplished nothing soaking us as surely as our own sweat. The sun burned relentlessly on our backs, each step up the steep hill making us all the more irritable.

The sparse conversation was littered with statements about her impending move-in. Underneath all of the day's frustrations lay the fact that she would be moving into my flat properly. It would be official, then, going steady, living together, joined at the hip. Although this seemed only sound, and was, in fact something we had been talking about, it scared her beyond words. Today, the Sous Chef was supposed to pick us up and we would move her scant room full of belongings into the apartment from her girlfriend's. If the punters were taking odds at the moment, all bets would be off.

Instead, I kicked stones down the hill past a church overflowing with a hymn, organ and choir shaking the building, the words indiscernible through the brick and glass. I wandered past the library and the Y, across Fulton, and into the Festival. Gospel music filtered through the buildings, the food tents were just coming to life, streets were being swept and the scatter of people walking seemed as aimless as myself. Sunday mornings always seem to begin in a tired and off-hand way for those of us who don't attend the church of our choice.

Upon arriving at the pub, it was as expected: locked up tight. Not even the mice were about.

"No whiskey for you, Wiley," I whispered to myself, and shuffled in the direction of *Amazing Grace*.

I decided that if I couldn't drink her off my mind, then I would eat myself into a stupor, or at least until the bar opened. The Festival has over forty food tents, all run by volunteers, all from charities or churches, none of which sells the same thing. A simple menu of three or four items anchored by one specialty. I began my wandering buffet with a hot dog.

In Calder Plaza lies the main stage, the areas reserved for children, and two enormous tents housing all of the artwork that is for sale. Despite my best efforts and in spite of going from food tent to food tent, art booth to art booth, stage to stage, my mind would continually return to the Waitress. It was like trying to dig a hole at the beach and finding that the water will always seep into it. The Waitress, the picture of my brother, the gnawing feeling that I had not lived up to what she wanted, pried its way into every thought. I purchased an elephant ear and returned to the tent to see if I had missed something.

It was then, the sugar from the confection, my own distractions, and a press of people pushing me off to one side, I found myself staring at a painting I hadn't seen earlier. There was a haunting feeling of déjà vu. Framed in weathered barn wood and double matted perfectly was an acrylic of a meadow hidden in a forest. The light was from an unseen moon. There was a dusting of stars just at the top, the trees, lush, full and dark, were bookends at the sides, the bottom of the scene was the meadow floor, as dark as the trees yet somehow warmer, grassier, inviting. Centered in the frame was a large flat rock the size of a dining room table. Mossy and slightly damp, it had the dark look of limestone, the light of the moon seeming to shine directly upon it. Atop this, sitting up, looking out toward the edge of the meadow, was a calico cat. The style was like *Hughes*, the edges of objects slightly diffused, the tones of the colors not quite real. It had a dream-like quality and I stared at it for fifteen minutes as if remembering or trying to remember a place I had been before.

"Hey, mister. Do you like it? Wanna buy it?"

I blinked and looked over at a young man of perhaps twenty.

"You painted this?"

"It didn't paint itself. It has great light, doesn't it?"

"Yes it does. It's remarkable," I looked over at the price, "I only wish I could afford it."

"Yeah, well there's a lot of work in there. I understand though, money's money, you know."

There was a pause filled with the murmurs of the ever-growing crowds, announcements from a more distant stage, and nearer the opening riff to *Surfin' USA*.

"Thank God," he exclaimed. "I don't know how much more church music I could've listened to."

"That place in the painting, is it real?"

"Only in our dreams, mister, only in our dreams."

"Thank you," I said, giving the painting one last look, looking back to the artist and realizing he was special, challenged, the eyes set too wide, slanting at the corners. My stare held itself for that one uncomfortable second too long, and he looked away sheepishly.

I shuffled on, the elephant ear falling to my side, falling into a rubbish bin, wondering what time it was and if the pub was open. Somewhere close-by someone's watch chimed noon, the frequency high enough to be heard over *'bushy, bushy blonde hairdo, surfin' USA.'*

The first pint went straight to the bottom, bypassing the souvlaki, the meat pie, the egg rolls, the barbequed beef, pulled pork and chicken. The second pint followed in rapid succession, a Jameson thrown in to truly separate myself from this day. When the third arrived I looked over in mid-swallow to see the Sous Chef standing beside me.

"I take it the move is off."

"What was your first clue?"

"Well, it could have been the empty apartment with the front door wide open. I locked it back up for ya."

"Thanks."

"Or, it could have been the sight of the Waitress walking down the sidewalk on her way to her girlfriend's. I didn't bother to stop and chat."

"Thanks."

"Or, hey Jimbo," he looked over to the barman, "Happy Festival, Bud and a shot of Crown. Or it could be that the proposed gentleman in this relationship is at the bar getting plowed. But! The real tip-off in solving this mystery is probably in here." He held up an envelope with my name scratched on the front. "What do you think Mrs. Wiley has to say? Would you like me to read it?"

"Please."

He slid his thumb underneath the flap and pulled out a small stack of yellow post-it notes.

"Not one to stand on decorum, is she," Jimbo pointed out.

"No," I agreed, finishing my pint.

The Sous took a pull from his bottle of Bud, set it down and cleared his throat. "Dear, Wiley. Things seem a bit strained at the moment," he peeled off a post-it note, "I can't thank you enough for helping me recover," off went another post-it, "there was no one else I could turn to," peel, "and the sacrifices you made, you made out of love," peel, "but I'm feeling a bit trapped right now," another note, "and I feel like I need to find my own two feet," he held up the last post-it note, "so, I'm moving back in with Sally. I still love you very much and hope you will call me. Thanks, again." He handed me the pile of notes, sat down, and reacquainted himself with his beer.

"Well," was all that I could manage, my fourth pint reaching to join its friends.

"You're going to be better off, Wiley. Finally. What you couldn't see for yourself, the gods have finally made large enough that ya can't miss it."

"I somehow think this isn't quite over," I admitted.

"No," Jimbo nodded. "These things take a while to finally sort themselves out, and let's face it, she's really unpredictable."

"I have an idea," the Sous said, "Jimbo, when are you done?"

"I will be on the correct side of the bar as soon as you want me to be."

"Now will do. Your competition up the block has an open air seating area located precisely at the choke point for both sides of Festival."

"I understand where you're going with this and it's just what our Irish friend here needs."

"I don't understand and I seem to be pretty comfortable."

"Don't argue, and finish that up."

We downed our drinks, Jimbo joining us with a quick Jaegermeister, left the pub, and walked up the street. It was early enough that we had our pick of tables on the sidewalk. There beside us was a never-ending river of humanity, half of which were female, all of whom were dressed in shorts or skirts. The point of the exercise was not lost on me.

I humored them as best I could, my heart not in it, my thoughts far away. The whiskey turned into tequila, slid into Jaeger, and then became whiskey once again. The afternoon tumbled into evening as Festival was packed away before our bleary eyes, traffic returning to streets now filled with shadows. Around Ten I bid my friends a goodnight, staggered from the bar past the dark library, the empty church, and up the hill to an equally empty apartment.

At the top of my steps, sitting on the porch as if queen of the world, sat a cat. I knelt down, my balance causing some concern, and stroked her head. I whispered little cat noises and was rewarded with a condescending look. She rubbed against my legs and then darted up to the ledge beneath my window. I stood, swaying to an imaginary breeze, looked up at the bright moon wishing I were in the meadow on the rock in the painting.

Inside, everything was as it was when I left. I stumbled off toward the bedroom with the full effects of the alcohol hitting me like a bat, gravity pulling me toward the ground, my hips careening off of walls, off of furniture. The wine box lay there, nothing replaced, the life of Wiley looking like so much rubbish. I looked it over as best I could, a weekend's worth of rage coming to a head, and realized she had taken the picture of my brother.

I tried to clear the table. I tried to flip it over. I tried to hurl it across the room, but being so drunk only succeeded in losing my balance. For one hopeful second, I hopped on one foot, but this only provided more momentum for my head-long crash into the bricked-over fireplace. My last thought was not of the Waitress, or of my brother, or of the painting, or of my friends, it was that I knew the chicken at one particular barbeque had been undercooked. My right temple struck the bricks, there was a flash of bright lights, and I promptly began to throw up.

Before I passed out, the last thing I saw was the moon in the window silhouetting the cat, both her paws scratching furiously at the pane like a boxer working over a speed bag, her mouth mewing open in silence from beyond the glass, crazy eyes asking if I'm alright.

41

Through the window of my local, past the streams of mummers thronging by on the sidewalk, the fires of St. John's can be seen on the hillsides, silhouetted stick figures leaping over the flames in rites as old as mankind. It seems odd, sitting here, that we aren't with them, the distant bonfires glowing like the eyes of dragons, the raucousness of the scene muted by the thick glass. The Sous Chef and I, celebrating the Solstice in our own secular way, sit sipping on pints of Guinness and smoking way too many cigarettes. The air conditioning has failed, and for the dozen or so patrons it has become truly uncomfortable.

"I don't know how many times I told you, a dozen, maybe more, but that Waitress was trouble from the word go," the Sous Chef shouts to be heard over the roar of an enormous fan standing in the corner. Sans shroud, it is spinning and oscillating back and forth like the propeller of a vintage war bird.

"You're talking about the woman I love, you know."

"Wiley you dolt, she runs out in wind storms. She's walked out on you time and again. Wake-up!"

The conversation has gone on like this for what seems hours, the Sous Chef fading in and out, eerily reminding me of my dear mother back in dear, old Donegal. My mind seems to be reeling as if on a narcotic, the heat in the room softening the edges of my consciousness, the drink no more than bricks in the Grand Canyon.

Glancing around the pub I notice that it is no longer simply the bar on the corner of Pearl and Monroe, but an amalgamation of numerous bars I have been in throughout my Bacchanalian career. Beer mats lying on the bar just like in the British Isles, the same tattered old dart boards as in the small pub in Boston, and just outside the window the view of the hill and sea grass across the road from The Strand View Bar in Maghery. The sudden realization of this is making me a bit dizzy as the barmaid places two pints of lager in front of us.

"Where's the Guinness!" I demand.

"You've been cut-off. You'll have to drink lager."

"By orders of who?"

"Local ordinance. Sorry."

"You're famous, Wiley," the Sous Chef says, shaking his head, "you have your own stout law."

At that instant, a man walks into the pub through the swinging doors. His head is down, concealed by a black, knit cap pulled over his brow. He has on an unbuttoned pea jacket with one hand tucked in under the left side. In his visible hand dangling beside him is a glossy picture of a woman, a head and shoulders shot like a model would have in a portfolio.

"My God, that guy's gotta be baking in that thing. Man, Wiley, did you see this guy?"

"I'm looking right at him."

"It must be one hundred degrees in here."

"Maybe he has a cold," I offer.

"Maybe he has a problem."

I take a drink from the pint of lager and nearly gag when I come to find out it's a pint of poteen. "How in Christ did this turn into this!"

"Shut-up and drink your moonshine, ya Mickorpatorwiley," the Sous says, myself taken aback by this oddly familiar epithet.

Outside the window a dwarf walks by. In his hands he holds a dead duck, a fishing line around the creature's neck. Beside him is a mongoloid with paint smeared over unnatural features, an elephant's ear clutched from a twisted hand. They stop to look inside, the dwarf's eyes seeming to fall right on me. "Did you do this to him, Wiley," he mouths through the pane, lifting the duck up for all to see.

The bar suddenly feels too large, the exits too far away. An acid-like taste of fear rises in my mouth even over the taste of the poteen.

"There are a lot of weird people in the world, Wiley," the Sous Chef points out, the pair at the window drifting away.

The man in the pea coat is slowly walking from table to table, showing each person the photograph of the woman. People methodically shake their heads 'no', returning to drinks and muffled conversations. Smoke seems to blanket the ceiling, a fog exhaled by a dozen sets of burning lungs. I light another cigarette.

The man turns toward the Sous Chef and I, the barmaid nodding her head and pointing to us. I feel a pit open in my stomach, my heart skip a beat. He walks behind us, circling, until he is standing on our left, the Sous Chef's body blocking my view.

The Sous Chef suddenly leaps to his feet, turning his face to me, his pint of lager falling to the floor from his hand. My friend looks at me, eyes wide with terror, and screams my name.

The man in the pea coat holds up the photo, his voice seems to gurgle, the smell of his breath is rotten, "Have ya seen my girlfriend, Wiley?"

To my horror, the woman in the picture is the Waitress, her face distorted by bruises, bumps and cuts. Locks of hair falling over purple skin and black eyes, she stares away in defeat, eyes avoiding the lens.

I look up from the picture to the man in the pea coat. In the half-light of the bar I can begin to make out his face. The dark eyes that are almost black, the pug of a nose misshapen from being broke, the scars around the mouth and along the right temple, and by the corner of his left eye a tattooed tear that falls forever.

It is my older brother.

He hisses without moving his lips, "Who gave you the right to touch my woman, little brother!"

From his coat he pulls a revolver. I fall from my seat, pushing myself away in the same instant, barstools toppling out of the way. I am already trying to back away before I land on the floor. The sudden jar of tailbone hitting hard ground, my hands slipping, gaining no purchase. He lifts the weapon so that it is pointed at my face, the tips of the large bullets shining in their chambers, babies awaiting the sudden pangs of birth.

"Wiley? Are you alright!" An incongruous statement from a man about to blow my head off. I look from his lips, to the barrel, to his finger as he squeezes the trigger, the heat enveloping the weapon seeming to separate concussively, the flash blinding, I shriek without realizing I've done so.

My scream echoes around me like a gunshot across a valley. The sharp smell in the air is not cordite, but vomit and urine. I am disoriented, my face wet, my body wet, the ground too close, the light all wrong. There is a knocking on a door, desperate pleas. I rise to my knees, stagger to my feet and realize I am in my apartment.

Shaking, chest heaving, my head on a swivel trying to provide any clarity at all, shame and fear resting on either shoulder, my heart pounding so hard it feels as if someone is squeezing it in cupped hands.

"Wiley, are you alright in there?"

"I'm sorry!"

"I said, Wiley, are you alright?"

"Yes. Yes, who is that? Who are you? I'm fine."

"It's Lois and Phil from upstairs. We heard some awful noises and wanted to make sure you were okay. Can we come in?" I can feel their weight pressing against the door. Rapping, knocking, twisting the knob.

"No, no, just a bad dream. Bit too much to drink. I'm quite fine. Thanks for your concern," I try to dissuade them, the puddle of vomit at my feet, my legs shaking, body swooning, pants stained from having wet myself. I catch my reflection in the mirror and know there is no way I can let anyone see me.

"It would mean a great deal to us if we could make sure you're really okay, Wiley," Lois again, insistent.

In the other room, as if from oblivion, the phone begins to ring. The abruptness of it jars me. I slip, lose my balance once more and topple over swearing.

"Wiley, are you okay?"

"Goddamn it! I'm fine! Where's the bloody phone?"

The phone is ringing incessantly. I'm beginning to clear tables, throw things, swearing in Irish, stripping off soiled clothes.

"Well you seem to be okay, we'll leave you to it," Lois.

"Yeah, Wiley, hope your day gets better," Phil.

"Hello?" the phone for some reason is under the table.

"Wiley?"

"I'm sorry."

"Wiley, it's me."

"Ma? Is that you?"

"Yes. How are you, son."

"I'm not sure. The phone gave me quite a start."

"I'm sorry love, I know it's early there, but I had to call."

"Why? What is it? Has there been a bombing?"

"No son, nothing like that at all.

She pauses. I can hear her catch her breath as if from a great sob.

"It's your brother, Wiley. He's being released in less than a fortnight. We're going to London to meet him."

"What? How come he never wrote us, isn't he in the Maze, or Long Kesh?"

"No love, from Parkhurst, on the Isle of Wight. It's part of the agreement. Early release. He's been in since Eighty-Nine."

It was my turn to pause, the dream still burned into my mind's eye. I hadn't seen nor heard from my brother in over sixteen years. I ask the obvious only to break the silence.

"Who'd he kill? How many?"

"I don't know, Wiley. But he was in with the lads, for all those years. You had to suspect, son. At least he's alive, eh?"

"Aye."

"Son, could you meet us in London. Please."

What can I say, "Yes, I'll ring you tomorrow, when my head's cleared."

"Thanks, son. All the best."

I cradle the phone and set it down on the floor. I stand naked in the half-darkness, wet and afraid, the room feeling as if it could go on for an eternity.

Always before my eyes, no matter how hard I rub them, lay the image of my brother firing the gun, the hot, white light rushing to greet my forehead. All I can hear, as if itself was from a dream, is the warbling of a calliope and the warning from the dwarf at the carnival, 'Don't go to England.'

42

Sleep patters at my consciousness like raindrops on a windowpane. In vain, I am trying to prolong the pause that occurs just before you succumb, like the moments before a rainstorm when the sky seems to sigh and a peace falls over the world. Each waking moment gives hope that dreams have been washed away on a tide of Heineken, driven by trade winds that smell faintly like whiskey.

Below me, as the jet rolls out of its bank and continues to climb, Detroit spreads out as a grid of lights, the dizziness of height and space buoyed by the aircraft's stability. The things that are at once familiar spin away as the planet turns beneath the plane. The faces, buildings, and neighborhoods become images tucked beneath a blanket of clouds. There is that feeling of being alone, of there being nothing but sky, plane, and self.

It is the memories that pull us from this womb. All too human, we take these unhurried moments to catalogue, to reflect, and in this exercise we dredge up all the feelings, the love as well as the pain.

I wonder which of these streets the Waitress grew up on. Where it was that all her memories had been formed. Friends, first loves, battles won and battles lost, somewhere below is where all that took place.

I have barely heard from her. The space she had asked for seeming as wide as this city, my last image of her is in my flat, holding that picture of my brother, her lips whispering words I could not hear from across the room.

I settle back into my seat, pull myself closer together from the chill, and return to the window. The dense, cold plastic is beginning to reflect my face, as well as the cabin. It always seems so odd that so thin a surface separates us from the vacuum, from thirty thousand feet.

My brother's impending release from prison in England has caused me a great deal of soul searching. The snapshots of growing-up mixing all too well with the images from the nightmare I had a fortnight ago. The gun aimed at my head, the picture of the Waitress in his left hand, and the warning from the dwarf are as surreal as watching my father and brother fight on top of the Christmas tree.

I can still see his face appearing from the alley, still feel his strong hand pulling me into a Dublin pub as a wanted man, the smell of endless cigarettes clinging to him. The strangeness of it all makes me question my own existence, pinch the fat of my hand, echo a prayer.

Pulling a pint of Polish vodka from my pocket, an odd look from the gentleman sitting beside me, I let the clear liquid fall into my mouth, "Nastrovia," I say to him in a hoarse voice with a skewed accent, eyelids partly shrouding eyes that are red and far-off. I turn from him to look back out the window and watch the world slide further away.

The Sous Chef had slipped the bottle into my jacket pocket as we hugged each other good-bye. My friend having been kind enough to drive me to Detroit the day previous, we had stayed with relatives of his who lived in Hamtramck, their generosity as thick as the butter we spread on home-made potato pancakes.

When they learned I was from Ireland, they insisted on taking me to every Irish pub in Detroit. All it did was remind me where I was going, and why. The pictures on the walls not unlike those in the Republican Clubs back in The North; my accent turning the conversations into the same dialogue, like an old nag continually walking from the cottage to the pub.

"Do you know the Marching Season is starting this week-end?"

"What do you think will happen at Drumcree this year?"

"D'ya think Gerry's gettin' the job done?"

"I myself am lookin' for a change."

"Do you have a few extra bob for some o' Rory's boys?"

"There'll never be peace, not there."

No, there'll never be peace, what the hell would we have to sing about?

The Sous Chef, sensing the change of mood in me, clapped me on the back and mentioned perhaps a change of venue. We dove into his cousin's van and made our way back to Hamtramck, pulling up in front of a nondescript red brick building.

"What's this?" I asked, smiles spreading over the wide, Slavic faces surrounding me.

"It's the Polish-Falcon hall. The drinking's not so heavy in here."

It was one of those nights that never seem to end. The blinds being pulled, pitchers of beer sloshing to the one, two, three of dozens of different polkas, the lyrics benignly tucked behind the veil of another language. Here were a people to which smiling comes easy.

In the morning when we arrived at his Aunt's house, a breakfast of eggs, sausages and breads, golabki, pierogis and placki awaited. The smells from the kitchen as welcome as an embrace from an old friend, the ghosts of the past kept safely at bay, there was no talk of Ireland, of war, or of grief. They spoke only of football, their jobs, and where which relatives would be celebrating the Fourth of July.

Because of the holiday, the Sous Chef decided to drop me off at the airport rather early. He felt so bad about leaving me hours before my flight that he bought me the half pint of Wyborowa.

"I'm sorry Wiley, but I can't see you off any more than this. I don't get to see these folks very often and it would be rude not to spend some time with them."

"It's no worries, man. I'm sure there'll be a bar in here somewhere."

He looked at me with concern.

"Wiley, the last time you left, I thought you'd never come back. This time is different. There's a change in you. Like you're too afraid to fight. Like you know you're not coming back no matter what."

I pulled back from him a bit, my eyes narrowing as sunlight glinted off a car bonnet.

"You take care of yourself, man. You understand?" I was taken aback, his arms enfolding me in a great bear hug. "Don't do anything stupid, Wiley. Gut it out. Do the right thing. And then come home. Right?"

"Aye," was all I could say, and then he was gone. His ancient car disappearing around a corner of the car park, the belt still slipping, the muffler still filled with holes and the engine sounding too much like a polka.

After a slow walk through the international terminal, a train to the main terminal, and then another long walk, I sat at The Innkeeper's bar drinking Heineken and shots of Bushmills. Behind me, for hours, I watched the workday of uncountable jets as the world went about its business. They could have all disintegrated in flames and still not pulled me from my thoughts.

Several hours before my flight, I returned to the international terminal, checked in my bag, and received my boarding pass, the flights of stairs leading up to the waiting area testing my heart as surely as the lack of sleep and the numerous glasses of beer. I settled into the next-to-last stool in the crowded bar with thoughts of metal detectors, check points, and interrogations spinning in my head.

What had my brother really been through? How had he survived in prison? On the street. As a volunteer. How had he survived at all?

They had approached me as they had approached him. First with questions about what was going on in the Six Counties. When my feigned diffidence did not brush them aside, they picked at my guilt, the assembly line need for volunteers giving rise to baser forms of recruitment.

"How can ya just sit and watch while they kick the livin' shite out of yer own people."

"You've relatives in Omagh. What d'ya think is happening to them?"

"Isn't it time ya did yer bit, Wiley?"

"Ya have ta, it's yer duty. Every generation."

"Why not son. Are ya afraid?"

"Or is it because you've got an English heart?"

"You drink too much."

"I beg yer pardon?" I stammered, shaken abruptly from the mists of time by a Mid-western twang.

"I said," she cocked a tiny, worn face at me with a perfect look down the nose, "you drink too much. I've been watching you. Seen a thousand like you. You'll drink yourself to death."

"I'm afraid I don't know what business of yours it truly is."

"Ah, you're Irish. I had an Irish husband once."

"Did ya now."

"He was a drinker as well. Nearly killed him. All the men in my life have been drinkers."

"You should stop meeting your husbands in bars."

I paused to finish my Heineken, this puritan interruption to my thoughts going past annoying on nerves well past frayed.

"You know, you'll never find what you're looking for in the bottom of a bottle."

"I love that phrase, but it sounds much nicer in Irish."

"Really." She seemed interested, so as the last call for my flight came over the PA, I slid off my bar stool, laid down a tip, and turned to face her.

"Aye, pogue mahone."

Now, that exchange offering both a smile and a shake of the head, I take one last look out the window of the plane before sleep pulls me into her fold. Fireworks reach up from the Detroit River like tiny colored mushrooms. Red, white, and blue, framed in gold and green, they appear and silently recede. Independence Day. Oh, how things change in a year.

The lights have dimmed, the soft hush of snoring, of sleeping people, the oxygen tweaked just so, in-flight service over until morning, I give up the ghost of waking, of consciousness, and surrender.

There is then, suddenly, that one startling, all-at-once bright moment, a flash of a second in which disbelief and recognition are fused, the horror of the immediate, jarring reality plainly there in front of my own unbelieving eyes. Impact followed by a car crash followed by a gut-lifting drop, hope for a split second as a feeling of calm gives way to tearing and then that awful wind deafening even the screams of the people around me. Jagged swaths of cold blackness cut across the blinking lights of the cabin and I realize it is the outside, that I am miles above the earth and the glow of orange is jet fuel alight, engulfing the plane before it breaks up entirely. The roar of this chaos suddenly ends, the fuselage now in pieces, the white noise of air rushing by as I fall, terrified but free, burning sections lighting the night, streaking flames reminding me of Bosch. I tumble as if on a roller coaster until the wind rips at my belt, and in one great tug I feel myself pulled from my seat, pulled into blackness, into the dark, into whatever execution God has planned for me.

But it doesn't end. In one moment I am tumbling blind, and now, the very next moment, I am lying in wet grass, rain upon my face, my clothes soaked, my body shivering. I blink hard, turning my face from the falling water. The night sky is too dark to discern how wide the sky has opened. It smells familiar, haunting, a memory of it begins to emerge, the violence of the plane ripping apart giving way to a different violence. The recognition grows, takes a form that becomes malignant. I turn my head and see the apple tree, the broken barracks. My heart sinks. I sense something very old, something horrible approaching. Hands grab at my bedclothes so quickly I shriek. I look up into the face, fear then giving way to hate, to anger, and punch once, twice, again.

"Sir. Sir! Are you all right? Sir!"

Once again there is the confusion, the panic, the embarrassment.

"I, I'm sorry. So very sorry. I, I just hate flying. Not good at it."

"It's okay. Relax. Would you like a water?" The stewardess is very close, hiding me from the concerned passengers. The man next to me can't get far enough away.

"That would be lovely," I say to her, thinking to myself of uisce beatha, the water of life.

Calm is restored. Apologies made with a silent nod and submissive eyes, I return to my vigil of staring out the window into the blackness, my reflected face hanging there above the clouds.

When the man beside me falls back asleep, I pull the vodka from my coat, fill my mouth, and ask Saint Christopher to protect me. I do this until it is empty, chasing it with a bottle of white wine left over from a dinner I didn't eat.

As the plane skips across the firmament, the throb of the engines becoming a lullaby, just before I slip into dreamless sleep, a melody and its lyrics are the last thing I remember. A tune from the other side of the ocean, from the other side of my life, heard earlier in someone's Tipperary Lounge, it causes me to pause, its relevance ringing not quite clearly enough:

To and fro in my dreams I go,
And I kneel and pray for you
Where slavery fled all the rebel dead,
Where they fell in the Foggy Dew

43

There is a gentle hand upon my shoulder, quiet words pulling me from distant shores, a glass of water, a smile and an understanding countenance from having dealt with all manner of passengers. I stretch, as best as one can in coach, sip water that burns on a dry throat, and wonder just where we are.

Out the window, blinking eyes disoriented from a broken night's sleep, parting clouds reveal the English countryside as dawn throws a faint glow on villages and fields. My ears make adjustments to the decreasing altitude, my perception just as fuzzy during descent as it was last night during departure.

The approach to Heathrow takes the plane over the center of London. The Tower and the Bridge are golden with the rising sun; the same sun that once never set on the British Empire, now greets the snarls of traffic that wends its way into Chelsea, Westminster, and The City. Tufts of clouds momentarily hide the buildings and boroughs I once called home, a place as wrapped up in history as it is with the fog that creeps up the Thames. Violent, vibrant and ancient, exuding an aura of wealth and dynasty, this town moves to a rhythm as old as the tide.

It is no wonder that the Irish have flocked here in such great numbers. The ones who were seeking glory and fame, luck and fortune, those who were hiding from home, from pregnancy and shame, from priests who rule over villages that seem like glass beehives. Or those who were just trying to dig for gold in the streets.

It drew me here, a young man keen to set his mark, eager to leave the bog lands and pubs of Donegal for the concrete and clubs of Soho. I spent many a night in blissful, drunken ignorance, but more's the time that I would sit up with the light on, a chair against the door, writing my mother on how scared I truly was.

I gather my thoughts while I can, the nervous seconds before wheels reach Earth, let go a sigh and try to ground myself as the plane touches down. I tell myself, 'no worries, relax, just go with the flow'. The image and words of the dwarf flickering in my mind's eye like an old News Reel.

The lights come on brighter, we stretch and search for carry-on. Eyes barely meeting mine, the man beside me smiles politely. I offer him a tired excuse of my not flying well, which he accepts with a 'good luck' and a 'cheery-o.'

I have unexplained jitters, as if I had drunk several cups of coffee too many, the long walk and wait for baggage seeming even longer. Tired circles are spinning at the corners of my eyes, the shreds of a migraine trying to piece itself together. I begin breathing deeply and evenly, fingers massaging temples, waiting for the tendrils of pain to recede, only to jump as a klaxon announces the arrival of our baggage.

In the queue, waiting for the immigration officer to check my passport, the heel of my right thumb working pressure points on the palm of my left hand, I notice the uneasiness amongst the staff. I remember what it was like being Irish in London before the IRA's ceasefire, when your accent would make even the kindest of people suspicious. With the Good Friday Agreement collapsing and the threat of a renewed and vigorous campaign, security seemed a bit edgy as I approached the thick, shock resistant glass and metal booth.

"So, you're not American, you're from Donegal. How long have you resided in the States? Six years? Do you have your papers? Is O'Wary your actual name? Rather infamous name at the moment, you know. As I recall, he's from Donegal as well."

He picked up a phone, there was a brief exchange and then he held the line. The queue of people behind me growing impatient, a woman in uniform began motioning them toward the other booths. It felt like every eye was on me, assumptions running through their heads: illegal alien, drugs runner, terrorist. I wondered how many remembered me punching the seat in front of me, a shriek from bad dreams, assistance.

After a lengthy conversation on the phone, the officer flipping through my passport very methodically, he set the receiver down and stared at me with a blank and accusing look, contempt turning up the corners of his mouth like a small dog.

Two officers, one with a German shepherd, the other with a short black rifle, turned the corner and approached the booth.

"Are you O'Wary?" the one without the dog asked.

"He is," the immigration officer replied.

"If you would, please."

I was taken along a narrow corridor to an empty room that had a gray metal table, two metal folding chairs that were long since rubbed away to a dull gray, and a picture of the Queen on one wall. The two officers took my suitcase and carry-on, looked me up and down curiously, and then left me alone for quite some time.

So, this is the way it's going to be. Go with the flow, huh? It never fails, no matter how far from home you wander, home lands right back in your lap.

I rested my elbows on the table, rubbed temples and breathed very slowly, the tendrils of migraine thickening, spreading. Beneath this I could hear quite clearly the calliope, the dwarf, and the sound of rain on canvas tents.

A short, stout man with dark receding hair and deep-set eyes entered the room, the sound of the door opening beginning a drum-like throb at the base of my skull. Two large men walked in behind him. He sat down opposite me, tapping and flipping a nub of chewed pencil on the table's surface. He had an easy-going manner that didn't seem to fit him, and he looked alarmingly like Bob Hoskins. There was a sense of something coiled tightly inside, like one of those cans of nuts that snakes jump out of once you've undone the top. He smiled, teeth stained with nicotine and coffee, and sat forward in his chair. With a nod, the two uniforms shut the door and stood behind me.

"My name is Nigel, I'm head of security for this terminal. How was your flight? You flew British Air, right? What part of the States? Great Rapids? Oh, right, near Chicago. One of the big lakes is near there, isn't it? Nice. Would you like a cigarette?"

Before I could answer he had already pulled one out for himself, then tossed the pack to me. My puzzled look caused him half a smile, the pencil in his hand still tapping.

"You're from Donegal. You lived here, in England, didn't you? London What part? West end, really. What did you do? A chef. What part of Donegal? Dun what? Not Letterkenny? No. Relatives in the North? Omagh. Shame what happened there, isn't it."

He scratched at the table with the point of his pencil, illegible graffiti making a doodle that was barely discernible from the faded metal. One of the men behind me rocked from foot to foot.

"Your sister lives here in London, doesn't she? West Ham. Very good. When's the last time you spoke with your brother? Then how'd you know he was being released? Your mam. Lovely. How Irish. So the whole clan is here, then. Not your Da, right. Passed on now, hasn't he."

He locked eyes with me, cold eyes, the affable, nonchalance suddenly smudged away like chalk from a blackboard.

"Your brother's associates. They ever talk to you? Not once. Not in Boston? Not in Chicago? Not ever. You've never seen the hat passed on St. Pats Day, stood for the Soldier's

Song and dropped some bucks in a tin can? Not at all. Just a chef, huh. When your brother left home, he never came back to you? His bosses never tried to swing you aboard? Am I knocking on any doors here, Wiley?" his thick knuckles rapping the table, the pencil nub squeezed in his other hand.

"Do you know why he's in prison? Are you familiar with Battersea, near the park? Very popular. You were living here then. Do you remember? Come on, now. Think about it."

I didn't have to. I knew right where he was going. There was a small pub on Latchmere that had been blown-up one summer night. It was a place frequented by soldiers and sailors. One of the officers opened up a folder and set a dozen black and white photographs in front of me. I couldn't look away fast enough.

"He had materials traced to that bomb," his voice began to rise, an eyelid twitched. "Bloody good barrister, not all the charges stuck. Three people died. Look, Wiley. Look at what's left of this one. Twenty-nine years old, Wiley. Lindsay was her name. She'd just named her daughter a fortnight before. Look, Wiley! Its bloody hard to tell she was a woman, isn't it."

I went to stand up, the bile rising in my throat, the migraine becoming a freight train, my stomach clenching and unclenching involuntarily. The officer on my right slammed me back down into the chair, the force of it sending a shock up my back. He kept his hand on my shoulder, thumb and forefinger squeezing the bit of muscle that runs along the top.

"I hate the fact he's being released. I hate the whole, bloody agreement, and I hate Tony fucking Blair. But mostly,

Wiley, I hate the fact that you've all come to greet him. That you've all come here to make merry over your terrorist brother and his sick fucking friends."

And with that, as if on cue, the officer on my left brought the back of his hand across my left temple. The room swam ever so slightly, spots gathering before my eyes like a distant flock of birds, the light flickering like an old movie on the periphery. I lost my balance from the blow, half-sitting, half falling out of the chair. I tried to catch myself by grabbing the table, my fingernails bending backward as they just caught the edge

The stout man continued to talk, though I don't know what it was he was saying. I wanted to look away, but the plain white walls made me dizzy. I looked down only to see the half-corpses in the pictures spread out on the table, so instead I looked up at the picture of Queen Elizabeth, a deigned smile falling upon her subjects.

At some point, my eyes watering from the headache, blurring my vision, a set of hands pointed my head in the direction of the man.

"We know all about you. We will be right behind you. One slip and you'll spend more time in rooms like this with people who possess a lot less restraint. Got me, Pat?"

I nodded, the three of them leaving me there, the dossier left open, the photos as grisly as ever. My eyes ground with the feel of sandpaper, my temple throbbed on its own, and an out-of-tune orchestra hammering Stravinsky began to ring in both my ears, salty tears landing on the metal table not unlike raindrops on canvas tents.

After an hour or so, the two large men returned. One collected up the folder while the other hauled me out of my seat and led me to the door. I tried to say something in my own defense, but the words would not form. I was led down a different corridor where we walked through a door and out into a hallway that connected to the main lobby.

There, waiting for me, was my mother and my sister, a young woman in uniform standing beside them. My mother, the tears clouding her eyes, pulled out a hanky and dabbed at the blood that had dried on my temple. With her other hand, she gently touched my chin so as to hold my face still when I winced. It was a thing that only a mother could do, a gesture filled with love, concern and understanding.

As we turned to leave, the ringing in my ears beginning to fade, the snake-like fingers of the migraine pulling back beneath their rock, I could hear behind me a hissed aside from one of the officers, "Fucking Irish," To which, we walked away from them, away from the terminal, and out into the gray clouds of London.

44

In England this time of year, night falls with the softness of a very clever thief. The planet's northern half, tilted ever so slightly further toward the sun, slips into evenings that are nearly as light as day; and then, like your wallet, the sun is taken from you before you even realize.

Now, in the dreamy haze of dusk as a few stars dimly shine above the trees in Kensington Park, I rub my swollen temple and stare past a statue into space. The day was as long as any I can remember, and it was one I would just as soon forget. My eyes shut against the headache, only to see the course of the day unfold once more.

In the taxi on the way from the airport, I learned that my brother would not be released for a day or two. A last-minute drive to repeal the commutation of his sentence had been pushed through by the conservatives. They were trying to prove that the Good Friday Agreement was no longer being honored by the IRA, and therefore that all provisions were null and void. A rally was planned on his behalf at a St. Patrick's Club in Chelsea. It was to this that we were headed.

The driver was kind enough to take The Great West Road, a slower and more relaxing trip into London. The road winds through a series of towns that were once villages, and a handful of farms holding out to the sprawl of the city. In a short time the River Thames appeared beside us, rolling to sea with a dignity that could be felt as well as seen. If there is a spring from which comes England, it surely must be the source of this great river.

The St. Patrick's Club is on a small lane that connects to Cromwell Road. It has been raided innumerable times in the past, and a half dozen black cars sat parked across the street, men with short hair taking pictures and notes of all who entered. The taxi came to a stop, the driver out very quickly, curious looks on his Indian face as he wrestled my bags from the boot.

A security camera above the door stared at us, a red light illuminating a spider web. I rang the bell; a buzzer sounded, the click of a bolt, and we entered the club.

There was a hail in Irish, laughter from another corner, and the sound of a pint glass hitting the old, stone floor. We blinked hard against the darkness, our eyes adjusting slowly to the change in light. I held my bags out before me in order to feel my way, the sound of canvas brushing brick.

I felt the clap of a hand on my back, and a palm upon my cheek, slapping it ever so gently.

"Wiley, *conas ta tu? An bhfuil aithne agat orm?*"

I stared at him for a long moment, my own language slow to me, my eyes still focusing.

"No, I don't. Wait. Donovan. I thought you were dead."

"No, just old. I've been here in London for a very long time."

"The last time I saw you I was twelve. Do you know there are still trout in that hole near Crocknafarragh," I said to him, my mouth agape at the apparition before me.

"You're like your father and your brother, you never forget a thing. So. ya've come to see him out. There's a lot of mixed feelings on this, there is. There's people on both sides who want ta see 'im dead. But in 'ere, he's a hero."

The pictures of the bombing still fresh in my mind, the twisted bodies burnt beyond recognition, I couldn't help what followed.

"A hero? Are ya 'aving me on? Blowing up a wee mother and some sailors who'd never set foot in Ireland in their lives. What kind of fucking hero does that?" I couldn't hold back the hate. My eyes exploding in fresh tears, I flung my bag to the side knocking over a chair and a table. I held my hands up to challenge anyone and everyone, the tension of this long day finally about to release itself from my chest. It seemed my destiny to now reduce myself to the same mindset.

A man dressed like a dandy came around from the side of the bar, his hands up, palms open, trying to calm me down.

"Young man, young man, please. This is a happy occasion. These folks have come a long way to be here. Please. Whether you agree or disagree, support or don't support, it has nothing to do with you, not today. Have a jar and relax, right?"

He took a step closer laying a hand on my shoulder, a cheesy smile across a ruddy face. It felt like he was selling me a particularly bad car. I would have none of it. I swung wildly at him, happy to be on common ground and have someone to go at. He ducked the half-hearted punch with ease, shaking his head at my folly and at the same time giving a wink to someone outside the fray.

Before I knew what had happened, two massive arms had plucked me off the floor and spun me around. I was looking at what had to be the largest head I had ever seen, its forehead already rushing towards my left temple.

The room swam ever so slightly, spots gathering once more like birds on the horizon. My knees buckled and I started to fall. I could hear Donovan trying to explain that I was an O'Wary and in fact the very brother of the man the rally was for in the first place.

My mother, the only soul with any sense on this rough and tumble day, brought me a glass of Jameson's and once more tended to my wounds. The tears in her eyes from before were replaced with a look of wry sagacity.

"Ack Jaysus, Wiley, you and your soddin' mouth. Don't you know who these people are?"

Deliberations on my behalf had not held up. This was a joyous occasion, a comrade in arms being released from the jaws of the enemy, and my behavior would not be tolerated. If I wanted to cool off for a couple hours, that might be allowed; however, under the circumstances, another day would probably be more acceptable.

Donovan made a purchase from the barman, grabbed me by the arm, and led me out of the club. My mother told me to catch a taxi back to the club tonight for the dance, or the key would be under the mat at my sister's in West Ham. I turned from the sea of curious faces, Irish smiles and laughter following me out the door, and Donovan and I staggered past the row of cops and into London.

We wandered through Chelsea to the Thames, stopping to stare at the slow-moving brown water, gulls turning lazy circles in the sky, a handful of boats slugging their way up and down the river.

"Jaysus, what an eejit I am," I said, leaning against a stone railing over the river.

"Aye, ya haven't changed much," Donovan agreed, a smirk spreading across a wizened face. He reached inside his coat and produced a bottle of Power's. "'Ere's lookin' up yer old address."

I joined him, the tension ebbing, the whiskey acting doubly strong on the lack of sleep, silence interrupted by a river tug leaving its berth, three long whistles followed by two short.

"Have ya seen him?" I asked Donovan.

"No. I tried for years, but he was always in solitary and his regular status had too many restrictions. They don't like him very much. He wrote a few letters. Haphazard, like. But they just seemed to get more distant, further apart, stranger."

I thought of the postcard he had sent my mother, the writing in crayon.

"How've ya been keepin', old friend?" I asked.

"Not well. My joints are nearly stiff with the rheumatism. Must be age."

"I'm sure it's not the drink."

"Oh God, no. Only thing that keeps me alive." He took a pull of Power's. "I do miss Ireland, but I love this town." He handed me the bottle and smiled, "Would ya mind very much for a bit of a stroll with an old geezer?"

"I'd be delighted," I replied, and took him by the arm as the old chums we were.

We followed the river, stopping at several pubs in Pimlico, to the City, crossing and re-crossing the Thames, bridge after bridge, as if the very act of fording the water was a blessing. Soon, the late afternoon sun was casting the first shadows since morning, we then wandered back through Mayfair, along the Bayswater Road to Hyde Park.

Donovan chatted away. Stories of youth, of being a young man, of growing up and old in London, he was happy that fortune had provided him with an audience. I suspected he knew where we were going, that there was ultimately a destination in mind, but it sure didn't seem like it, the points of the compass seeming cast to the wind. We left Bayswater for the Ring Road, called West Carriage Drive once upon a time, and entered the park, dusk settling behind us between the buildings, streetlamps beginning to glow before us.

We stopped on the bridge over the Long Water, swans gliding below us, their long necks moving like soft metronomes. Two Bobbies walked past, Donovan's hand leaving the bottle inside his jacket, a conspiratorial sideways glance at them to me.

"This is the last place I saw your brother, Wiley, over there, a ways, by the statue. Two nights before they picked him up. I couldn't believe he was still in London."

I turned and looked back out across the pond, "Then he did it, didn't he?"

"Yes, I believe so. That and probably much more."

"How, why? I mean all those innocent people," I protested.

"Ack, Jaysus Wiley, you've turned all your hatred inwards, he turned his outwards. I don't know the reasons. God only knows. But you O'Warys have always been a fiercely confusing lot. Bloody angry. Angry and confusing."

There was a long pause, the sting of the words lying bright before us. He extended the bottle, cap off, an apology already written on his face. When I took the bottle, his hand patted my shoulder, "Not that ya's wouldn't do anything for anyone, to be sure Whenever I was in need, of recent or way back when, your sister, your mother, your aunt, they was always there. Always," he made an emphatic nod of the head, an hrumph! of sureness.

We resumed walking across the bridge, turning to the right at the other side.

"How did he seem?" I asked.

"He wasn't scared, or desperate, or panicked, not at all. No last stands, no. I'd say he seemed tired, as if the fight had left him and he was ready to rest. I mean, it had to be exhausting, the stress and all. Understand, he was on the run for nearly twenty years, most of that living in shit hole safe houses alone."

"I just don't understand what would drive him to that for so long a time. I mean, in the early years, when the marches had all ended so bloody and the North was in chaos, yeah, sure, but for all that time. Where does that kind of hate come from?"

"For most of the lads, Wiley, it's from having no alternatives. No jobs, no hope. For others, it's the eight hundred years of humiliation, exploitation, and repression. I myself was a volunteer, back in Ireland, back in the fifties."

"You? Really?"

"We were a desperate lot, inept, unorganized. Oh by Christ we were bad," he placed a hand on my chest, "stand back John James, there's a wee mistake," he shook his head at some private memory, "Somehow we managed to survive," he froze for a moment, looked at me leaning in close, " I can't say for sure what drove your brother, but it was deeper. I don't think it had anything to do with the Brits or the troubles. He woulda fought any army in front of him, but to this day I could not tell you why."

We turned left, away from the water, dusk settling into night. The bottle was passed again, its contents nearly empty, our gait becoming a stagger. Donovan began to lean heavily into me, his head tilting toward my shoulder, and I wondered how many Irishmen had slept in this park. I found a bench and eased him onto the seat. He looked up, "This is the last place I saw your brother. He led me here from the bridge then, and I lead you here today," and with that, Donovan closed his eyes.

I sat down beside him, placed my jacket around his shoulders, and looked up at the dim shape of the statue before me, soft snores beginning to emanate from his chest. I took the bottle of John Power's and filled my mouth with the last swallow.

Above, the early stars look down at me with cold indifference. The hum of London, like its glow, hangs beyond the trees. Crickets and frogs are playing the oldest of symphonies, night-noise like lightly brushed tympani. The park is empty, still, only that odd summer breeze that comes about each evening.

I let my eyes focus on the statue of Peter Pan, the grace of his feigned movement implied perfectly. He stands on a bronze stump while fairies and woodsy creatures ring the bottom. I let out a deep sigh, the smell of the whiskey hanging just below my nose.

Enough of bombs, security and corpses, of police, resistance and hate, this is as close to Never-Never Land as I will get. And as night nestles in beside us, that wonderful hush of dusk like a living blanket, I try to find that one happy thought.

45

In the North, when the skins on the drums of war were being tightened, and men in smithies were pounding steel edges keen, a lone piper would take up the Pipes and prepare to call the lads to arms. The thin, haunting whine from atop mountains, near the entrance to passes, at the confluence of rivers wending through glens, would prick the hairs on the backs of a hundred necks.

On this day, the Glens of Antrim lying across the Irish Sea, the lone piper stands in front of a dartboard. The call of his pipes, deafening in the enclosed space, carries through no mountain mist, but hangs in the air with cigarette smoke. The hearts of dozens of Northern Gaels in this St. Pat's Club having heard the call to arms, and of those here, many have answered.

I leaned against the doorframe to the snooker room, looking more like an adolescent at a wedding than the brother of a man being released from prison. The crowd, nervous with anticipation, milled about in front of me, pints in everyone's hands despite it being only ten in the morning.

My mother, two solicitors, and a representative from Sinn Fein were the only ones allowed to greet him outside the prison. Thankfully, England's attention had been turned to the heavens for a solar event. The front-page condemnations of my brother for his conviction in the bombing were relegated to back pages. The Daily Mirror carried the only front-page article, 'A Total Eclipse of The Heart.'

The empty billiard room beckoned, my eyes suddenly rapt upon someone staring at me from an ancient picture. It was a 1920 photograph of Michael Collins, your man standing nearly at attention, head casting a piercing gaze over his shoulder past the camera, he nonchalantly tugs his gloves tighter, the sheer will of the man emanating from the print. History has been kind to the big fella. His cold, shrewd tactics and his strength of deliberation having been softened by the years, make no mistake, as hard a man has not lived, ask his enemies. But then, there would be no Ireland without him.

My escape into yesteryear is broken by a wave that ripples through the crowd, crashing before me as if I stood at the end of a pier. There are a couple of shouts from upfront and the smell of exhaust issuing through the club. The pipes begin to keen The Foggy Dew, voices soften, and necks crane for a view.

He cuts through the throng like a rock star, two large men moving people out of the way. My mother, right behind him, seems a bit flushed with all the excitement, and looks very much out of place. There was instantly a volley of hails and welcomes falling around him like shells. A glass of whiskey thrust into one hand, a cigar placed in the other. The crowd applauds; their hero has returned.

A gentleman steps out from behind the bar, crosses all the way along its length, and embraces my brother. He whispers something in my brother's ear that yields a smile. The dandy then motions to the barman who quickly reaches beneath the bar and pulls out an unmarked bottle of purplish liquid. The barman pours two fine crystal glasses full, the crowd quieting as the two men receive them. The dandy looks my brother in the eye, narrows his own, raises his glass of poteen, and offers a toast in Irish. "*Beannact De leat. Ta failte romhat. Coladh slan.*"

They down the plum-colored spirits, neither taking their eyes off the other, drop the glasses to the floor, the tiny explosions of crystal popping in our ears, and embrace once more. Then, as quick as that, the dandy leaves with the two large men, not out the front but by way of the back.

It was then that my brother spotted me. He had the barman draw two pints of Guinness, looks back to me and gives me a sideways nod. I smile back wanly and duck around the corner to the snooker tables.

The room feels cloistered. The pantheon of Republican stars staring at me from walls filled with photographs and paintings Wolfe Tone. Emmett. Parnell. Connolly. Pierce. Sands. You could almost feel their pulse, smell the powder burning and hear their raspy voices reaching out from the grave, 'Join us.'

I turn to find my brother standing right behind me.

"Jaysus! You'll scare a man to death creepin' around like that."

"Sorry, man. So, little brother, why aren't ya in with the rest of the lads?"

"Ack, it's just not my crowd."

"What if we were all a load of cooks and chefs, like. Then would ya belly up to the bar and greet yer long, lost brother?"

"You a chef? Ya'd still be in prison."

He laughed. A great, loud laugh that sent him into a fit of coughing. So much coughing that his face turned red and he reached inside his sport coat for a puffer.

"Jaysuss, sorry, Wiley. Don't ever go to prison, little brother."

He regained himself quickly, fixing me with a grave look.

"It's hell, Wiley. It really is. On the way here I just started to cry. Not over any crimes, or years lost, or things I could have done, girls I could have married. No. It's the space. The brilliant sight of wide, open spaces. And just seeing people walk through them, with no realization, without ever thinking about the marvelous space around them." He looked down at the floor, muttered something to himself, and then downed his pint in one go. "By God, I'll die before I go back again."

A silence fell over the two of us. The pall of the situation, of his past, of the blank, staring faces in the pictures that surrounded us, it felt like an eddy beginning to widen.

"So, little brother," he said, looking over his shoulder, a nervous tic tugging at his right cheek, "I understand you're in Amerikay. What's that like then," his empty hand received another pint, a barman having come and gone as quietly as a ghost.

"It's alright. It's different. It's not a bit like Donegal."

"Tank, fukin' God fer dat, den," he said, trying to sound as if he'd just walked off the bog. Once more we laughed, the joy in it chased out of the room by the dead soldier's faces.

"No really, is it nice? I mean, there's loads of space there, isn't there?"

I nodded.

"There's loads of money there too, aye?"

"Aye."

"Girls?"

I blushed.

"Wiley! Have ya a sweet Yankee back in the States?"

He knew he had me, and as any older brother would, he went in for the kill. First, by rubbing my hair. Then, by tapping me with his great fists in my ribs. Finally, by picking me up straight away. At that point I had had it, and we went to the ground, Guinness splashing the floor, my pint glass crashing beneath a picture of Mairead Farrell, heads spinning around to see the commotion. Before I knew what had happened, he was standing over me, my wallet in his hands. I was stunned to see how good he could still move.

"Wiley, ya have a picture of Mom in 'ere. You're not thinking about joining the seminary, are ya?"

I feigned a punch to his groin as I picked myself up off the floor, instead cursing him in Irish. He turned the page in my wallet to the one picture I had of The Waitress.

"Wiley, who is this? Is this her? Unbelievable. I've seen her face somewhere. In a dream," his voice trailed off, his eyes looking through the picture, through the wallet, past me. He turned his head to the ceiling as if he expected God himself to answer.

"Wiley, do ya believe in dreams? Do ya have any dreams?" he implored, eyes wide, child-like.

"Dreams?" I replied, shaky images of stairs, blackthorn, a face not quite all there, "Oh yeah, lots of 'em."

"Well, that's that then," he said to no one about him, "it was in the cards, as they say."

He flipped my wallet back to me after removing the photo and turned to head into the bar.

"What the hell are ya going on about? Hey, where are ya going?"

He turned, the size of him filling the doorway, a halo of smoky, blue light outlining his head.

"I'm going with you."

"What?"

"I'm going with you. To America." And with that, he walked into the bar.

I stood there beside the heroes, a buzz in my ears as if someone had fired a rifle. The worst of all possible conclusions spreading as quickly as a cancer, I felt helpless, as if everything I had worked for, had loved, hoped and dreamed about, was going to blow up in my face.

Why should I feel this? I loved my brother. I had looked up to him. He was really the only sibling I had grown up with.

Still, there was something deeper. Something I couldn't guess at gnawing inside me. A distrust of all things O'Wary lingered in the shadows. The feeling there is something big, yet unseen. Like knowing there is someone in the house, but you can't find them.

I looked around the room for solace, but found only the faces of the dead. Their eyes, as empty and dark as coal, burned holes through me. Everywhere I turned there was another martyr; and in that instant, I felt the first twinge of hate.

46

I'm going with you, to America," he had said over and over, in every corner of London. My brother hardly talked about anything else. I could only smile and nod, be the sounding board. I knew there was no way to convince him otherwise, not yet, not as worked up as he was. I watched him with the kind of fascination you reserve for people who are touched.

There was a moment, sitting in a small diner in Soho, the seats and tables covered with a thin layer of grease, the walls filled with photos of London from during the Blitz, all of them tilted as if a V2 had detonated a few blocks away, when he took me aback. He had eaten his breakfast in a most compulsive way, fingers carefully arranging and rearranging the plates and cutlery as if there were a plan. It seemed each piece of flatware, each plate and glass, had places at his setting that were more than custom. At times he would softly speak to himself. At other times his brow would furrow and he would look to his left or right. It was then that I realized how much the time alone in prison had changed him.

He asked question after question about America, his face lighting up with each of my answers like a child sitting around a campfire. The thought of so much space, of being able to go where you want, when you want, it seemed to make him high. I can still see him dabbing at the yellow liquid of a broken egg with a bit of toast, his eyes closed, marveling at the flavor, mumbling something crazy about the yolk of freedom.

London had become our treadmill. For hours we would walk through the streets and alleys, the cobbled stones turning to brick, to tar, to concrete. He would sip on small bottles of gin, light cigarettes furiously, and swear at the walls that announced a cul-de-sac. In a stand of trees in Regent's Park, his hand on the trunk of a great oak, he had stood there sobbing. His massive shoulders shaking up and down, the soft sounds of a man weeping being swallowed by the forest. When I went to reach out to him he had knocked me to the ground.

That unexpected, single act of violence now seems prophetic. Sitting here, in a corner pub not far from Battersea, not far from the bar that he had blown up, dabbing at my swollen eye, my bloody nose, my split lip with the corner of a wet towel, I begin to feel the earth slip away. What will be, will be, I say to myself, clearly seeing that I have no control over what will transpire, and it is this that frustrates me so much. I dip the towel into a glass of Jameson, suck the corner as I can't sip, and wince as the alcohol touches open skin. How did this all happen and what did I do to deserve it?

A day after he was released, our Mother had put on an old-fashioned Donegal feed at the sister's. A Limerick ham, roast chicken and breaded plaice with all the trimmings, cooked as only a mom can cook. There was claret with the meal, sherry and port with trifle for after, the good china and Waterford crystal. Donovan had to stand and shout the toast above the din of my brother's sobs, telling him that if he didn't stop the blubbering he would stuff his gob with the ham.

My brother had eaten like a horse, his compulsiveness causing us all to stare, mom and sis wiping tears away with their embroidered napkins. He spent the entire dinner arranging and rearranging his setting, continually turning his water and wine glasses to a spot that hadn't been drunk from, separating all the food into neat piles, and then, with a shudder and a smile of abandon, pushing them all into one heap, gravy over the top. I looked over to see if my mother was noticing the same thing. She had, and I think this is what set off the tears. It had to be difficult seeing your son act like this. Prison or no prison, she surely remembered the postcard from Australia written in crayon.

When we had finished, two hours later, not a crumb left, my brother having eaten five full plates of food, the women cleared and cleaned while the men went to the garden to smoke. Donovan and I swirled goblets of sherry, my brother a glass of gin. He lit smokes for each of us, drew hard on his, and then leveled his black eyes at me.

"So, young Wiley. Tell me more about Amerikay."

"What haven't I told you already?" I said, hoping to turn the conversation from the outset, "did either of you catch Celtic ta other night? Brilliant job by the mid-fielder."

"Not so fast, little brother. I have questions before I move in with ya."

"You're going to America? With Wiley? That's grand! The brothers reunited after all these years," Donovan exclaimed.

"Tis an incredible thing. Wiley here has been hounding me about this ever since the release," my brother shot me a glance and a sideways nod.

"That's not true." I pointed at him and held a palm up at Donovan to stop jabbering about how wonderful this was. "I think you should take some time, settle in, shake-off the years, and then figure out what to do."

"Ah there's the voice of reason. Little brother's never rushed headlong into anything, aye? No shotgun weddings or quick moves in the middle of the night, not young Wiley," Donovan was laughing, the brother's volume increased, I shook my head at the ground. "Oh, no, Wiley has always planned everything out to a fare-thee-well. Now what about this waitress," my eyes shot up, "do tell us how you met."

"That's my business," I blurted, way too quickly.

"Wiley, you can't be jealous of your own brother?" asked Donovan.

"Yes I can, the bastard," I was serious, but the two of them nearly fell on the ground laughing. My brother started a coughing fit, Donovan did as well and they passed the puffer back and forth until they could both breathe.

"Jaysus, Wiley, don't do that again, I'm too old. The ticker's liable to explode," Donovan gasped, grabbing at his breast.

"Wiley, seriously, what is up with you? Let me ask some simple questions."

"Fair play," giving in, arms crossing in front of my chest.

"Now then, which state is it ya live in?" he asked, hands behind his back assuming the role of solicitor.

"Mississippi," I deadpanned.

"I thought it was Michigan," corrected Donovan, earning him a look.

"Yes, that's right, Mitch-e-gan. Please, Wiley, you've only said sixty words to me in three days and I fairly much have this all sussed out as it is. Now then, which city in Michigan is it?"

"Detroit."

"Not true again, little brother, it's Great something. Great River. Great Rapids."

"Grand Rapids!" shouted Donovan, "this is just like a game show."

"'Tis indeed a game, isn't it, little brother. Grand Rapids on the Grand River, eh, Wiley?"

"If you know already, then why the charade?" I asked, a weariness settling into my voice, sherry settling into my mouth.

"The answers verify the information, the delivery verifies intent."

And then I understood, another day in London, another interrogation.

"Now listen, there has to be something here we're missing, right, I mean you can't just leave prison from being in the IRA and then travel abroad? Right?" I stopped for just a second, finally feeling like I had found the solution to derailing this nonsense. "You have to have a passport, be allowed to leave the country, clear parole. Right?"

"Ah, Wiley, all those things were traded away between America, England, and Ireland before the ceasefire. The nouns don't matter, Wiley, we're all just chips being bartered by state departments And you have to understand, the IRA and Sinn Fein aren't going to let me just walk these streets. I'd be killed within a fortnight. So my safety helps cement further deals, greases the wheels of commerce, and helps England get out of Ireland altogether."

"And what does America get out of the deal?"

"Wiley, really, its time to put down the cookbooks and read some history. You could walk from one end of America to the other on the backs of freedom fighters from all over the world. What's one more rebel in the Yankee Stew?" He leaned against the tool shed, a stern look on his face, the wheels of his mind making the connection, bringing the conversation back around. He looked over to me, his black eyes holding mine, "You can't stop dreams, Wiley. They have a will of their own. They slowly build up steam and then, like a train, they have to run the track that's laid out before them, and all we can do is ride along."

"Very wise, very true. Say, Wiley, you should just be happy with the fact that you can both begin again, far away. No chains, no ties, let the memories fade like I did when

I moved here. Say goodbye to the bog for good," Donovan rested a hand on my shoulder. I felt like I was the subject of an intervention.

"I have begun again. I am happy. Leave me alone," I protested, but only to the sound of the door opening, an invitation to look at some old photographs by the sister, something none of us wished to do. The two of them trudged in, the door slamming metallically. I stood for an empty moment in the garden alone. The air filled with evening birdsong, traffic a white noise in the background, the sound of a jet. I lit a cigarette and contemplated what to do. Dreams. Memories. Love and hate. What did it matter?

"Wiley," shouted my brother, "Jaysus, they even have one of us from Christmas. Man you were an ugly child."

I squeezed my eyes shut and wished myself away, knowing it was fruitless, the smoke in my lungs burning as I held it, the sound of a nearby crow laughing from an electrical line.

"Fuck's sake," I answered to the bird, and turned to relive the past once more.

The treadmill continued. The gin continued. The pints continued. The day after the dinner he and I again covered vast sections of London. I followed his lead in a chaotic ramble that only he fathomed. We walked ever onward, through museums, places of history, places of note, through the one hundred neighborhoods that supported, lifted, trudged, built, toted, fought, fell, cried, swooned, rejoiced, suffered and died to make this town. The crushing history of England as thick as the clouds, as real as the rain, as heavy as the ancient buildings falling against each other. From one corner to the other and back again, it seemed inevitable that I would end up once more in Kensington Park, the bridge behind us, Peter Pan before us, my brother slumped in the same seat on the same bench that Donovan had been in just a few nights ago.

"Gawd, I love this place. This bench, that statue, I've dreamed of sitting here for years. The smell of the trees mixing with the smell of London," he paused, stretched, took it in, continued, "In prison, I saw a picture, a newer one, about Peter Pan. Except they didn't even name it after him, they named it after the bad guy. Seems these days everyone wants to be the bad guy," he paused again, looked over to me standing before Peter Pan, "maybe that's what happened to me!" he laughed, coughed, puffed.

"What did happen to you?"

He shifted in his seat, looked the other way, looked up at the statue, "What do you suppose his one happy thought is, Wiley? What's yours?"

I answered with only silence, stared at the ground, the color of the grass, the walkway.

"Jesus Christ, Wiley, are ya ever going to talk to me? I'm not the one to hate. Don't you know where you come from? Don't you know who you are? Who we are?"

I looked away, far away, toward the sky. Tears were welling up in my eyes, my jaws clenching and unclenching.

"What's your one happy thought, Wiley? Or fuck that, what's the black spot on yer heart? What's it look like, Wiley? Does it look familiar?"

"I don't fucking know, okay! Why don't you tell me?" I moved toward him and in one motion he sat up, brushed me aside and resumed the treadmill. A fresh bottle of gin, a fresh smoke, an air of hostile indifference, and I followed, knowing he had said something important, something profound, something I needed to know.

From that moment the difference in us became as wide as the city. Our words were short, angry jabs that turned into outright insults. We did our best to walk each other into the ground, nearly coming to blows in every shop or pub on who would stand the round.

We were a pair of angry Irish bulls, all of London our paddock, we curb-stomped through the worst of neighborhoods hoping for an altercation, for a chance to tear hell out of something other than each other. In Brixton, the rainbow sea of faces parted, foreign curses hurled along with disbelieving stares, a volley of rotten tomatoes nearly sparked a riot as we overturned tables of produce, Pakis scattering, lettuce leaves fluttering like feathers in the air. We ran, the warble of police sirens in the distance, our faces red, tempers stoked further.

All of this ended at a spot beside the Thames on a lonely pier off Salter Road, gulls tracing circles in the sky, the brown water circling below. We stared at each other with a recklessness that can only come from two people about to collide. My feet were sore from over nine hours of walking, my clothes drenched in sweat. The sweet smell of alcohol permeated the air, my brother finished yet another pint of gin and casually tossed it into the river.

"You love her, don't you Wiley."

This was the first time he had mentioned the Waitress all day, but his thoughts of her, like my own, had lain just below the surface. On the day he was released he had taken my picture of her and it had ignited something in him. On a street corner bank of bright red phone boxes, I had pretended to call her, leaving the door ajar so he could hear me say, 'I love you too', a confused Sous Chef on the other end of the line, of the Atlantic.

I turned from him, leaned against the railing, and stared out over the water toward Canary Wharf. The late afternoon sun was reflected in a thousand windows with such glare that it looked as if London was burning.

"Aye, I do, and I don't see what she has to do with you at all."

He laughed hard, a thin wheeze at the end of each explosion. Himself doubled over, hands on his knees.

"Are ya scared, little brother, scared of your own flesh and blood?"

He stopped suddenly, the bright light of inspiration, or memory aglow in his eyes.

"But then, are we really flesh and blood? I don't think we are. Do you?" And with that, he returned to his delirium of laughter.

I turned to go.

"You hang on a minute, little brother, I'm nowhere near finished with you."

"Why do you have to come to the States? Why can't you just leave me be. Why can't you just get on with your life? I mean it's not like we were a family anyhow."

"Family. Well, you can pick your friends, but you can't," he just trailed off, leaned against the railing as I had, his lips trembling. "Wiley, do you know what it's like to have something stolen from you when you're just a child? Not a toy, or a bicycle, or a watch, but something inside you. That special, little spark that makes you a child. Taken from you. Not gently, like a thief would, but ripped from you."

I looked at him and saw the fear in his eyes. He was staring at an eddy of water in the river, but he was looking past it. If it were possible to see to hell, that was where he was staring. His eyes filled with tears, his face twisting.

"Every single day of your life, you remember exactly when it happened. You remember the icy hands around your heart, the fist closing around it, and the suck of wind in your hollow chest as that spark is torn out. Every day you stare at your face in the mirror and relive it. That's when you start to hate. That's when the tide in you turns black. That's when," he turned away, whatever it was he said only the gulls and the waves could hear.

"I still don't see what it has to do with me, or my life in Michigan, or the Waitress."

"Do you believe in dreams, little brother, because in prison that's all you have, dreams and memories. The dreams keep you going. The dreams in the daytime carry you from meal to meal through the hours of the day. The dreams at night carry you outside the prison walls. And the memories, well, you can imagine, I suppose," he paused, then, "I dreamed a little dream one time, about a girl and a place where the sun seemed to never set, and the sky was as large as the land, and you kick dust up in the air so it would become a wee cyclone. I stood there in the middle of the desert, on a hopeless ranch, but filled with hope, and she loved me and I loved her and the world could spin itself crazy and I could care less," he grabbed me by the shoulders, those black eyes flaring, "Wiley, she's that girl."

As he turned and took several steps away from me, I could feel the snap in the back of my head. All of it, each little piece of it, every single second, needed to be released. The tension, the police at the airport, the pictures of the dead, the republican club, all of it was just too much. His constant bantering, the way he lurched as he walked, the ridiculous repositioning of every single piece of place setting, his pointed references to our home back in Donegal, knowing he knew something that I didn't, it had me seething. But more than anything, as men will do when they are hopelessly in love, it was the picture in my head of him sleeping with the Waitress that pushed me over the edge. So, I charged him.

He knew it. He could feel it. His instincts were still too keen. Just before I could lay my hands on him, he wheeled, a great fist hitting me square in the middle of my face. The London twilight disintegrated. I did not even feel the ground when gravity claimed me.

I have no idea how long I laid there. An old man splashed beer in my face to rouse me, his weathered hand carefully touching my cheek. The dull ache that I came to with was soon outright pain, my face frozen stiff in a mask of dried blood, a tooth hanging just above my tongue.

"Jaysus, son, how many of them was it?"

I tried to stand, my head spinning like the water, like the dirt devils in my brother's dream, and threw-up. I reached into the puddle and pulled out my tooth. Staggered over to the railing and let the strong river air wash over me.

My brother was long gone. I knew I would not see him again on this side of the Atlantic. Whatever would be, whatever it was that would happen, had been fated long ago, or so the Vikings believed.

I looked out across the dark Thames toward Canary Wharf, the street lamps of the docks muffled by a light fog that had traveled up the river and was now spreading through the city. I reached inside my jacket for a cigarette and came out with a note. I lit a match so I could read it, my eyes slipping in and out of focus.

The words had been written in crayon, the scrawl of a child. The note simply read: Dear Little Brother, Fee Fi Fo Fum.

I set the bloody towel aside, finish the glass in a single stinging go, and call for one more whiskey. My headache rages, my ears are still ringing, and the back of my head feels like so much cottage cheese from where it hit the ground. Another successful day has come to an end for the O'Wary's.

"Hey, lad," it was the barman, setting a glass of Jameson before me, ice in the drink to numb the pain, "I'm going to be locking up here in a moment, this one's on the house. If there's anything else I can get you, I'll be right through that door. The door will lock on your way out. Hey, man, sorry for your troubles."

"Thank-you," I slur, pulling the glass closer. Lifting, drinking, wincing. The few remaining lights cast the pub in shadows, wood older than two centuries making sinister faces. There is that familiar heavy stillness in the empty room, one million moments suppressed by time, distant yet just under the surface. I stand slowly, bones creaking to attention, and finish the whiskey. My face in the mirror looks like Lon Chaney's. I don my muddy coat, push the heavy door open to the street, and walk out into London after midnight.

47

I had never been so happy to leave England in my life. The pressing confines of London, the ravings of my brother, and the inability to reach the Waitress had done me in. I left the city for Heathrow, adjusting my flight schedule on the way, breakfast and lunch being discarded to save time. It is as if I were a starving waif shivering on Liverpool docks, gladly boarding even the most rat-infested ship just to escape to America.

Yet isn't it true, that no matter where you go, there you are, and the past seems to always have a way of shadowing you. My reflection in the side mirror reminds me of the Waitress, a bruised and purple face, the salt of my tears stinging as they fell just moments ago.

The endless roll of cornfields thrum past the window, my eyes heavy from the flight, the Sous Chef drives us onward toward Grand Rapids, the Michigan farm scape blissfully uneventful, soothing in repetition. I shake my head without realizing it, saying 'no' unconsciously to the ghosts chasing me across the Atlantic, crowding my heart, imploring me to open my eyes to truths that are dimly discernible.

After I had left the pub into the dark, London streets, I had checked my pockets for a bottle, for a flask, and found none. The whiskey in the pub in Battersea was the last drink I've had. That was only thirty-odd hours ago and already my hands are shaking. Nothing at the sister's, nothing at Heathrow, nothing on the flight, the drink is an affliction I keep at bay, pistol, whip, and chair at the ready, I look out the window and think of better uses for all that corn.

"Wiley, Jesus man, if I'd known what rough shape you'd be in I would've brought a bottle of something," the Sous Chef said, being diplomatic.

"Christ, I can barely drink as it is," my hand lightly touches a purple cheek, "better I tuck the sauce away for a while and figure out what's going on."

"I can't believe your own brother would do that to you," disbelief as he looks my busted face over again. I turn away to deflect his stare.

"I don't even know if he's my brother anymore. Gawd, what a mess," I shook my head, returning my gaze to the fields floating past. "And you say you haven't seen the Waitress."

"Not at all. They keep hiring her back and she keeps taking off. It's been a few days, but then she doesn't work the front of the week."

"No unusually large and violent foreigners hanging about?" I asked, trying to create some levity.

"Everything's steady as she goes. Summer slow at work. There've been some break-ins up in the Hill, around your neighborhood, but that's been going on since before you left.

It's the same every summer, hot, muggy, windows left open. That's just life in the big city."

"And Jimbo at the bar hasn't seen anyone out of the ordinary?"

"All's the same, Wiley. We haven't seen anything weird. But remember, he only punched you, what, a couple days ago. How could he get here that fast? You should call your mom, or your sister, or that Donovan guy. They'd probably know more over there than us here."

"Yeah, you're right. My head's all fogged up, ears still ringing, hands shaking. Worrying for nothing," I said, hoping to return to just that.

"Do you want to stop for a drink? I'm sure there's some podunk farmer bar around here somewhere."

"No, no, that's quite all right. Thanks, though. Just a little rest 'till we get to town," he nodded approval, both of us knowing there wasn't much two drinking buddies could do other than drink.

A town sped past the window, an Irish name, more corn-fields acting as bookends. I thought about the flight, staring down through cloudless skies at the dark blue of the Atlantic. Even on such a perfect day the wind made white streaks on the waves, an undulation that could be seen from seven miles up. How many of us slipped beneath those waves, cattle ships meant to cross the Irish Sea used to ply human stock. Hunger so desperate it drove them through three thousand miles of fear.

I looked down to the gray blur of the expressway, listened to the white noise of the tires on the road, closed my eyes

while leaning my head against the glass, the vibration soothing for just a second, then making me nauseous.

My whole life it's seemed that I've been stuck in motion,
unable to control the events around me, just along for the
ride. The Buddhist chef in London whom I had worked with,
who had explained that you simply step out of the stream
and then observe the river of life flowing by. Opening my
eyes and looking again at the pavement, I fought the urge to
open the door and try just that.

"Hey, is that thing charged up?" I asked the Sous Chef,
turning from the window, pointing at his cell phone sitting
on the console, plugged into the lighter.

"Yeah, go for it."

"You mind if I call England?"

"Whatever you need, buddy."

"Thanks," I said, unplugging the phone and flipping open
the top, digging in my pocket for my wallet and my sister's
number in West Ham.

My mother had dropped me off at Heathrow. The airport
seemed exhausted, like a carnival after the weekend, the
party over and the hangover of cleaning up just settling in.
No cheery hullos, only the endless queues, the waiting. It
seemed all of England was happy to see me leave. The police
at the airport barely looked me over. Not even an odd glance
at my bruised face.

We were much the same. My mother was very quiet, seeing me off only as far as she had to. When it came time for
us to part, she took me in her arms, hands then cupping my
cheeks, she told me how sorry she was. Then, oddly, stopped

abruptly, as if there was so much more she had to say, but could not find the strength to do so.

On the flight this tormented me, how she had acted, the feeling of something horrible just beneath the surface. The things my brother had said, this continual undercurrent of past events I couldn't remember. I thought back to my last visit to Ireland, my father's funeral, nearly drowning.

"Jaysus, but that's a tough part of the world."

"I'm sorry, what's that?" The Sous asked. I hadn't realized I'd spoken aloud. "Wiley, you know how to work that thing?"

"Not really. This sends it, right?"

"Yeah."

"Thanks," I said, turning slightly to make the call, the familiar English ring chiming in my ear.

"Hullo?" It was my sister.

"Hey sis, it's Wiley. Is mom there?"

"Right-o, let me put her on. Jaysus, Wiley, I'm so sorry for what's happened. He's just not the same, huh? I do hope your next visit will be a little less dramatic."

"Me too."

"Right, here she is. Mom, it's Wiley."

"Wiley, ya've made it safe and sound?"

"Aye."

"Thank you so much for calling and letting me know."

"Not a problem, its just nice to hear your voice. Say, mom, have either of you seen or heard from him?"

There was a pause. In my mind I could see my mom fretting, looking at my sister for help, shrugging her shoulders It was then that the pop in my head happened, the ringing stopped, ears opened. It physically hurt causing me to jerk, the Sous suddenly looking over.

"Son, I'm not sure how to put this, but you're both adults and you're brothers, and things always have a way of working out."

She went on, but I had stopped listening. When we said our good-byes I think the phone was already moving away from mouth. I set it down and looked out the window, suburbs creeping up on the city of Lansing.

"Well, what gives, what the hell? Wiley?"

I closed my eyes and held up one finger.

There would be no storm-ravaged, three-week crossing in a leaking ship for him. No, that ten percent chance of foundering off of Sable Island, another group of Irish ghosts sharing the landscape with the wild horses, an incessant wind crying a lament, that happy thought simply no longer existed. He would face the same sterile flight that I had just finished, following the sun over the horizon until the old world falls away and the new world rises up.

"Wiley, dammit, tell me what the hell is going on!"

Was he already in touch with the Waitress? Would she be picking him up from Detroit Metro or O'Hare? Would he clamber on board a bus as I had so many months ago, the slow and uncomfortable trip to Western Michigan, the banal questions about your accent from people who had only seen Ireland in *Darby O'Gill and The Little People*.

And when he arrived? What then? Was Grand Rapids big enough for two O'Wary's? Maybe we'd work together. He could use myself as a reference. Do dishes. Hell, we could even live together. With the Waitress. Kind of an Irish version of *Three's Company* with the IRA thrown in for cinematic effect.

"Wiley! Goddammit! What the fuck is going on?"

I stopped tapping my forehead against the window. I may even have stopped repeating the word 'no'. I slowly turned to face my friend, "You'd better find that podunk farmer bar, he's on his way."

48

I sit pressed against an enormous rock, drenched from the rain that lashes at the ground, light from street lamps on Fulton Street cutting through the trees casting jagged shadows across the cemetery. The rain creates a muffled silence, the sounds of the city enveloped, only my heart can be heard above the shower. I catch a sob in my throat, tears lost in the rain, confusion driven by jealousy, by hatred.

Oh how I wish I could light a cigarette. The brandy in the flask is much easier to apply, though nearly finished. I lightly tap my head against the giant grave-marker, a boulder that rests upon some fellow named John Ball, hoping some sense will be driven into it.

Sitting here in the downpour, his voice seems to rise above the rain, imploring me to stop running, that it's all a mistake, that he's sorry, he hadn't known it was me. He yells after me, his accent out of place here, that he's sorry for the fist, it was all due to too much drink, too much pressure and too much prison. These are the excuses that follow his footfalls in the puddles.

I wouldn't stop. I refused to listen. It was easier to run. The whistle of the bat splitting the air is still singing in my ears, washing out his voice, his explanations. The night promises to hide me, darkness and rain providing the cover, I figure I have a handful of hours to think this through, find the reasons, find a plan.

The flask tipped all the way back, the brandy igniting some warmth, some clarity, I try to recall the past week and find where it all went wrong.

I had, by all appearances, neatly settled back into a routine. I worked, or at least acted as though I was working, my mind never far from the reality of what could happen, the maze of possibilities being worried into exponents. I read, the words dissolving before me, the text lost in a mind not fully focused. I tried to write, outlining projects long dormant and not far from that even in study.

And I drank. Pints followed pints, shot after shot, the beverage lists of bars, restaurants and markets suddenly seeming too short, too antiquated. The drug of choice, packaged in any form, was chosen to keep the wolves at the door and the dreams from returning.

For the first week after returning from London, I had rung the Waitress five or six times a day, her message machine filled with my trying to make contact. I stopped by her flat as often, but there was never anyone there.

My friend the Sous Chef kept telling me I was a fool. That I needed to just relax, let her go, let him go, move on. His patience worn thin, he grabbed me once by the shoulders behind the line, the tickets flying in and chaos ensuing, my focus not there at all, his eyes trying to bore sense into mine, "Goddamnit, Wiley, pull your head out of your ass. These head games are killing you and you're killing us. Get to work!"

I tried to explain what had happened over there, but he would have none of it. "Give it up, Wiley," he would say, "she's nuts, and she's making you nuts as well. Forget the two of them. Forget it. Nothing good will come of this."

No matter how hard he tried, I would continue to call her, harboring even the most remote chance to win her heart. He decided that in this extreme of a case, the only tonic was to take me down to the local once more, ply sense into me with the aid of stout, and pawn me off on an unsuspecting barfly.

As we sat there at the bar, the day's last sunlight having long since fallen through the low, scudding clouds on to Pearl Street, my mind continued to follow the well-trodden, con-voluted paths of the past week. The Sous Chef, seeing my face twisted in thought, slapped me on the back and leaned forward clinking his pint with mine.

"Give it up," he implored.

I took a long drink, set down the empty glass, and ran my face through my hands. I wanted to still myself long enough to see the sense of what he was saying. Hoping to feel the bright shining light of reason cutting through the blinders.

"That's the way," he said to me. Then to Jimbo behind the bar, "two more, please. Whiskeys as well," he pushed the empty glasses forward, leaned back and stretched his arms to the ceiling.

"So, Wiley, what's your brother look like anyway?" Jimbo asked, setting us up with the Jameson's and letting the pints cook.

"He doesn't look anything like me at all. He's bigger, over six feet tall, maybe seventeen stone. His hair is black and a bit unruly. But it's his eyes," he turned to look at me more closely, an expression slowly painting itself over his face, "they seem to take everything in. It's as if his eyes are all pupils, they seem almost," his expression froze me, the painting complete.

"They seem almost black, don't they? And he mutters. He talks to himself, doesn't he Oh my God, Wiley. You were right. He was here. Right here, in this bar. Say," he called out to the other barman, "Tommy, you remember that weird guy who was in here the other night."

"What guy?" Tommy set down what he was doing and walked over to us.

"That one drinking gin and talking to himself."

"Yeah, I remember him. Hey you know what, he talked a bit like you, Wiley. I wonder if he's Irish?"

The dots had finished connecting. I had at this moment that rare opportunity to be able to see my life from a slight distance. The many paths that could have been chosen again appeared beside the path that had been selected, illuminated by my own incomprehensible footprints. If only If only. If only. All I could do was smack myself in the forehead with the palm of my hand.

I stood up from the barstool slowly, my eyes focusing far from here, seeing eddies in the Thames, pictures of the dead, blackthorn and an apple tree. I could feel the bile rising in my throat, yet finished the whiskey anyway, determination, fear, and practice coalescing for one moment.

"Hey, where you going, your pint is ready?" Jimbo called.

I turned and walked slowly toward the door.

"Wiley," called the Sous Chef, "c'mon, man. Let it go. No worries. Like you say, no worries. Wiley!"

I stepped into the breezeway.

"Wiley!" they all called.

And I made my way outside.

The sky seemed very close, street lamps wanly casting a glow on the shadows filling the streets. I hadn't realized how long we had been in the pub, how much we had drunk.

I ran the short distance up the hill to the Waitress's apartment, my lungs burning within my ribs. Slowed to a walk, stopped, and bent over breathing deep. I felt a painful lump in my hip and discovered my flask. This propelled me to the small market where I bought a half pint of brandy.

In a small alley not a block from her flat I filled the flask, finishing what wouldn't fit, and put together a plan to circle around the block and place myself in front of her building. A few drops of rain began to fall, the summer day nearly eclipsed, the city streets only occasionally interrupted by a lone car, I hesitantly and not so steadily walked the long way round.

A single light shone from her bedroom, a soft yellow that was only bright enough to outline shapes inside the window. I stopped across the street not knowing quite what to do. The wind kicked up leaves and bits of paper, their scuffling the loudest sound. I stood for a long time on the far side of the walkway beside an old oak, it's bark rough against my face.

A shape crossed the room to the window, and paused long enough to part the curtains. I pressed myself close to the trunk of the tree, my eyes squinting to better make out the identity. When it seemed the figure had left the window, I walked down the block, crossed the street, and then went back up to the apartment.

Great evergreens covered the entrance to the large, old house. A half dozen different letter boxes hung beside the main door, the hallway lit by a small bulb, the porch light itself either switched off or burned out. I opened the door, it feeling heavier than I remembered, and entered the house.

The hallway was covered with dust, empty save for a hutch that held mail no one wanted. From one of the apartments came the mumbled sounds of a telly, louder than this a buzz coming from the hallway light. I walked to her door, a feeble orange glow coming from the ringer. The number of the apartment had fallen off, but the shape of the numeral 'five' remained.

As I reached for the handle, my ears now tuned to any sound that might come from behind the door, I looked up at the eyepiece, which was set just below the missing number.

That instant, that minute piece of time, as palpable as any single moment in my life, could not have been any longer. So long it seemed, that the full thought of what would happen next crossed in its entirety through my mind.

The metal of the handle was just barely on my palm, when I realized that there was a black eye looking out from the eyepiece. The door was opened inward hard and fast, and as I had my weight leaning against it, I lost balance and fell into the apartment.

I heard the shriek of the Waitress, my eyes focusing in the dark to see if she was safe. I saw her standing in only her favorite nightshirt, a glass of wine in her hand. I followed her eyes to what was above me, my brother, his arms high over his head, a baseball bat in hand. It was just beginning the arc toward my head. I rolled to my left, the whack of the lumber hitting the floor, the shaft splitting in a sharp crack.

Before he could regain his balance, I was on my feet and out the door, down the hallway, and out into the night, his voice behind me yelling to stop. The Waitress was calling after me as well, lights brightening the once dark windows of the other apartments.

The sky opened. Rain falling from clouds so close it felt as though they would smother me. The dry clap of my boot falls turning into the splash of puddles. I ran from them, from myself, from the whole twisted mess.

The gates of the cemetery, the tall trees touching the black sky, the neat rows of tombstones seemed as inviting as a warm hearth. I stopped for breath beside this large rock, and fell beside it in exhaustion.

As sleep reached up from the earth, pulling at my eyelids with soft, silent hands, I heard in the distance my name being called. The accent, even amidst the rain, was unmistakable. And then, before I lost consciousness, for the first time in years, I prayed to God.

49

At the end of the lane, itself more dirt and mud than a proper street, stood the parish church. It lay protected by a wrought iron fence, a cemetery, and three enormous yews. I walked to the gate beneath an orange sky where black clouds seemed to swirl in several directions at once, the effect making me a bit dizzy, as I hadn't eaten in days.

Sitting propped up against the rails were other children, equally gaunt, their lips stained green from the grass. One of them tried to hail me, a sad salute that ended in a thin arm lifting only several inches from her lap. Her eyes, only a year ago as bright as stars, now empty and set far back beyond her cheekbones. I walked on through the gate, a sexton opening it for me, and toward the priest who beckoned me from the rectory's front door.

Inside it smelled of incense, the pungent odor trying to hide the stench of the dead and dying laying beyond the fence. Underneath this, crouching there in wait, the smell of home-baked bread, roast pratties, and stew. My stomach tightened, and if it were possible I would have cried.

"*Beannacht na Fheile Padraig leat.*"

"Go mbeannai Dia dhuit."

"You are welcome here, young man. Please sit here beside me at the table while the food finishes cooking."

I sat down in the wooden chair. Its back was very straight and the seat so high off the floor that my feet dangled in the air. He moved his seat beside mine, the nearness of him making me feel ill at ease. He had the smell of someone very old who had not washed in quite some time.

I stared at the table, a bright blue place mat in front of me with a large oval plate in the middle of it. They were the two cleanest things I had ever seen. Around me, on cupboards, shelves, on window ledges, filling the place in a crowded and uncomfortable way, were statues of saints, of Mary and of Christ. There had to be hundreds; their eyes staring holes in my soul.

"I know that some of your family are too weak to come to mass. If you'd like, you could work with me around here, doing odd things, and I could pay you in food you could take back to your home," he said, his upper-class accent making the word 'home' sound anything but.

"We would really like you to stay here with us," his voice began to hiss, a lisp that wrapped certain consonants in saliva. He placed his hand on my knee. "If you're as hungry as we are," his hand sliding up my thigh, "and work really, really hard," his hand nearly at the top of my leg, "you can eat all the food you want."

I tried to jump off the giant chair, the anguish in me coming out in a muffled squeal, but was too afraid to move. I turned from the plate, from the place setting, from the rows of statuary, to look up at him.

His neck seemed to be swelling in his collar, black hair choking out the dingy whiteness of it. His chin was pointed like an elbow and his mouth seemed to be all teeth with a thin, red tongue licking gray lips. Above this, like a rotten acorn, stood his nose. His eyes, as black as holes, sat on the end of his eyelashes which were not lashes at all but great black flies. And then, the tingle rising in me with the scream, his hand went to squeeze me where no man should ever touch.

I awoke, it seemed, dripping wet, blood stiff on arms and cheeks from what felt like a thousand cuts. The moon leered at me, its light setting aglow the ancient apple tree, the walls of the dilapidated barracks, and the thick wet grass in which I lay. As I came to, I felt dampness on my legs, on my backside, and realized my trousers had been pulled down. There was a slow-to-rise soreness, the feeling of grass on my face and then the laughter. A great figure stood over me brushing grass off his knees, the light of the moon rimming his head, hiding his face. His snigger sent shivers through me, I scrambled to lift my trousers, to scurry away, to dig a hole and hide. He turned to walk away, but not before I saw his face, a second scream tearing through my lips, ripping open the night, my heart, my soul.

I awoke, the chill on my cheeks telling me so, dripping wet, the sound of my voice echoing throughout the cemetery, carrying itself out onto Fulton Street. There was no movement. No voice answered my shout, turned to face my blinking eyes. Only the blind stare of a statue on a tombstone, a ship's captain forever looking out to a sea that does not exist. It is the soft patter of raindrops falling from the leaves of the oaks, and the damp, stone presence of this rock I had fallen asleep against, that connects me to this moment.

I left the cemetery staggering in the direction of my flat. I had a slight chill and a cough from having spent the night in the cold, wet air. I needed a drink. I needed a smoke. I needed some time to collect myself and shake the dreams. I had no idea what I looked like, but it had to be disarming. My feelings were coming from someplace deep within me, a place that hadn't seen light in an age, if ever. The actual world around me seemed nothing more than wet tissue, a veneer painted on the truth by gods with nothing better to do.

A block from home it dawned on me that my brother would likely be waiting for me there. My narrow escape from him the night before now fresh in mind, I decided to walk downtown instead. Without even realizing it, my head swimming in scattered thoughts of famine, priests, and brothers swinging baseball bats, I headed for my local. The normal aspects of life seemed of little consequence, living having been reduced to the basest elements.

The distance between my flat and the city center evaporated, my head too confused to notice simple things like time and space. I stopped before the town clock by the great hotel, the dark sky both close and removed like a low ceiling you learn to live with. The lateness of the hour surprised me. I must have slept beside that rock for hours.

The city seemed empty, no cars, no people, only a home-less man gesticulating wildly at a bank of phones. I squinched my brow thinking I was in another nightmare, looked down at the puddled-pavement, and numbly moved on. At the corner I hesitated, again looking around at the apparent ghost town, a particularly strange feeling of being out of one's own dimension tapping me on the shoulder. I slowly continued a few more steps, my breath catching in my throat, and walked into the pub.

Jimbo stood behind the bar, his hands working a rag around a glass in the mantra of barmen all over the world. When he noticed me he nodded.

"Jimbo, whiskey please. A lot."

"Wiley, what gives? You raced out of here last night like you'd seen the devil. And today, you've had your own brother waiting here for hours."

I stood up before I had even fully sat down, my heart skipping a beat.

"My brother was here, today? When?"

"When? He's right there walking toward you."

I turned to see him, his great hands pushing chairs out of the way. The Waitress was right behind him, pulling at his arm and saying something. I turned toward the door, stepping back as he reached out for me. His momentum pitched him too far forward, and I caught him with a full fist on the side of the head. This sent him reeling, belly-first into a table. As he lay sprawled across it, his arms and legs swimming in the air, I punched him in the back and made for the door.

"Wiley! Ya feckin' eejet, give me half a second," he yelled at the back of me.

I ran down Pearl toward the river. The streets still slick, the sky still dark and close, a lone valet stood by the curb beside the great hotel, his head turning with me as I ran, the broom and dustpan in his hands as frozen as his expression.

Stopping just before the bridge, breathing deep, I looked right, straight, up, down and turned left to get on the boardwalk. As I hit the bottom of the steps, the soles of my boots thudding on old, river-worn wood, I thought to myself how absurd this had all become. I remembered my brother in a different light, not the seeming terror who couldn't finish a sentence without mumbling, but the young man who climbed Mount Errigal with me as a child. With this in mind, I came to a halt.

How could this have come to this! One dart thrown at a map in Boston, one restaurant in a city filled with restaurants, one waitress out of dozens, my mother who I hadn't seen in years and my brother who I hadn't heard from in even longer, somehow all dovetailing into an Irish Stew that had become the ridiculous side of absurd.

I inhaled deeply, exhaled slowly, and turned to see where he was.

He was right on top of me. Both arms extended, he tackled me with all the force of a large man running down a flight of stairs. This sent the two of us flying onto the boardwalk, the concussion knocking the wind out of me, my head smashing back and bouncing off the wood. I winced hard from the pain, my chest on fire trying to breathe, blood beginning to mat my hair.

With what strength I had left I shoved him aside, kicking, clawing, and screaming. I could hear his voice, but it was growing more distant, a ringing rising in my ears like church bells reverberating up close. Small black dots began to fill my vision, the light at my periphery flashing.

I rolled over and crawled to my feet, the sudden rising sending a wave of dizziness and nausea, tried to make a dash for it but ran squarely into the guard rail, the force of my momentum sending me head over heels over the low railing and into the river.

The light of day is gone. I inhale deeply as I roll, brown, brackish, slow, lazy summer river water filling my lungs. The mud of the bottom holds me close, it is an embrace that can last forever. No thoughts, no struggle, only acceptance.

Then, in one sudden upward motion, there is great pain, the return of light and I hear my gargled screaming. I fight to stay conscious, fear flickering thoughts through my head in no distinct pattern, but settled on one image cast in a new light. I thought about the Christmas day he had left home. The fight he had had with our father, the tree knocked aside, ornaments strewn, furniture toppled. My brother had said one last thing to my mother, something I couldn't have known then, but now understood fully. As he pulled me from the river, I heard the one thing he bade my mother to do before he left for Belfast, 'tell that buggerin' bastard to keep his hands off of Wiley'.

And with that, I stopped trying to fight. The sky beyond the tangled locks of my brother's hair looked Irish: close, dark and filled with rain. My heart felt Irish: closed, dark and filled with pain.

50

Before I came to, I walked to the edge of a field in the middle of a very old forest. The trunks of the trees seemed as big as houses, ferns spreading from the field deep into the maze of oaks, pines, and birch. It was night, but the hidden moon cast enough light to make it feel like dusk. I passed through the ferns, my fingertips outstretched tracing across their tops. The Milky Way spilled out from between the clouds, which seemed like perfect paintbrush strokes of cotton.

There, in a small clearing in the center of the field, sat the Sous Chef's cat, long since dead, looking up at the stars on a large granite rock.

"Where am I?" I asked.

"You're standing in a field, by a great forest, talking to a cat."

"I thought you had died."

"No, I just had to leave. You'll have to leave one day as well."

She turned, arched her back in a great stretch, and then jumped down into the ferns. I felt a handful of raindrops land on my hair, and looked up hoping some would land on my cheeks.

"Well, I guess I'll follow you then," I said, and began to step toward the forest.

"No, no, no," smiled the calico, "you still have to go home."

"To Ireland?"

"Yes, to Ireland."

"When?"

"Soon," and the cat turned and left.

I turned the other way, out toward the expanse of the field, and looked up at the sky. The clouds scuttled like sheep, working their way from one horizon to the other, rain fell in whispers, and the wind, almost as distinct as an old friend's voice, pulled at the corners of my eyes.

"Wiley," it seemed to say, "Wiley, wake-up."

And I did.

I awoke to my brother kneeling over me, one giant hand patting my cheek, the other lifting my head above the boardwalk. As I drifted away from the field, I remembered him tackling me, the wind rushing out of my lungs, my head slamming against the wood. The sounds of the river swallowing me as light slipped away.

Only now, the light had returned. The sun shone from behind clouds heavy with rain, the sky a yellowish-gray, the sort of color that implies bad weather, my mind suddenly thinking of forests and windstorms, waitresses, and running.

Coming to, I was greeted with drops of rain, the saltiness of which caused me to look up. I closed my eyes against them, realizing it wasn't rain at all but my brother's tears.

"Wiley! Jaysus. Wake de feck up, would ya," he held me in his great arms, rocking back and forth, his face twisted with grief. "Ah, c'mon lad. Where's your spirit, man. Yer from Donegal, come on, man. Jaysus, but ya have ta wake-up, please! If ya wake up I'll buy ya an ocean of stout. An ocean of stout and an island of whiskey."

It was then that it all came rushing in. A river unto itself, my soul flooding with the waters of guilt, shame, and rage. I wanted to make myself small. The smallest thing possible. A grain of sand lost on a beach. An unnoticeable mote of dust; a breath hiding in a hurricane. I wanted not to be. As if God's hand could undo his work, rip a page from this mortal book. In the dots connecting, in the tracery of stars in my own personal heaven finally making a recognizable constellation, all I wanted was to be back on the bottom of the river.

The dream was real. The heavy steps on the stairs, the weight of intent, the heart filling with terror, the escape and the sprint through thorns to Hooker's Hill, it was more than an oft-visited nightmare. I could feel my eyes darting as fast as my mind was racing: *was it the only time?* How many times had this happened? Was my entire childhood smeared with this profanity?

I began to sob, great silent tears falling from cloudy eyes. My brother, realizing my thoughts, began to keen. "I am so sorry, Wiley. I am so sorry. I knew. I knew, I knew, I knew. It happened to me, it happened to us all."

His words rang out, a gunshot across an empty valley. I could feel the birds within me scattering. *All of us? My sister? Him?* What sort of monster was it that had raised us?

"I should have stayed. I wish I could go back and stay. Protect all of you. They should have sent all of us away, not just our sister. They never thought it'd be us too. We were boys, I mean, for fuck's sake, we were boys."

He shook with such violence I nearly catapulted from his arms. Sheets of tears falling in a deluge, the guilt that had haunted him for so long, decades of self-hate spilling out onto my face, my breast, onto this boardwalk and soaking into the American soil.

"I should have killed him. I was so close. These hands," he held them up before his face, "were wrapped around his throat. I wish I could trade all the lives I destroyed for his worthless soul. Done my time, carried the shame of killing my own blood. A hundred thousand years would have been worth his death."

The chance now existed to put it all together, to begin to understand the enigma that had always been my brother, the shadow that hung over our family, and that darkness which dwelled within me. His words presented an opportunity to stop the train wreck of my own self-loathing. Here was an escape from descending further down the helix of the pit.

I began to understand his hatred, his anger. How did the Brits ever stand a chance? A warrior as committed as any berserker, as any martyr. The wrath in him a shield, he had no concern at all for his own life. He had driven the force of his emotions outward at whatever stood before him. I remembered in a flash that afternoon in Dublin, many Christmases ago, the shock waves of fury pulsing from him.

And I? Oh, it was quite internal. I could feel it burning now, deep in my core, dim and obscure like a failed star. Hiding beneath clouds of hate, shame, and guilt, behind years of carefully layered chaos. The detritus of a life wasted, each drink helping to suppress, each failed relationship an excuse, running from them for fear of finding myself.

With the light as dim as it was, I could see the outline of his features without the detail, the difference in the way he looked and the way I looked. The epiphany came all at once, the sudden truth hitting me in the forehead. It had only happened once, that one time on the Hill. There had been close calls, many, but only once. Someone had stood between us, protected my mother and I against him.

"We're not related at all, are we?"

He sighed, as if about to give up a ghost that had been trapped a very long time.

"Yes and no."

I furrowed my brow; he took a moment, struggling with something he didn't want to share but now felt he had to.

"The man ya buried last year in Dunloe was my father. For my whole life I've hated him. I thought it had faded, but seeing you only reminded me of that Christmas morning, and it all came back up inside of me."

He stood, turned his back to me and walked to the railing, his silhouette against the black river. I rose, finding my feet and making to follow, but stood still. His words, his voice, were as heavy as the rocks in the current. Nothing could sweep them away.

"He was a man who puffed himself up. Who hid behind great deeds and tasks that other men couldn't do. He'd had to prove himself over and over. But people knew. People always know. I thought they did, anyway. It just wasn't something that was talked about. I mean, it was our business, right? It was as if the shame of it would sink the town, or cause bad luck, like the time our uncle drowned. That's how it's always associated."

He paused, his face buried in his left hand. Thumb and forefinger rubbing each temple so hard I could hear it from six feet away.

"I remember his shoes on the stairs. They were half covered in muck from the field and with his weight it made them sound like a slippery thumping. It sounded like a monster, and by Christ if it wasn't. When I was young, it wasn't so bad. I could block it out by thinking of the stand of blackthorns where I would hide during the day. When I was older, and less compliant, that's when the beatings would happen. My body covered in black and blue. A wee child walking like he had polio. My eyes never meeting anyone else's."

I could hear his tears now. They landed on the boardwalk with wet, heavy thuds, as if blood itself fell from his eyes. The sounds of the city were all but gone, as if the town had drawn and held a collective breath.

"When you were born it stopped. People remarked how lucky we were to have another child after so many years of being barren. I'd become a young man then, nearly fourteen, and I vowed it would never happen to you, that I would never leave your side. But the hate inside of me, for all those years he had stolen from my childhood, I just couldn't control it. And so I left. I left before I could kill myself. Before I'd walk up Errigal one last time and throw myself off the north face."

He turned to face me, his cheeks glistening with tears, lips quivering as the sentence choked in his throat.

"I'm sorry, Wiley. I'm so sorry. Please God in heaven forgive me. I should have been there. I should have been there for you," he sank into my arms, a man suddenly half his size, his sobs muffled by my shoulder and neck. I guided him over to a bench where the two of us collapsed. The weight of all those years, of all those repressed memories, of all the violence, the hatred, the crippling thoughts of revenge, the way it all shaped us, changed us, drove us into lives of self-loathing and self-destruction, it broke on us like a squall at sea, sudden, unforgiving and then gone.

We stayed there for hours, the sound of his crying giving way to a peace that only a river can bring, night settling around us like a quilt. A mist rose up from the water and gave the streetlights halos.

I felt nearly at rest for the first time in longer than I could remember. The ever-present white noise that filled my head had gone, replaced with calm silence, stillness, as if someone had finally turned off the television, the channel long since off the air. In knowing there is understanding, and in understanding there is peace, in the same way we look beneath the bed, open the closet door, or check all the rooms of the house before we sleep.

My childhood had been nowhere near as bad as his. There were times when I too had to hide in the stand of blackthorn, but unlike my big brother, I had someone who looked after me, someone whom my mother and I could trust.

"So, who is my father?"

"Ack, Jaysus, Wiley, think on it. Think about whom you really look like. Remember that one kind soul who always seemed to be about, was always there, suddenly like, when ya needed him to be."

I stood up from the bench and walked closer to the bridge I had seen on the first day I came to Grand Rapids. I saw in my mind the face of a man who was the one who really raised me. Kind. Strong. Making a living from the field. His weathered hands so large I could place my whole face in his palm, yet they were always gentle with me.

John Gallagher. No longer Uncle John, but my father.

"Didn't anyone know?"

"I think they knew," he said, rising from the bench, "but they were as happy as mom to have someone standing guard."

"Why didn't anyone tell me?"

"By the time you were old enough, I had left. By the time I saw you again, it was too late."

"What about mom?"

"Ask her yourself, Wiley," he said, sitting back down on the bench in exhaustion, a great sigh issuing forth, "I think you'll be seeing her soon."

My hands gesticulated without my voice, no words for the gestures to underscore. I was at a loss, my expression of imploring confusion visible even in the waning light.

"Christ, Wiley, give it a rest now. This must be the longest-running soap opera in history Be a good lad and put on a comedy," he turned, settled into the bench and began to doze.

I turned to the Grand, and stood there for a long time watching the river while he slept, the water dark and gently rolling, its sound filling my ears with the softest of phrases. I know this moment is profound, that my life has changed, has begun to come together, to heal. The simple bliss of the river keeps my head from filling too fast with thoughts, rushing too far, too soon. The lights from the bridge twinkle across the river's surface, the arch is reflected as a smile. I close my eyes and return the favor.

51

The rails no longer give our ears that wonderful, free sound of a train moving through the countryside. The sleepers and coaches are too quiet, the wheels beneath the cars travel over the separations between the tracks and we hear nothing but the sounds of people sleeping. Deep within us, as if recalling a memory that we all have come to share, we feel the motion of the train, and conjure the clickety-clack to satisfy its absence.

The lights in the car have been dimmed, and outside the window morning slowly begins to rise upon the endless fields of corn stalks, fragile autumn sunlight reaching out across the bottoms of the clouds with purple and indigo fingers. A flock of crows scatters from telephone lines, their reflections echoed briefly in standing water. I pull out a flask that had been given to me by the Sous Chef, remove the cap, and take a long drink of Jameson. It is a sup, a tear, and a fare-thee-well, my thoughts returning to the party of the day before.

The Sous and I had arrived at the pub before noon, lingering over lunch and exchanging our cokes for stouts. These were the first proper pints in weeks, the time since the river filled with thoughts of home, plans for tomorrow, and hours of walking the city with my brother. My train didn't leave for Chicago until very early the next morning, so we figured a bit of a gathering was in order.

"Alright, Wiley, before the first whiskeys pass our gums lets go over the list one last time," the Sous said as he stood up from his chair, pulled a list from his pocket and smoothed it out on the table.

"Right-o. Are we caught up, yet?"

"Let's see. Boxes and bags packed?"

"Check," I replied.

"Boxes taken to the post office for shipping?"

"Check."

"Your whites, aprons and other work-shit returned?"

"Happily."

"All interested parties informed of today's party?"

"Not a clue. Its my party, you're in charge."

"I'm pretty sure every greasy line-monkey in town knows you're leaving and today we get sauced," he finished while signaling for whiskey from Jimbo. "I think we're all set, my friend. Good to have a drink with you. It's been a while."

"Indeed. Thanks for the kind schedule. Needed those hours for my brother. Time goes fast, aye?"

"Yeah, too fast. What's that line from that book you always quote: It's not how much time you have, but how much whiskey you can drink before your time is up."

"That's close. Hey, looky here, whiskey," I said, standing up to meet the proffered libations.

Jimbo set the glasses down, took one up and cleared his throat. "Now, Mr. O'Wary, to your health and good fortune. And if you can't find those, to whatever poor fucker finds you." We downed the glasses. "I took it upon myself to arrange some Irish music," Jimbo said, "didn't think you'd mind," he gave me a wink and collected up the glasses.

"Half three, as you would say," the Sous announced, looking up at the clock above the bar, "the gang should be rollin' in."

And on cue, they did. The autumn fresh in their cheeks, a number of cooks from the restaurant walked into our shouts, a blustery rush of leaves and cold air following them in. My brother, the Waitress, and some other wait staff were right behind, smiles and hails, hugs and kisses as the throng increased. Soon all the denizens of the local were milling about, folks wishing to say 'so long' and enjoy a bloody, good excuse for an afternoon off.

As in all moments like this, we exchanged addresses, promised to visit, swore to stay in touch, and then, as the afternoon slowly unfolded, recalled events and services that were singularly hilarious or tragic. The recollection of battles won and lost by the foot soldiers of the culinary wars. Men and women who live paycheck to paycheck, gladly buying rounds, happy to not be in chef's whites, the laughter filling the room with the sunshine.

A tumble of loud voices announced the arrival of the band. They quickly set up their gear, called for jars, and began to play. The beat of the bodhran, the whine of Irish pipes beside the accompanying guitar, mandolin, and fiddle, stirred blood within me that had been well kindled. The pulse and weave of the reel pulling me back to the pier head in Dungloe, to the words of my mother, 'Follow the setting sun, Wiley,' she had said to me when I was a child, 'don't ever be afraid to follow it, he will always bring you home'.

On a dart board in the back of the bar, fixed to the cork by the splintered pieces of an Irish pound coin, is a map of America from the Mississippi west. Before the day was over, my eyes closed, a dart would be thrown and fate would take over.

A little over a year and a half ago, I had done the same thing in my local back in Boston. The dart struck Grand Rapids on this very same map held in place with the same broken punt, my eyes at the time opening to a new land, new people and new adventures; how was I to know that so much of my past would make the trek along side me.

My brother walks over to me, tugs on a shoulder and motions to the bar. It seems a wee dram is in order. In the time since we had come to terms on the boardwalk by the river, we have spent much of it together. Laughter replacing tears, the lightness of his self having returned, he seems years younger, more like the lad I had had a snowball fight with on Errigal. As if thinking the same thing, he has two glasses filled with a type of poteen now bottled and sold by a company in Ireland. He raises his and reminds me of that time, of telling me that poteen comes from snow. We share the drink, the moment and the memory, a bond re-fastened, brothers once more.

As the music continues, more people join the group. The bodhran player begins to sing *In The Rare Oul Times* and I can feel myself drifting back to Dublin. The way the sunlight filters into the pub, the music, the round happy faces, heads cocked searching for their own meaning from the lyrics, I could almost be there. 'Jaysus,' I think to myself, 'it's not long before I'm home again'.

"Ireland," I say softly to myself, and the gentleman across the aisle of the coach stirs in his sleep.

Outside the window, patches of sunlight appear through the breaks in the clouds, the sun's morning song erasing the shadows. My train plunges ever southward, toward tomorrow, toward the future that is written yet not written. I think back to the hoolie, only hours past, and feel the heart pull from leaving so many friends.

They had asked me to dance a jig, but mercifully for all, the Waitress insisted on a dance. We were asked if we had 'our song', which we didn't and if we did it would probably have been by Pantera. So instead, they played *Misty Morning, Albert Bridge*, by our old friends The Pogues. As I held her close to me, I felt the warmth of a friendship, not the passion which I let burn for far too long. When we looked into each other's eyes there was an understanding. Though no words were really shared, no regrets spoken, she wished me luck with a smile and returned to my brother's side when the song had ended.

Time slipped away in the way that it only can in pubs, and the nearness of departures was made apparent.

"Wiley," the Sous Chef called out in as close to a brogue as he could manage, "stand-up ya shaggin' git."

"Are ya talkin' ta me," I drawled out in the best mid-western nasal I could manage.

"Aye that I am," he paused, reached into his coat pocket, which was draped over his chair, and produced a gift. He handed it to me, one tear rolling down his cheek, and hugged me as if it were the last time on earth he would ever see me again. He shook my hand with both of his, declaring, "You're the worst damn card player who ever lived and a lousy cook, but you're one helluva friend, and for that, I thank-you."

I opened the package and found my own tear. Beneath a silver flask was a small-framed picture of he and I and the calico kitten, taken several days before she had died. Before I could say anything he called loudly for a speech, a demand that was taken up by the rest of the lads.

I have never been very good at these things, despite the fact that parting is a uniquely Irish custom. So, I always leave it to the moment, the muses of both sorrow and hope penning the words as they fall from my lips.

"You know in your gut when it's time to leave, at least I do, anyway. I have reached the end of the day, as they say, and must bid you all farewell But that is a word that is too final for my Donegal nature, so instead, I will say *Slan Abhaile, beannacht Dé leat.* Safe home and God bless. In my heart, as sure as that man there keeps time with the bodhran, you will all be there, each and every day.

This is one of those bittersweet days that life serves up to us, whether we want it or not. If we hadn't lived life to its fullest, it's likely we never would have met. I think it's that passion for living that drew us all together, and now sends us spinning in different directions. I have learned and experienced much since arriving in Grand Rapids, and wouldn't trade one sloppy sauté pan, cigarette, pint, shot, card game or memory for all the Irish wood in England. I'm a better man for having been here, and it is to all of you that I must say thanks. *Go raibh maith agat. Slan agat.*"

And then, I was turned toward the dartboard.

Now there is something very liberating about not having a plan, and not giving two shakes whether you have one or not. Sitting here on this train, a fraction of a day removed from the moment when two people chose not to choose their life's next chapter, I have only my reflection in the window to keep me company. The rhythm of the train as reassuring as the rocking a woman will do to quiet a frightened child, a smile warms my face at the thought of yesterday's spectacle.

I can see the dartboard before me as it was in the pub. The map a bit crooked. The shards of the pound coin shining with the wee spot lamps that illuminate the target. Lining up on either side of me, all the way from the point where I was standing to the board on the wall, stood the lads, pints in hand, howling and cheering as if they were betting on the ponies. I lined up the dart with the map. I looked over at the Sous Chef, a great, giant glass of Jameson in his fist, he gave me a wink and a sideways nod.

My brother was on the other side of me, his giant right hand squeezing my shoulder, patting me on the back in the way a trainer would coax a boxer before a round. On the other side of him was the Waitress, her face furrowed with concern, destiny no longer cloudy hopes and dreams, but about to become very real. "Alright, Wiley," he said to me, "hone right in on it. We're counting on ya, Wiley. Our future is in yer hands. Pick some place brilliant, close yer eyes and send the dart true. True, mind you. You've got to throw it true."

"Well how de feck do you think I'm going to throw it," I replied, my eyes returning to the map, the dart starting to slip a little from sweat.

The lads yelled us on. The Sous took a swig and nodded. My brother tapped a fist on my shoulder, gave me a look of confidence, and backed a step away as the bodhran player feigned a drum roll.

I closed my eyes, the image of the map seared upon my retinas, and I took a deep breath. As I exhaled, so very slowly, I thought how trusting my brother and the Waitress were to let me choose the next place they would call home. Then, composed, I let fly the dart to a cheer and then a collective gasp.

Now, the subtleties of my throw: the flights of the dart, the weight of the dart, my grip, or lack of grip, the eddies and differing directions on how the air moves through the room, the strength of my throw, the spin of the dart as it leaves the tip of my index finger, all of these conspired to the destination of not only the dart, but my brother and the Waitress as well. When silence followed the gasp, I opened my eyes. "Jaysus," I said softly to myself, shaking my head, "how strange this life. Strange and wonderful."

"Where in the fuck did you just send us?" my brother asked, the crowd still stunned.

I blinked, narrowed my eyes, and tried to read the nearest place-name from where I stood. My brother walked tentatively toward the board. The Sous Chef let out a howl of laughter and the Waitress hung her head.

"Are ya out of yer feckin' mind!" my brother shouted, "how about two outta three!"

"You knew the rules when you let Wiley throw the dart. You've got to at least go to the place and give it a chance," explained the Sous.

We walked up to the board, the dart casting an awkward shadow from the spotlight. Its grip on the board was tenuous at best, the tip just penetrating the map.

"There's nothing there," I said softly.

"No shit, little brother. We may as well be bears."

"I want to be a state park ranger," it was the Sous, singing at the top of his lungs, guffawing so hard that he slapped his thighs.

"I am truly sorry," I stammered.

"Live a life of sex and danger," the Sous continued, walking to the bar for more of something.

"No you're not. You knew bloody well where you were throwing that dart."

"I aimed for San Francisco," I said, defending myself. "Besides, I'm sure there's a town or a ranger station nearby."

He sighed and jotted down the nearest towns to the dart. Finished his drink, motioned to the Waitress and made to leave. Outside a taxi was waiting. They were on their way to a hotel by the airport.

"Well, little brother, that's that then. I'll ring you when we get to a phone out there and let you know what Timbuktu, Wyoming looks like," he smiled, hugged me, and with a hand on each of my shoulders, "thank-you for finding room in your heart to forgive me." The door opened and closed. I stood for the longest moment staring at the empty vestibule between the doors and watched the cab depart. Two people who had so influenced my life, one in the recent past, one for all time, they had trusted me to decide their fate. I wondered when I would see them again.

"And then there was one," the Sous, glasses in hand. "There's a ride waiting for you, we all pitched in and got you a room at the Grand. That old apartment was just too empty for your last night in Grand Rapids. You know, this would all be more exciting if you were to throw a dart as well."

"I'm afraid my aim is a bit off. Liable to end up in Death Valley."

"Your train is way too early in the morning, so this is it."

We stood there, whiskey in hand, tears streaming down our faces, the crowd giving us a little room, but looking on, sobs, sighs and more tears.

"What a pair of manly men we make," I said, the room laughing, the Irish deflection of humor easing the pain we all felt.

"I'm going to miss you, buddy."

"Aye, I'm going to miss you too," and with that, the hug, the handshake and the door.

Full on morning, bright sunshine fills the car, the gentle rocking as the train makes its way to Chicago. An *Aer Lingus* flight is on tap for this evening, proceeded by another train out to O'Hare. The flask has held out remarkably well, I take a sip of Jameson and close my eyes, my head gently touching the window, the cold of the glass numbing my forehead. In a matter of hours I will be home. Why? I'm not sure. It just seems like the thing to do. Back to Éire, to Donegal, to Dungloe, the circle of a lifetime coming to a close. I wonder what lies ahead, what is waiting for me in those hills, along those shores. Maybe just peace. Maybe just life. Wonderful, simple, frustrating thank God for every moment life.

My eyes water, the face of the Sous comes to mind. The line, the cooks, the tickets and all the pain-in-the-ass-servers with all their pain-in-the-ass requests and the royal pain-in-the-ass Chef and suddenly the weight of the moment makes me bury my tear-sodden face into the window.

Damn I'm going to miss them. Them. The town. The way it seemed there was a church on every corner and a restaurant across the street. The nearness and distance of the whole place, like you could walk for hours and not see one person you know and then see the same homeless person from hours before. A town that will forever be trying to grow up into a city, but will never shake its provincial charm, and right then I know what I will miss the most: that first beer with my brothers after service. What a crew. What a great friend.

And I open my eyes to East Chicago and know that I am flying home, and know that I may never see America again.

52

The waves curl in from the west, past the islands of Aranmore, Inishfree, Inishmeal, and Rutland, the pier head dividing the swell, foam bunching up around the pilings, the sound of the breakers bringing dreams and the promises of tomorrow. The setting sun hangs just above the Atlantic, imbuing the sky and sea in an orange-red glow, the lazy evening call of gulls as hypnotic as the surf. I stand here on this pier in Dungloe, the ocean breeze stiff, cold, and true, knowing now that it is here where I will remain, in Donegal. The heart of my life is once more working to a rhythm as ancient as the swell, I have returned to roots that had been waiting to embrace me.

In a few moments the circle will be complete. I can only shake my head at how strange and wonderful this journey has been, how odd the subtleties that determine the flights of darts and also that of men.

"And then to see a welcome face, for travelers one and all," I sing softly, the lyrics rising up from the whitecaps with the mist, "for your hearts are like your mountains, in the homes of Donegal."

"Who are you talking to, Wiley?"

"Only the waves."

"We should be going. Your man will be leaving the hotel soon and I'm too old for days as long as this one," she sighed, "I still have to go home and make tea."

"Just a couple more minutes, Ma."

"You said that ten minutes ago. My couch misses me."

I look back to see she's okay, watch as she buries her face in the flowers I bought for her at Shannon, and then return to the water. It seems strange that I am here, the going-away party only two days removed, the absence of so many friends tugging at my heart. Closing my eyes, I can hear the Sous Chef's great laugh, picture the Waitress, and feel the nearness of my brother though thousands of miles away. A quiet prayer goes out to each and all, their faces tucked in my heart like pictures in a locket.

A sudden jolt of wind brings me back, eyes narrowed against the spray off the tops of the rollers, another set of lyrics from that sweet song surfacing: "For there's rest for weary wanderers, in the homes of Donegal."

I give the waves a sideways nod and a wink, then turn to face the shore, bracing myself to complete the reel, finish the dance, close the circle. "One last chore there, Mister O'Wary, one last chore."

"Ready, son?"

"Aye."

She had picked me up at Shannon Airport, the same beat-up old car filled with half-finished projects, books for resale shops and books recently purchased, half a bagel, a partial cup of coffee beside a partial cup of tea. I could sense my mother's nervousness from across the room. What do you say to the son you have raised, without ever having told him his life's deepest secret?

I had come to terms with all of it, my quiet perseverance and suddenly sober outlook anchoring me with fresh perspective. The old joke is about the Irishman with amnesia who forgot everything but the grudge, yet from my experience we have always been the first to let the water flow under the bridge; choose the path of least resistance. That is how I felt about it all, the whole bloody mess, now that it was out in the open; now that the nightmares had ceased and the dawn broken bright and clear, it was time to forgive and move on. At the very least, this is what I keep telling myself.

I could tell, as I exited the door separating customs from the reception area in the terminal, that my mother was quite well bursting at the seams. Bouncing from one foot to the other, spinning a ring perpetually around her finger unless brushing a lock of hair away from her forehead. I could see she was rehearsing a speech, trying to figure out how to say something she never really anticipated having to say.

"Hullo, mom. You look great."

"Ack, Wiley, I look like an alley cat that hasn't been inside in a fortnight."

"You do seem nervous," I gave her a great hug, one of those crushing son hugs, "it's no worries, mom, we have thousands of days in front of us, each one better than the one before."

"You're drunk. Or you're in denial. Which is it, or both," she stepped back to look at me, hands on my shoulders. I just smiled, one of those heart softening son smiles. "Gad, but you're all impossible," and a hug returned, one of those mom hugs that says everything's going to be okay. She locked her arm in mine and we headed toward the exit, my bags rolling beside me in a trolley.

We stopped at a kiosk for water, a snack, and the *Irish Independent*, her eyes not far from a rack filled with bouquets of flowers. As we left, I told her I'd forgotten something, purchased a bouquet, and somehow managed to surprise her. Upon reaching the car, we cleared a spot for my luggage and myself, replaced the old cups of coffee with new ones, and settled in for the drive to Donegal. There was an air of anticipation, her nervousness spilling forth as we entered the motorway.

"Well, Wiley, first I must say I'm sorry for not having told you everything about everything. You must understand, I didn't know the depths to which the man had sunk. In those days we were all very afraid of him, and had to give him a wide berth. Perhaps if your Uncle Colm hadn't drowned, or your brother hadn't left, there would have been someone to stand up to him sooner," she glanced out her window, tears welling in her eyes, hands wringing answers from the steering wheel, "but that wasn't to be."

Silence. The wheels on the pavement. Clare FM. What was there to say?

"I hope you can forgive me, Wiley. I did the best I could. You have to understand that. If I had known more, then I'd have sent you to London or to Armagh," she paused, "I'm so sorry." She paused again, a catch in her throat. "John and I had had that conversation so many times. Omagh. Omagh. Omagh. But then, what would have happened there, with the war and all."

"Mom, it's okay. Really. I love you," and I took her hand, the tears in both our eyes blurring the road, the horn from a BMW bringing us back to the N18.

We drove from Ennis to Sligo, bursts of confession on her part, a story she had buried beneath the surface now finally able to be told. It was almost as if we were meeting for the first time, her love affair with John Gallagher, the pregnancy, the quiet, brooding drama of it all enfolding along the coast of Donegal. The emotions tucked as tightly to her breast as the town to the cliff. It was hard to believe it had happened and harder to believe I was a part of it.

We stopped for tea and a sandwich at the foot of Ben Bulben, a wee cottage selling snacks and sundries to tourists in coaches. Yeats' grave was only a hundred yards away. The break from driving gave us the opportunity to talk about the poet, the bread, and the late-season travelers. It was a welcome respite from the seriousness of the last four hours. Arm and arm in step, the two of us walked to the cemetery, glanced once more down at the tomb of Ireland's poet laureate, and read again the epitaph: *Cast a cold eye on life, on death: horseman, pass by!* The mountain loomed into the mist, a verdant mesa that stretches into the Dartry Mountains, it's nearly sheer sides lit by the early afternoon sun, a beautiful but somber setting. We heeded Yeats' advice and returned to the car.

The road to Donegal Town just barely hugs the coast, the ocean appearing and disappearing on the left while the hills rise on the right, the two suddenly coming together where the Eske flows into Donegal Bay. We stopped in the middle of town at a place called The Diamond, found a corner pub, and braced ourselves for the winding road to Dungloe, my mother doing her best to buy me a pint or a dram.

"Are ya nervous?" she asked.

"Aye, a mite," I said, knowing she was hinting at meeting my real father, but then feigning different, "you know, new job, new boss, my first kitchen."

"That's not what I meant."

"Aye, I know, and no I won't have a drink. There's not a straight road in the whole county."

She smiled, "I'm very proud of you, Wiley."

"I've driven before, you know."

"That's not what I meant," her fist tapped my hand, "bravery doesn't always hold a sword." She rose, walked through a door to find the bathrooms, and left me to once more shake my head at so profound a woman.

The pier sits at the bottom of three hills beside the confluence of three roads, one leading to Burtonport as you drive away from Dungloe, the other being the steep main street of town, a third road rising sharply on the shore side leading up to the new hotel and conference center. Sweeny's Hotel and Restaurant is shore side at the bottom of the old main drag, protected from the Atlantic by a good-sized building that sits on the corner. There is a wee stream that flows beneath the road beside Sweeny's, the clear mountain water tumbling down to the ocean in a burble that says everything is as it should be.

"Is Danny O'Donnel in town?" I asked, looking up at the new hotel as my mother and I left the pier, referring to Dungloe's most famous resident and the new hotel's owner.

"Not sure. Probably on tour. He was on Aranmore last week for a benefit, then off to America I suppose."

"Too busy a life for me. Give me a kitchen, a prep list, and the promise of a pint afterward."

We turned the corner, walked up the right-hand side of the street, past The Bridge Inn, and stopped at the steps that followed the falls. I stepped down, my mother hesitating, rolling her eyes at my very obvious stalling.

"Wiley, you can't put this off much longer. You need to drop your kit off in your new kitchen, meet the manager, and then back to the house, right."

"Aye, I know, but it's not as easy as it sounds."

She walked down beside me, pulled out a pound coin and offered it to me. "Make a wish."

"There's a good idea," I dug in my pocket, "save your punt, I have one here I won't be needing again," and then removed the splintered pound coin I had used twice before for holding maps. I closed my eyes, composed myself, exhaled, and then wished, "dear God in Heaven and the spirits of these falls, I wish for peace for all those who have touched my life, safety for this village, long life for my mother, sister, and brother, and a swift conclusion to the rest of the evening," and then tossed the pound coin pieces into the burble, the glints of silver disappearing into the stream.

"Very nice, Wiley, and thanks for the mention," she then pointed to the 'Sweeny's' sign just visible above the sidewalk, "now."

I turned, sighed, trudged up the steps and over to her car. I pulled out one of my bags, and took out my knife kit, my chef's coat, and work shoes. I looked up at the hotel's sign, as if I wasn't sure this was the place, and then walked up to the door. It opened just as I was reaching for it, the manager all smiles and handshakes, a clap on the back and a hearty failte!

"Mr. O'Wary it is a pleasure. We look so forward to your getting started. I trust you know where the kitchen is located. It's quiet now, as we're closed until you can get us up-and-running once more. We'll go over the details in the morning, say nine. Feel free to look around. I would stay and chat, but it's later than what I expected and I'm late for my pint up at O'Donnel's. Cherrie-o, 'till tomorrow," and then off he dashed, out the door and up the hill, touching his cap as my mother shot me a look.

"You'll be late for your own funeral. Hurry on, we're expected back at the house."

I sighed, butterflies turning into condors, and closed the door behind me. The hotel was dark, new paint smell still hanging in the air. They had closed for three months and remodeled the entire hotel: reception, guestrooms, lounge, bar, dining room and hopefully, the kitchen. It was a remarkable makeover. What had once been an austere, stuffy collection of rooms, the hotel now flowed with light, charm, and elegance. I was already changing the menu in my head, preconceived notions being cast aside, the dining room begging me to push the cuisine further than I had hoped.

It was in this revelry that I entered the kitchen. I backed into the swinging door, my mind spinning with big nights, gushing patrons, servers screaming and chef's swearing. As I turned, the last of the day's light spilling in from a side window and glinting off the new stainless steel, I jumped at the sight of a man leaning against the server-side of the line, arms folded across his chest, a smile on his face.

He wore an old fisherman's sweater, a gray tam, blue jeans and wellies, his arms opening up, the smile growing larger, his giant hands outstretched. I caught the sobs in my throat, the tears hitting the new tile as I dropped my gear and ran into those arms, the embrace like a bear's. I didn't know whether to call him Mr. Gallagher, John, or Dad, so I didn't say anything at all, the moment too perfect the way it was.

We held each other like that for a moment, the tears subsiding, a compressor somewhere shutting off returning the room to an absolute quiet. He then took me by the shoulders, staring into my eyes at arm's distance, his smile as bright as the sun reflecting off a heart as big as the ocean.

"Welcome home, Wiley, welcome home."

Liam Sean is a writer, musician, and chef who dwells deep in the boreal forests of the upper Great Lakes. For projects and info, please wander to: www.liamsean.com

CPSIA information can be obtained
at www.ICGtesting.com
Printed in the USA
FSHW010623060720
71816FS